Raid of Souls

RAID OF SOULS

KALEN VAUGHAN JOHNSON

FIVE STAR

A part of Gale, a Cengage Company

LIBRARY OF CONGRESS CATALOGING-IN-PUBLICATION DATA

Names: Johnson, Kalen Vaughan, author.
Title: Raid of souls / Kalen Vaughan Johnson.
Description: First edition. [Waterville : Maine] : Five Star, a part of Gale, a Cengage Company January [2021] | Series: The Empire Barons; book 2
Identifiers: LCCN 2020016611 | ISBN 9781432877392 (hardcover)
Classification: LCC PS3610.O3576 R35 | DDC 813/.6—dc23
LC record available at https://lccn.loc.gov/2020016611

First Edition. First Printing: July 2021
Find us on Facebook—https://www.facebook.com/FiveStarCengage
Visit our website—http://www.gale.cengage.com/fivestar
Contact Five Star Publishing at FiveStar@cengage.com

Printed in Mexico
Print Number: 01   Print Year: 2021

To Gary—my best friend, confidant,
and dearest love of my life.
To the rest of my growing family, you guys are my heart!
Your love and support mean everything.
Kristin and Brian, Kelly and Jamar, Matt and Diana,
Aidan, Wyatt, Maddi Jo, Connor, and Amy.

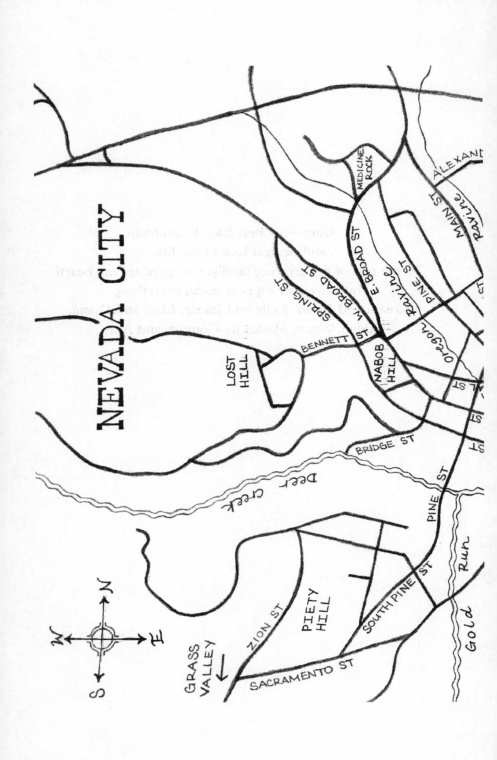

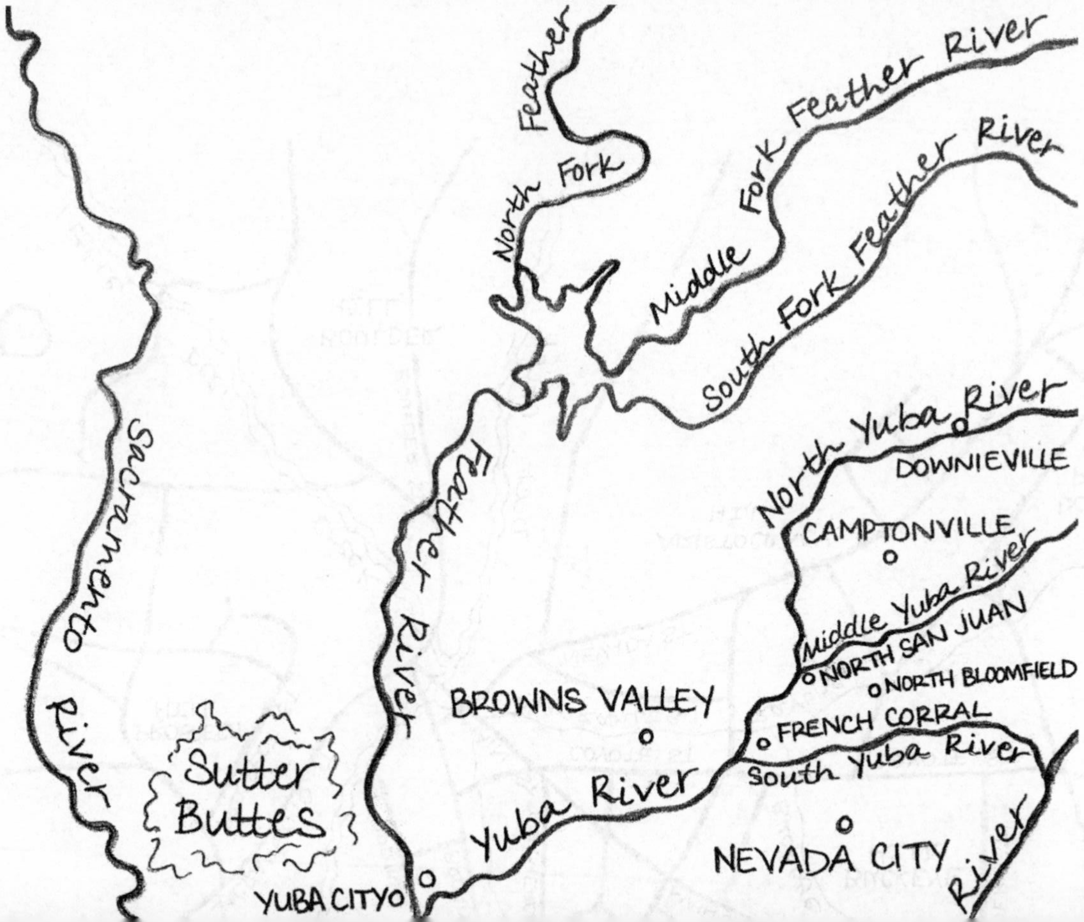

North Fork Feather
Middle Fork Feather River
South Fork Feather River
North Yuba River
DOWNIEVILLE
CAMPTONVILLE
Middle Yuba River
NORTH SAN JUAN
NORTH BLOOMFIELD
FRENCH CORRAL
South Yuba River
Feather River
BROWNS VALLEY
Yuba River
NEVADA CITY
River
Sacramento River
Sutter Buttes
YUBA CITY

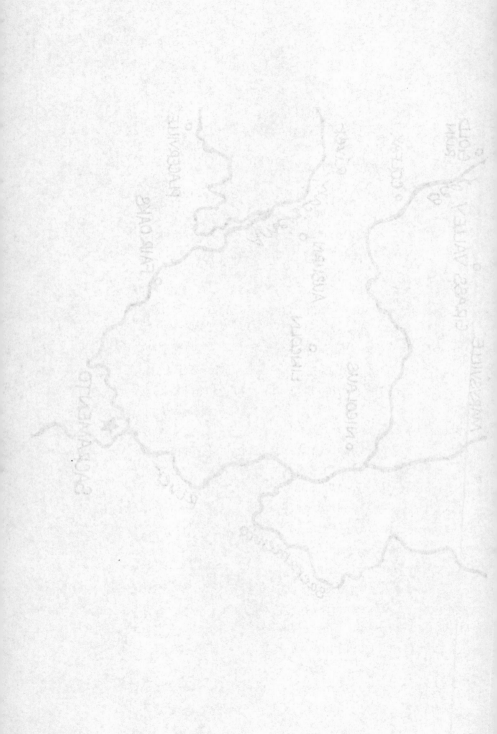

CHAPTER 1

Nevada City, California, The Silver Moon Tavern, June 1866
The conflict now rising was not so much amongst men, but of battles first waged in dark hearts. Hostilities proved a mere hiccup to California, isolation being its sanctuary and its curse. The nation survived a war, faced reconstruction, and the race of railroad titans culminates to link a beleaguered land.

And yet, a savvy, subtle enemy hovers as a will-o'-the-wisp. In the best of mortal man, good intentions meander. Covetous notions, curtained from view, fester. Justification feeds reason, building its case to devour the unguarded.

Man's eye side glances to the inner workings of his heart, exaggerating his own honor. His soul is an assailed entity, searching for nobility in a rash and reckless world. The weak tremble under temptations of the influential. Few lions arise to protect the pride.

James MacLaren felt as though the stone of Sisyphus rolled against his braced back. He returned from Sacramento with new evidence and a string of mares, only to be faced with the emptiness of Justin's departure. Spring's heavy rains yielded a bumper crop of alfalfa awaiting harvest in his fields. Althea's slow recuperation, and the shock of the accident that nearly killed her, still pierced his core. Worse yet, he found Lodie's agitation over phantom manipulation of the gold mines to be warranted.

He hoped Sean, as a new foreman at Empire, possessed

11

enough insider knowledge to untangle the twisted path he discovered in Sacramento's public record. A grab for controlling interest in the Empire mine began long before the rumors. Claims trailed to the San Francisco Stock Exchange, where speculators gobbled up mining shares. Leads appeared as tossed marbles in a roulette wheel, leaving James to guess where they might bounce out again.

And now, ensconced at their customary corner table at the Silver Moon, James bestowed his bundled enigma of field work upon his former mining partners, Sean Miller and Lodie Glenn. Ignoring the raucous noise of afternoon patrons, Sean studied a sheath of papers. He shoved their abandoned beverages aside, the last of the deflated froth clinging to sour smelling mugs.

"I'm not sure what this means." Lodie sat, elbows on the table, his head resting between his large hands as he stared at the scattered files. His fingers furrowed rows through his white-blond hair.

"Nor I," answered James. "I followed a horrific paper chain, one filing after another. All transactions ended up under ownership of Empire mines, ta be sure."

Sean muttered, "I coulda told you as much. As quick as small mines fail, they show up on my list as holdings to be inspected."

"But, who's behind this?"

Escalating woes of independent miners inflamed old wounds James fought to keep hidden. Rules of engagement had changed over the dozen years since their partnership of four flourished. The slow and calculated march of progress failed to alarm early pioneers besotted with newly acquired autonomy. He could find no face behind the advance, only that there were many. But he knew they wielded common weapons—power, money, and position—in their bid for takeover.

Surfaces picked clean of profitable ore now required heavy equipment to penetrate unreachable depths. Empire's investment in machinery pushed independents with title to choose between abandoning claims or teetering on the edge of financial abyss. Even worse was legal confusion created by gold-laden veins stretching their spiderlike spread into areas both claimed and poached by independent miners—areas that Sean warned months ago nested on land now titled to Empire.

"We need names." James reached abruptly into Lodie's fanned out pile to snatch a particular page. "One peculiar item . . . I traced the newest holdings ta a separate entity, a finance network called *Coleridge Sierra*. And them unrelated ta large bundles of stock William Bourn owns. Apparently, Coleridge Sierra put up the money, ultimately causing failure for our independent friends. They did na waste time calling in their loans."

Lodie frowned. "What's Bourn's part in this?"

"Nothing new as far as I cu tell. He's invested for years, gradually buying up stock. A businessman with many interests—I cu na find anything ta suggest he's got any portion of what's happening here."

"But how does this tie into Empire?" asked Sean.

"Coleridge Sierra owns the largest block of stock, other than Bourn. They're calling the shots, and it's na just mines. Coleridge Sierra acquired a small railway servicing old Dog Run Mine near Camptonville and the Miner's Foundry here in Nevada City. Then, there's our stamp mill."

"Damn." Lodie looked surprised. "They're moving right into town. What the hell else do they intend to own?"

"Well, I do na suggest borrowing money for *any* reason."

"I don't like this at all; it's bad enough when independent mines fold all around us. Older towns than ours die out for lack of business. I'm all for chasing dreams, but, if more collapse, it hurts the reputation of the town. Everything I own is tied to Nevada City. In fact, this affects all our livelihoods." Lodie shook his head in disgust. "Maybe, if the miners sold out earlier, this fiasco wouldn't be raining down on our heads."

"That ain't quite fair, Lodie. We all put hopes on pulling rocks outta the ground. How much sense does that make? When manna from heaven quits, it ain't our call," said Sean.

They sat in silence, each struggling for answers like a drowning man grasps at a trailing rope.

Sean rocked his chair back on two legs. "Question is: what now?"

"Well, it's clear we can't sit on this," stated Lodie.

"No, but we can na explain it, either. Someone's making big moves on our whole area. We've got ta come up with a plan."

"This is why we need the union, to put up a united front."

"We need *names*. We've *got* ta kin who we're up against."

Silence hung over the table once again.

Sean let the front of his chair hit the floor. "I'll see what I can dig up at the main office. But I gotta be up front about a union with the bosses. I'll shine it up like an apple at the fair—let 'em see a union's got advantages. I'd feel better with our own people in this thing so I know who to count on. Empire plans to bring in *experts.*" He spat the word. "Experts on theories, anyways . . . a bunch of educated blokes that ain't never raised a blister or broke a sweat. Nothing but a pain in the arse." He rubbed his brow above the eye-patch. He rarely seemed conscious of his souvenir of Vicksburg, but, when agitated, he swiped at it like an annoying insect.

James nodded. "Our own need ta be involved. It's crucial we get word ta every town, along every ridge, that ever found an ounce. We'll draw in the holdouts—miners still in operations we kin. Let's announce a meeting. Send curriers ta nearby taverns. If we organize, men cu have a say in their future and that of the town."

Lodie gave him a hard squint. "Then, you'll let me put you

14

forward as union chief?"

James scoffed at their old argument. "It'll take more than me ta make this work."

"It's a start. I'll talk to the bosses," offered Sean. "Ya know, Clancy worked independent long before *we* were partners; he knows most everybody. James, if you write up the notice, I'll get him to post it around."

"I'll address the Merchants Bureau, see if anyone's been offered loans," added Lodie. "And, local banks—they'll worry about competition, which will throw their support our way. I can draw up major points we aim to accomplish as a union. We three should meet in a day or two to go over it—add to it as we see fit. If we're done here, I'll get started." He pushed his chair back to rise.

Sean leaned towards James. "On a separate matter of sorts, I need to hire blasting help if you've got time." He grinned. "Wouldn't hurt you politically for the men to see you back amongst 'em."

"What ha ye got?"

"Cornish pumps pulling out eighteen thousand gallons of water per hour. Heavy spring rains done a number on stopes. Makes for future safety issues—a union concern, I might add. Need to open up some new tunnels. Trouble is, as we develop one area, another falls to rest until I can send more men in. The mining progression depth is falling below the water table. Where water sits, ceiling timbers show signs of rot and produce methane. Gets tricky, but we got to replace those beams."

Lodie turned. "You taking canaries down in the meantime?"

"Nah. The boys feed the rats to keep 'em around. We watch them."

"I'll have a look. When?"

James glanced past Lodie to watch Sheriff Shaw push through the doors of the Silver Moon. The lanky, gray-headed man

15

walked straight for their table. Stopping in front of Lodie, he pushed his hat back and greeted them with a quick head bob.

"Afternoon, fellas. Sean, I'm headin' to Althea's dress shop. She back at work yet?"

James answered, "She rode in with me this morning."

"Need to talk to her. Sean, you might wanna come along. Lodie, as mayor, I 'spect you ought to come, too."

Sean straightened. "Sounds official, Tom."

"Could say that. You know a miner by the name of Salty Scanlon?"

"Yeah, I know him. Nice enough fella. Worked up at North San Juan Ridge before he took off for Comstock—knew him there, too, as a matter of fact."

The sheriff nodded. "He just got back from Virginia City— been there a couple months now. Came in to see me today. Seems the last day he was here was the day of Mrs. Albright's accident. Wanted to know, did I catch the guy driving the wagon that hit her?"

"No one drove it," said James. "The driver was in a saloon and swore the brake was secure. He did na kin what spooked the team or how the hand brake came loose."

"That's just it. Salty came up behind the wagon and saw a man take the team and whip 'em up good, ran 'em hard down the street. Man still sittin' in the driver's seat when the wagon went outta his sight. Salty didn't know Althea'd been hit 'til he got back to town. Nobody else recalls seeing anybody driving. He got a pretty good look at the fella, too. Stranger. Never seen him before, but says he'd never forget—guy had both earlobes cut up like a bad horse."

"He jumped," she whispered.

Althea paled, clutching her throat. She stared into nothing-ness, struggling through jagged impressions. The circle of men around her waited.

"I . . . didn't recall until now. I saw a man jump off." She traced memory's steps in her mind. "I turned . . . I heard the wagon coming and . . . he jumped . . . as it ran me down."

"You get a look at him?" asked the sheriff.

"No. I barely remember seeing the movement. He . . . had long, dark hair. I didn't see his face."

"Witness said his earlobes been tore up."

She stared at the faces huddled around her, her panic rising. "Sean! That's the man who came after me that day."

"I recollected you sayin' so the minute Tom gave his description. I told him what happened."

"What does this mean?"

"It means he thinks you saw something in the alley that day," said Lodie grimly.

17

Justin Albright rode slowly. On a journey to nowhere in particular, it seemed absurd to rush. His leisurely pace allowed him plenty of thinking time. Even breathing came easier away from his family's constant watch for signs of how he felt. He wrestled with the peculiar realization that he now had an aunt in Boston, perhaps relatives in England. Lady Margaret would know if his father still lived. He hoped the man was dead. As dead as the father he grew up with. He steeled himself with the belief his family included only Althea, James, and Charlotte . . . and, with his mother's upcoming wedding, perhaps Sean.

Out of the seven hills of Nevada City and through Grass Valley, he picked his way to the far side of hill country, noting the slow change from evergreens to softer, fuller broadleaf trees. He absorbed the familiar landscape, committing it to memory as he absented. He felt oddly at peace with himself, resigning to push away sentiment and focus on his future. As much as he loved James, striking out on his own held great appeal. The man cast a long shadow.

Justin considered riding past Sutter Buttes, a solitary, mystical mountain range rising up in odd contradiction with the flat plains of the Central Valley. The Maidu revered it as a spiritual place of renewal; where Father Sky met with Mother Earth twice each day. He decided crossing the Feather River at that point took him too far out of his way.

He planned to spend his second night at the American Hotel

in Nicolas, a crossroads for travelers and information. Once the county seat, the town thrived as a ferry crossing for both cargo and passengers. James conducted business with Humphrey's freight company there, as his farm, Thistle Dew, had a growing reputation for fine horses. Justin hoped to chat up the proprietor as well as look into job postings at the inn. He counted off the farms he knew along the way, families and friends he had grown up with from Marysville days. He picked up a trail near the Bear River and followed it into Nicolas.

The bustling hotel teemed with miners, farmers, ranchers, and businessmen on their way to or from towns within a fifty-mile radius. Justin sat down for a hot meal in the dining hall and began studying people around him. He listened in on conversations, asked questions, and a few discussions led to names of outfits all the way to Sacramento. He strolled the streets after dinner, observing his surroundings as never before, as a young man on his own.

Nicolas was a modest sized town packed with transients. Justin enjoyed its energy and liveliness—and the way it awakened his senses as he contemplated his future.

The next morning, he continued his surveillance of the locals over a leisurely breakfast. As he sipped his coffee, he heard raised voices coming from the front desk. He paid his bill and went to stand in line behind a family of four, the father crying out to a frazzled hotel clerk. The mother, with two small boys clinging to her skirts, wore a deeply worried look. Justin heard the last bits of the exchange.

"I'm sorry, sir, I've already sent someone for the sheriff. You will have to report the loss to him; there is nothing more I can do."

"But it happened right outside your hotel! You don't understand; I can't afford to replace that horse. We cannot leave here without him!"

19

"Ah, look," said the relieved clerk. "Here's Sheriff Davis now. I'm certain he can help you." He looked past the man and waved Justin forward.

Justin turned to watch as the man and his family hurried towards the sheriff.

"Checking out?"

"Yes. Albright." He held out his cash for the clerk. "Horse thief?"

The clerk took his money. "Thank you, Mr. Albright. I trust your stay was satisfactory?" He lowered his voice, "Yes, unfortunately. A town this size with so many people coming and going . . . there's bound to be a number of unsavory elements lurking about."

Justin noticed the clerk frown as he put his wallet in his back pocket. The man shook his head. "No, son." He patted the front of his shirt. "Put that inside your coat. Lots of folks on the streets today—pickpockets."

Justin nodded. "Thank you."

He grew anxious to check on Baron at the livery.

After paying the stable boy, he ambled over to the freight yard for a brief hello. The owner, Mr. Humphrey, remembered him well from numerous trips accompanying James to deliver stock and eagerly offered him a job. Justin thanked him, stating truthfully his interest, if his journey brought him back this way. He left, encouraged with one good job prospect.

Justin picked up his pace with the anticipation of exploring Sacramento. He trotted Baron into the cool of a forest to escape the overhead sun. Jogging along, his mind wandered as he pictured what his family might be doing right now. He came upon a stream, and, after refilling his canteen, he let Baron satisfy his thirst. He decided to walk for a while to stretch his legs. He glimpsed a clearing ahead and noticed a man bent over, examining a horse's foot. Three horses were tied to a tree.

Justin called out, "Trouble?"

Before the man spoke, Justin saw his shoulders jerk, then straighten at the sound of Justin's approach. The man turned, gun drawn. He said, "Now, that depends."

Justin raised his hands. "Hey—I'm not armed." He thought wistfully of the old Sharp's rifle tucked in its scabbard on his saddle.

The man seemed not much older than himself. A lock of dark hair fell over one eye. His intensely unfriendly eyes glared at Justin, daring him to move. His square jaw clenched, and his stance suggested a readiness to fight. Justin did not move. He watched the man's gun hand . . . asking calmly, "What do you want?"

For a moment, the man looked confused. "What do *I* want?" He scrutinized Justin more closely. He squinted and barked, "What's your business here?"

Justin stated carefully, "I'm just passing through. I'm on my way to Sacramento."

"From where?"

"Came from Nicolas this morning. My family has a farm outside Nevada City."

The man lowered the pistol slightly. "You do look more like a farmer than a thief."

"Me? The way you turned on me, I thought you were after my horse."

"Can't be too careful." He holstered the gun. "Besides, you shouldn't come up behind a man like that."

Justin offered his hand. "Maybe you shouldn't turn your back to the trail. Justin Albright."

Maintaining his menacing stance, he clasped Justin's hand firmly, "Royce Collier."

"Nice string of horses you got there."

Royce sucked in an aggravated breath. "Just bought 'em. I

was preoccupied with that mare's split hoof when you showed up behind me. It's going to be a slow trip home."

"Mind if I take a look?"

Royce frowned. "You know anything about stock?"

"It's what I do all day." Justin walked over and leaned into the mare's shoulder until she let him pick up her foot. She stood patiently while he poked around inside the hoof.

"It's an ugly crack, all right. Did it come on all at once?"

Royce stood with his arms folded. "Looked her over good yesterday before I paid for her and didn't see a thing. Must be a weak spot. It'll take forever to heal—if I can get her home."

Justin studied the hoof. "The frog is swollen. I've got herbs in my bag to make a poultice, if you want to try. Might help keep it moist and prevent further cracking."

Royce looked surprised. "You carry that stuff with you?"

Justin smirked. "We farmers are a resourceful lot."

Royce chuckled and rubbed the back of his neck, conceding, "It's worth a shot."

While Justin mixed the poultice and secured it with a cloth, Royce checked the rest of his bunch. Satisfied, he returned to watch.

Justin looked up. "I trimmed the hoof back; she's sound otherwise. These things can flare up with no rhyme or reason. But, you're right. It'll be a frustrating wait for that hoof to grow out."

Royce grumbled. "She'll get a nice long rest before I can put her to work."

"Mind if I string along with you for a bit? If you're headed towards Sacramento, I mean. I'd like to pick your brain about the area."

"Sure. I'd like the company. I'll tell you what I can before you get tired of moving at a snail's pace."

"Great. I'll pack this stuff up, and we'll see how she travels."

Royce went to adjust his saddle just as Justin reached his stallion's side. Baron jerked his head up and snorted. Justin stepped back to see two riders race abruptly into the clearing. Royce spun around where he stood, drawing his pistol.

The lead rider reined in hard, his gun cocked and pointed at Royce. "Nope. Drop it!" he shouted. The rider behind covered Justin.

"I'd say we're even, friend." Royce kept his gun leveled.

"Not hardly. Your man's unarmed. We'll both plug you, before we worry about him. Now, drop it. I'm not itchin' to see blood, but I'll spill it, if I havta."

Royce hesitated.

Justin stood, his hands raised high. He noted the lead man's horse to be highly agitated, shuffling its feet and jittery as if unaccustomed to this rider and uncertain how to respond.

Royce lowered his pistol. Angrily, he tossed it to the ground.

The lead man snickered. "That's it. Get his gun, Harvey." He watched Royce carefully from his mount. "I been following you since this morning, boy. Good-looking bunch of animals—they'll bring a good price. Nice of ya to pick up a friend. His horse'll fetch a high price, too. You fellas made it a grand day's work for me, yes, sir."

Harvey dismounted, walking to where Royce's gun lay on the ground. Once out of Harvey's line of sight, Justin snatched the hat from his head and hurled it under the feet of the nervous horse. The startled animal screamed in alarm and reared back, unseating its rider. Royce dove for his gun. Harvey whipped around at the commotion, and Justin slammed into his midsection, causing him to drop his weapon. Justin sat on his chest and back swung his fist to deliver a knock-out blow. The lead rider scrambled out from under his mount and froze. Royce stood over him, the barrel of his gun aimed squarely between the man's eyes.

"Don't move," Royce growled. "Hey, farmer. I got a rope on my saddle; can you bring it over here?"

"On my way."

Justin tied him, while Royce covered him. Harvey had no complaints from where he lay.

"A man at the American Hotel had his horse stolen this morning," began Justin. He nodded towards the skittish steed a few feet away. "I'm betting that's the missing animal."

Royce pushed his hat back on his head. "Horse thieves in possession of stolen goods . . . as well as this attempt. I think we'll take a side trip to turn these boys in. Lincoln's closer than Nicolas—they have a sheriff. He'll get it all straight."

Securing the prisoners, Royce belted out instructions like a man accustomed to giving orders. "I'll lead with the string. We'll go slow with that mare. You watch them from behind for trouble. Okay by you?"

Justin nodded.

Royce gazed at him with respect. "Pretty good reaction for a farmer. What'd you say you were going to do in Sacramento?"

"Look for a job with a big spread."

Royce gave a deep laugh and clapped him on the shoulder. "Justin Albright! You just quit being a farmer and became a ranch hand—if you want. We'll talk after we make our drop at the jail!"

24

CHAPTER 3

Nevada City

Sean's discussions with Empire management bore mixed results. His immediate supervisor, Judd Olmstead, thought it prudent to bring in senior officers. The committee listened to Sean summarize conditions of the mines, as well as his ideas to draw reluctant independents into their fold. Management agreed: the rapidly growing company needed an outlet for men's concerns. Recognizing opportunities to present policies and safety measures on a large scale, they felt representation from Empire was key.

Overall, Empire consented to many of Sean's points, capitalizing on the potential to tap manpower in the area. James was disappointed, yet not surprised, when the committee rejected Sean as the liaison. Thanked for bringing matters to their attention, he was assigned to assist one of their own, Jim Schuester. Judd told Sean privately that his close personal ties to the proposed union chief were viewed as a conflict of interest.

Lodie consoled him. "Look at it this way: you gained their trust for presenting ideas to them directly, and you'll probably overhear more of their strategy because of it."

"Well, Schuester ain't gonna give opinions other than what he's told. I spend half my time answering to a man that's gotta ask me how things get done in the first place. Must be somebody's bloody nephew," grumbled Sean.

With tremendous territory to cover, Sean sent Clancy and a

bevy of couriers carrying notices of union meetings to towns, taverns, and mining camps. Sean's knowledge of far-flung outfits along the ridges flushed out groups of miners nestled deep in sequestered dugouts. Drawing them out proved easy. Fueled by rumors, the uncertainty of working land taken over by Empire created anxiety.

As the appointed day arrived, Nevada City was full to the gunwales. Amused, James witnessed local taverns and merchants revel in this union idea for the business it drew to town. He heard owners of the Silver Moon, Rob and Peter Stuben, toast the event as a long overdue payoff from the mines.

The Methodist Church hosted a standing room only crowd. James observed from the wings as Mayor Lodie Glenn opened with a genial speech. He nodded along as Lodie emphasized this gathering as the beginning of a fraternal organization of support. Concluding discussions, a vote to confirm James as the first union chief would be called. Failing that outcome, nominations for a future election would be taken. Excited shouts, whistles, and applause erupted as James received his introduction.

The rusty-haired Scot strode to the podium; his towering form dwarfed the lectern in front of him. He stood quietly scanning the crowd, his hawkish, green-gray eyes searching for familiar faces, striving to learn new ones. Satisfied with the assemblage, he gave a quick, sharp nod, and his authoritative voice boomed out to envelop the crowd.

"Think of *this* as a forum. Look around ye—at the men ye kin in this room. At the ones ye don't, but . . . look fairly much like ye. *This* group is where ye bring yer concerns. *This* place of brotherhood is safe. *No one* judges ye for matters ye bring here." He paused to absorb the stillness in the room.

"Safety issues, working conditions, compensation for job-related injury or loss—these are significant points. *This* is yer group ta work towards solutions. We present our challenges ta management in an orderly manner." James abandoned the lectern as he spoke, pacing back and forth across the stage, connecting with every part of the room.

"Look where most of us began. We came ta California ta make our fortunes. Opportunity rolled before us like gamblers' dice. Anyone. Anyone at all cu do it with hard work—a new start, in a new land, with no limit ta success. 'Twas a grand idea, for its time!" he thundered.

Whoops and hollers sang out from the crowd. James stopped and smiled, feeling his walk amongst kinsman. His invigorated pacing resumed.

"Those were the days, were they na? Every man free ta follow dreams, reap the benefits of his own sweat, his own ingenuity, and sometimes just dumb luck. But even then," he paused, "it required us ta work together ta bring it about. We worked shoulder ta shoulder, in icy rivers and hollowed out rooms of rock, and we each got our share. Look around . . . at what we've built! Our labor built these towns . . . our toil created businesses and farms . . . our effort established churches and schools. This far, fruitful land lay in wait for us courageous enough ta come and claim it, and we . . . the miners . . . did just that! We revolutionized everything ye see, and each of *us* . . . has been transformed by the land, the growth, and the times. Why must this change be something ta fear?" he challenged.

A shout came from the crowd, " 'Cos someone is holding a deed, and it ain't any of us." Laughter erupted, breaking nervous tension.

"True enough." He cocked his head. "Difficult times lie ahead. Grueling times, for the mining company as it tries ta organize massive holdings. Tougher still ta find enough experienced men. Demanding times are *here,* for the men whose claims have vanished or played out. So . . ."

James held out his hands like a scale attempting to balance.

"Yer choice then is nothing . . . or something . . . and it cu be a sizeable something if ye think a wee bigger." He stopped to regard the faces around the room.

"Lads . . . there's nothin' ta say ye can't ask for something along with yer wages . . . a bit of extra profit for those willing ta put in extra work, or more risk. *Now* is the time for asking. Na when workers are hired from other towns ta take plum jobs, and all rules become set. The owners need ye—*now*. They *need* yer experience; they *need* yer knowledge of the area." He strode across the stage, speaking urgently.

"They *need* ta kin the type of rock and soil and timber ye've dealt with up ta now. They've got experts. But their experts have na worked . . . *here*. Ye have. That's worth something. It's worth time . . . time na wasted chasing wrong solutions. Ye possess something of value. Ye've got knowledge it'll take them time ta accumulate, and time is money. Show them enough ta see *ye hold* their potential profits and ask ta be paid fairly, but accordingly."

Rumblings rolled through the crowd, excitement and hope building in weathered warriors, as James saw they now glimpsed options where none existed before.

"Do na demand," he cautioned. "Ye'll push them back ta their experts. And believe me, most *experts* do na relish getting their hands dirty. They bark orders from the sidelines. Experts cost more, long term, than ye. Once they've voiced whatever technical point they were hired ta make, show the owners ye can take it from there. No need for expensive experts anymore . . . because they have *ye*."

James charged along the front row, pointing to each man individually.

"Each and every one of ye: ye're local, ye're loyal, and ye're damn hard workers. They'll be hard pressed ta find better."

"All right, James," called out Clancy. "Say we get their attention. How do we go about this?"

"Ye organize. Put yerself in teams. Ye have team leaders. Ye can na all be shouting opinions like an unruly mob. Ye pull together, or they'll put their own in charge of ye whether they kin what they're doing or na. Trust each other, as neighbors. Elect team leaders for specific terms. Yer team leaders stay in touch with every team member and their opinion of every situation. Then leaders meet together and present their findings ta the bosses.

"Sean Miller is a foreman; that's an advantage. He knows ye. He can speak for ye with management. Ye elect someone amongst yerselves ta deal with him directly, or ta deal with the man in charge of the operation ye're stationed at."

The men began dialogues and queries amongst themselves, and he could see the buzz in the room charged with a new energy and optimism.

"So, why do *you* want to take this on?" came a call from the back of the room.

"Frankly, I don't." He breathed an exasperated laugh. "But I do na like the idea of a huge and faceless operation moving in and taking over. They're unknown. And they're quietly buying up businesses that affect us all. We need ta stand together."

"What do you want?"

"Me? I want our towns ta grow. I want more towns ta spring up, because this is a profitable area ta live. I want ta see more families. It's good for my business. It's good for everybody's business. There—that's the selfish bit I want."

Lodie stepped up behind him and placed a hand on James's shoulder.

"Men, you have the gist of it. It's a lot to sort through, granted. The decisions I'll ask of you today are twofold. One: are you with us? If so, there's a sign up sheet for membership in the Nevada City Miners' Union. Second: is James here the man to get us started? You each have paper under your seat to write yea or nay, simple as that. It's your future, gents. The more informed we are, the more we stick together, the better chance we all have for success. That's all I have to say."

The level of noise in the room mushroomed as men spoke with neighbors, moved about, asked opinions of one another. Their mood appeared buoyant; choices bloomed before them. Within half an hour, they confirmed James as union chief, and the Nevada City Miners' Union was born.

Their jubilation spilled into the streets, as they headed for taverns to discuss whom amongst them to put forward as team leaders. James and Lodie left the church and found Sean waiting outside with the new Empire representative. The short, red-faced man stood nervously beside Sean awaiting introduction.

"Congratulations on your election as union chief." The man stuck his hand out awkwardly close to James's face. "Jim Schuester, Empire representative. Happy to meet you, sir."

James squinted as he studied him. "And ye, as well."

"I was pleased to see that your topics were more or less positive. The men's welfare is, of course, of great importance to the company."

"I look forward ta meeting yer colleagues, to learn where Empire stands on the men's concerns."

Schuester cleared his throat. "Well . . . of course . . . for the time being anyway, it will be only me. Any questions I cannot answer, I will be happy to check with my supervisors. Everything must be done by the book, you know."

James gave him a measured look. "And what book would that be?"

The man tugged at his collar. "Well . . . not a book per se, but . . . well, I will be sure to let you know what the company wants me to let you know, in as timely a manner as possible."

"I see. I'm certain we'll be seeing a fair bit of each other, Mr. Schuester. Perhaps we can set up a time early next week ta get things started?"

"Of course. As soon as I check with my supervisors, I will let you know. I can send word through Mr. Miller here, if that suits?"

"I eagerly await yer summons."

"Very well. Again, good to meet you, Mr. MacLaren."

Schuester spun about, clumsily bumping into Sean.

"I'll see you back to your buggy, Mr. Schuester," said Sean. He turned back to James with an annoyed look. "I need to give him directions out of town, then I'll meet you at the Grubstake?"

James nodded.

Lodie sniggered behind him. "Directions out of town? How many ways are there?"

James stood with his arms folded, watching them leave. "I do na think I like him very much," he said, frowning.

"Of course not—he's the opposition. Hmmph . . . a good man to get close to though."

James looked at his friend and saw a twinkle in Lodie's eye. "Oh?"

Lodie shrugged. "Sure. I sense he's not but so bright."

James burst out laughing.

Lodie gave him a sideways glance. "Could be useful."

James raced Rusty out of town with a youthful exhilaration he had not felt in ages. The big bay drummed noisily over the wooden bridge, drowning out the rush of Deer Creek and, at James's urging, took the curves and ensuing hills at a pace that belied his years. Fueled by the hope and confidence of the brotherhood of miners, James attacked the road with a fervor. The heady scent of pine air filled his lungs, and he breathed deeply, feeling the release of burdens held too tightly.

Grand it was, to be a part of the working partnership again—even though his cherished Thistle Dew, the grail that drove him across an ocean and a continent, demanded his full attention. From the moment he set foot on the dock in Boston, the grasping hold of his past drifted aft, as if lost in a heavy Scottish mist.

His journey with Lodie began as the family's indentureship to Lord Vernon ended. An instant comradeship sparked with the young farmer from Pennsylvania. Their eleven-month pilgrimage by wagon train afforded them time to forge plans and banter ideas of how to seduce California's golden riches from the ground and stake their frontier empires. James's wife, Emma, and her childhood friend, the widowed Althea Albright, formed deep attachments with Lodie's wife, Matilda.

Once settled in the thriving river town of Marysville, Lodie found Sean Miller, a local miner through and through. Sean's knowledge and experience proved crucial to their start. For a hundred thousand pioneers and immigrants pouring into the state with the same lofty goals, success was fleeting and the pursuit of it, dangerous. Thanks to Sean, slowly and steadily, they banked a modest livelihood. But it wasn't until Vicente Sifuentes selected James as caretaker of his secret that their prosperity soared. James smiled, remembering that the little Mexican seemed to stalk him around town—watching and sizing him up.

They stood leaning against the hitching post in front of Murphy's Tavern. The sun had clearly won its battle over the early morning clouds and warmed their faces as they discussed replenishing provisions. Sean looked past James to see a Mexican man standing a few yards away, waiting patiently to be noticed.

Sean pointed at the man. "You know him?"

James turned. "Aye. Vicente. I bought a lariat from him a

few weeks ago. Does good work. His wife makes a pretty good tamale, she does."

"I think he wants to sell you somethin' else," said Sean as Vicente beckoned to James. *"Maybe you ought to run him off."*

"No harm in seeing what the man has ta barter. As I say, he does good work."

Sean followed closely as James approached the man. *"Good day ta ye, Vicente."*

The man smiled, humbly nodding. *"Buenos días, señor. Come, please . . ."* He backed up slowly until James followed him. He looked over James's shoulder at Sean and frowned. *"Please, only the señor."* Vicente bobbed his head.

Sean shrugged. *"No skin off my nose."*

James followed the Mexican down the street, where the man's donkey stood tethered to the railing. Vicente motioned again. *"Come close . . . please."* James watched him put his hand hesitantly on the saddlebag. Sean observed from a distance.

Vicente looked at James as if summoning his courage. *"I watch."* He pointed at James. *"You, good man. I want to trust."*

James shrugged. *"We've been fair—each ta the other."*

"Sí. I want partner."

"A partner?"

"I need partner."

James smiled kindly. *"What are ye needing a partner for, Vicente?"*

Vicente leaned on the donkey's side, blocking the view from passersby. James inclined his head as the man pulled something out of the saddlebag. His smile vanished. He glanced up the street at Sean with an expression of shock.

Sean wore an anxious frown.

James caught his breath and covered the Mexican's hand with his own larger one. *"I see yer concern."* He rubbed his jaw as he tried to think. *"Vicente"*—he indicated Sean with his head—"Sean is my partner. He, also, is an honest man. I think we may need him."

Vicente looked uncertain. He studied James's face and nodded reluctantly.

James called, trying to keep his voice even. "Sean, could ye come down for a minute."

Sean walked towards them grumbling. "What's he got in there, a severed head or something?"

James stared at him. "Try not ta react," he said and lifted his hand for Sean to see.

"Holy Mother of God!" he cried.

There, shielded by two hands, was the biggest lump of gold Sean had seen in a year.

"Good job not reacting, that. Would ye keep it down?"

Sean glanced around quickly. He smacked his head in disbelief.

"Remind me never ta count on ye if I decide ta rob a bank," muttered James. "Vicente, this is Sean. He'll be fine once he's located his wits."

"I think we need to move off the street to discuss this," said Sean.

"Ah, there, he's found them," said James. "I agree. Where can we go?"

"How 'bout we walk slowly out of town?"

"Is this all right with ye, Vicente? Say, have ye got another lariat?"

Vicente nodded, nervously.

"Perhaps ye should give it ta me as if I'm buying it, then, if anyone is watching, they'll see that we're conducting other business."

Vicente nodded, slipped the gold back in the bag, and pulled out a lariat. He unlashed the tether, and they led the donkey down the street.

34

James spoke in a low voice. "Do ye need help cashing something that size in? Is that it?"

"No, señor, there is more."

"Sean, stop lookin' wildly round like a gunfighter has got ye in his sights! Keep yer head about ye, man." He turned back to Vicente. "More? More like that?"

"Sí. I can do nothing with it. The tax . . ."

"Tax? What's he talking about?"

Recognition sprang into Sean's face. "Oh, the Foreign Miner's Tax."

"Sí, sí, sí!" Vicente nodded quickly.

"Folks got afraid they'd lose out on the best claims with so many Chinese and Mexicans filing. So, they started the Foreign Miner's Tax to drive 'em out. It's steep—twenty dollars a month. Most of 'em couldn't afford to pay and survive, so they left. The ones that stay get harassed from the other miners to prove they've paid."

"Mí familia . . . I send them back home. Too hard. It is not safe for them."

"That's why I have na seen yer wife around?"

He nodded. "I want to make my money. I need to make lots of money; then I send for them. There are many bad men, señor. They would take what I have found."

"You got a claim, then?" asked Sean.

Vicente shook his head. "The bad men, they would kill me and take it from me. And if I pay the tax, they know I have claim, and they kill and take." He pointed to the two of them. "We be partners. I can show you."

James looked to Sean, dumbfounded.

"Vicente. We have one more partner . . ."

He shrugged. "I see him, too, the smiling one. You trust, I trust."

Sean blew out a big breath of air. "I gotta hand it to you,

Vicente. You got huevos."

"*We have a lotta work out here. Ye need ta meet Lodie, and we don't want ta call too much attention ta ourselves meeting in the open.*" *James's face lit up.* "*What if ye come with us ta our claim? We'll make it look as if yer working with us, like we've hired ye on as a laborer. No one'll be suspicious of our spending time together.*"

Vicente grinned. "*I like this idea. It is safe for me.*"

"*It's good,*" *Sean agreed.*

"*Meet us Sunday evening at the boarding house, and we'll all ride out together. Is this good?*"

Vicente grabbed James's hand and pumped it vigorously, "*Muchas gracias. Sí, is good.*"

A decade ago, their four histories forged a kinship, an assimilation of cultures and ideals. Each sought a different ending to their glittering tale. No matter what squabbles arose amongst them, they possessed an ironclad bond—a common vision for themselves as men, despite individual goals.

James marveled at Lodie's uncanny cognizance, his ability to swiftly recognize trends, sum up opportunity, and act upon it. He had a bit of the gambler in him, abandoning his heritage to farm in order to leap headlong into the mercantile trade. As Nevada City's new mayor, Lodie clucked over his flock. Since he always seemed one step ahead of the crowd, many sought his advice.

Sean, on the other hand, proved an all or nothing sort—he led with his heart, jumped in the fray with both feet, and didn't look up from a task until it was conquered. Honed by years of experience, his tactical mastery as a miner was renowned. Yet, he suppressed an on-again, off-again battle with the bottle and the gaming tables, as well as his relationship with Althea. Currently, he was winning on all fronts.

Often overlooked as a simple peasant, Vicente possessed an

acuity that astounded James. Perhaps, he was the best of them all. As father of five, his paternal aura, patience, and quiet humor grounded them. He alone had held the key to their fortunes, the foundation to their current businesses. His fight to win a place in this new world, fraught with violence, mirrored James's own.

With this notion, James's attention drifted to the uncertainties of Coleridge Sierra. His exuberance from the union meeting cooled, as he settled Rusty into a more moderate stride. A passing cloud dimmed the brilliance on his horizon, so his thoughts turned moody.

He felt it, the general confusion. Unanswered questions usually meant something unseen, unexpected, and underhanded. And one only had to look up the ranks of privilege to find the source. Yes . . . there was a dragon in their village, as his grandfather would have said. Its size, intention, yet unknown. He had never heard of a benevolent dragon anymore than he had a generous king. His ancestors lived under the yoke of the rich, the powerful—his own experiences notwithstanding. The watchdog in his soul bayed a danger approaching.

Moving at a slow trot, James left the main road and followed the meandering lane of Thistle Dew. He needed to sort through the perplexities facing the miners, and he did not wish to carry the burden of it home to his haven. Growing gloomy, he knew his heaviness of heart was due to the gaping hole left by Justin's absence. Equipped with supplies for the tack room, he dreaded facing its disarray—another testament to Justin's quick departure. Far too soon, the boy he helped raise became a man. Justin had snatched the reins of his own life.

James nudged Rusty over to the white picket fence at the top of the hill. Sunset roses of pink, yellow, and coral were budding nicely around the perimeter of Emma's grave. Normally, he liked to visit her early in the morning before anyone awoke, when the mist of the earth emerged as the sun warmed the ground.

"Hello, luv," he murmured.

The view from here lifted his spirits as he surveyed the layout of the farm. He had created a large quadrangle, loosely closed in by the house, Althea's little cabin, two large barns, and a tack shed next to the corral. From this vista, he observed his small group of Percherons—he proudly traced his prime stud back to Louis Napoleon 281. A peace fell over him as he regarded the noble giants, a cluster of grays and blacks, clean-limbed and powerful, grazing in verdant pasture. Below the meadow, he saw his daughter leading a recently acquired black Morgan mare from one of the two training rings—a good match for Charlotte if she would ever consider a horse other than Banshee. He sighed, knowing he must face the chaotic jumble of equipment strewn about the tack shed.

Charlotte disappeared into the barn with her charge as he advanced down the lane. He lashed Rusty's reins loosely over a post, dismounted, and fished two bottles of liniment and a new curry comb from his bag. He frowned, seeing she had forgotten to latch the tack door. He pushed it open, stepped inside, and froze.

He gazed about the room in wonder. Shelves straightened, neat rows of halters, bridles, heavy harnesses, leads, and lariats, all hung in order along the back wall. A strong scent of leather greeted him as he noted saddles—cleaned, conditioned, and racked.

"I took an inventory as well."

James turned, shaking his head. "I can na begin ta tell ye . . ."

She smiled, her green-gray eyes acknowledging all that he felt in their softness.

"I miss him, too. Silly, but I felt closer to him, doing his chores."

"Well, for me, 'twould ha been opposite."

She smirked. "I know."

He scanned the nearest shelf for content before placing his purchases. "I best put these in the proper place, ta be sure. Nice ta ha a system again." He studied her face. "Did it help? His chores, I mean?"

She shrugged. "I feel like I lost half of myself. Justin's been at my side since I learned to walk."

"Understood. Imagine how Althea feels."

She did not answer for a long while. She glanced hesitantly at the floor, then her gaze shot up to lock eyes with his. "Da, *why* did she not tell him the truth about his father sooner?"

"Och. I'm sure now, she wishes she had. 'Twas bound ta be a shock, no matter. Ye have ta know, it was a life ye'll never understand living here. Stations in life, ye cu never hope ta attain because of yer birth. I do na blame her, in her foolish youth. She let her heart rule her head. She knew better, but she fell in love. He was na worthy of it. With a new beginning in America, it was preferable ta be a widow with a drowned husband."

"I'm sorry. I don't mean to drag up old baggage. It's just . . . I feel . . . off. It's odd, not to have him here for balance. Not that I asked his opinion, necessarily, but he freely gave it, anyway. Sometimes, I think he knows me better than I know myself."

James chuckled. "Ye gave as good as ye got."

"Yes, but I don't think he misses it from me."

"Men rarely do, darlin'." He tugged her into a bear hug. "Leastways, we *never* admit it. Come, now. What ha ye prepared for my supper?"

"Althea's cooking tonight."

"Ah, even better."

"Hey! That was a very Justin thing to say."

"I know; I try ta fill the gap. Why don't ye run inside ta help,

Kalen Vaughan Johnson

while I rub Rusty down?"

She pecked his cheek and turned for the house. He beamed, watching her go. That girl made all seem right with the world.

CHAPTER 4

Nevada City

The creaky sway of the wagon emblazoned with "Thistle Dew" on its sides lulled its three occupants into a reverie of their own thoughts. James navigated his team up Boulder Hill, following the road's rising twists and turns, and down again to meet the twin wooden bridges crossing Deer Creek. The sprawling vista of Nevada City's entryway never failed to spark optimism in his heart. The seven hills upon which the town was built displayed a queue of prosperous gold-fed businesses lining ascending streets and crowned at the top by Sugar Loaf Mountain. He crossed the gurgling rush of the creek, choosing the bridge on the right to the primary thoroughfare of Main Street, and was met by the heady scent of flowering fruit trees planted at regular intervals along the avenues.

Althea raised her chin skyward, allowing the sun's brief kiss to slip beneath the broad brim of her hat. The street was pleasant today. Last evening's rain had settled the dirt, abating the usual swarms of dust. Residents armed with marketing baskets strolled the timber walkways, enjoying the cool of morning.

As James halted the team in front of the post office, Althea declared, "I feel quite special being squired about so."

James looked into the bonny face of his oldest friend, unable to contain his delight at the rosy glow returning to her cheeks. "As well ye should. As long as I've union business in town, there's no reason my lovely ladies should lack an escort. I'm

41

glad ye're well enough ta get about."

Charlotte climbed down from the back row and hopped to the ground. "It's just the one package?"

"Yes, thank you, dear. It should be the new silk we've been waiting on from San Francisco." Althea watched Charlotte stroll inside and turned back to James. "I'm well, though not strong enough to rid myself of this silly walking stick. Normally, I'd welcome a brisk turn down the street. I'm afraid that hill is more than I can manage just yet."

"It'll come in time. For now, door ta door service, m'lady."

He made a swooping gesture with his hand, tumbling from his brow, to finish a mock bow. She laughed at him. They gazed at one another contentedly for a number of moments until she broke the bond by looking down. Weeks of tender care drew them even closer; he hoped not awkwardly so. She plucked at the fabric of her skirt. He decided on the safety of a popular topic.

"I hear wedding plans are resuming; that's good news. Sean is over the moon."

She did not look up but stated quietly, "Yes. Now that I'm better, we're speaking of it. Although Sean is quite consumed with his job and the union." She peeped up at him and teased, "I blame you for that."

He sat back abruptly. "Me? Och, blame Lodie! He's dragged us both inta this."

Charlotte rushed out of the post office with a bundle tucked under one arm and waving an envelope in her hand.

"Look!" She beamed. "A letter from Justin!"

He smiled, "And ye've torn inta it, already? Good tidings?"

"He has a job."

"Indeed. Whereabouts, my lovely?"

"Not far out of Sacramento. The Collier Ranch, he says. Maybe you can see him on your next trip to the horse market!"

James tilted his head. "Let's give him a chance ta settle in, shall we? Might not impress his new boss if I go checking up on the lad. Justin's his own man now."

Charlotte looked disappointed. James glanced at Althea.

Althea patted Charlotte's hand, "He's right, dear. But, I do think the next excursion warrants shopping in Sacramento. Then we can all go and say hello."

She brightened. "That's a wonderful idea." She buried her head in the letter, scanning for details.

James clucked to the horses and prompted a cut-through to Broad Street. "On ta yer dress shop before I'm late ta meet yer future husband."

Had he taken the left bridge over Deer Creek at the town's entrance, they would have passed the stately Nevada City Hotel, the Silver Moon Tavern, and Lodie Glenn's Emporium. Advancing up the thoroughfare was City Hall, the Nevada Theatre, Fire House Number Two, and the Methodist Church.

The team jingled in their traces as they labored up the hill to upper East Broad Street. James stopped in front of Althea's shop, secured the hand brake, and walked around the wagon to help the ladies down. When he turned, he caught sight of Lodie waiting on the porch. He noted the big man's grim expression. James frowned as Lodie spit out distressing details.

"I came to buy some white thread off you," he said, looking at Althea. "My suppliers are behind. When I got here . . ." He held up two objects—a hastily scrawled note and a rusty penknife. "I found this stuck in your door."

"What is it?"

"A threat." He handed the note to James. "Damn it, I knew we weren't done with that accident business."

James's jaw tightened. He looked around the streets and muttered, "Let's go inside."

He helped Althea to a chair and reread the note as Charlotte sat down beside her. He looked at Lodie. The women stared until Charlotte blurted out, "But what does it say?"

He read aloud, *"Keep yer mouth shut. I took care of ye, so ye know I mean business. Tell Miller and MacLaren don't cause no problems with this union. Next time I come for yer children."*

He shook his head. "This does na make sense. We had na started the union when ye were hit . . . at least no one knew we spoke of it."

Althea looked frightened. "They think I saw something to do with . . . what? Empire or this Coleridge Sierra?"

James's voice grew terse. "What *is it* they want? Or do na want? And who the hell is this bugger skulking about?"

They turned in unison as the bells on the door announced Sean's arrival.

"Hey! Saw your wagon out front. Wanna hear something odd?" He stopped short as he noted gloom on their faces. "What's wrong?"

James handed him the note; Lodie said, "Stuck to her door."

Sean's mouth fell open. "We gotta take this to Sheriff Shaw. Somebody's nervous about the town gettin' a say in who owns it." He nodded at the women. "What do we do to protect them?"

"Whoever it is is unaware Justin has gone." James stiffened. "I think it best ye both go, too. Until this blows over."

"Da, we can't leave you! Where would we go?"

"Maybe Sacramento for a time; be near Justin. Ye'd both like that."

Charlotte and Althea looked at one another, quietly considering.

Lodie broke the silence. "What *else* is odd, Sean?"

"I just came from Ott's assay office. He told me old man Hollister quit. Retired and moved out—gone from Nevada City."

Lodie huffed, "He's been in that assay office since they opened. Where'd he go? Why?"

"Some cabin he's got up in the mountains. Once he heard Althea was targeted, he spooked. Said this town was gettin' too dangerous."

CHAPTER 5

Sacramento

A tap. He swept the hat in hand alongside drab angola trousers, past the tailored frock coat, and gave it a resolute pat upon his dark head. Eyes, black as obsidian and even less revealing, peered out from beneath its stiff silk brim. A swift scan of I Street verified slim prospects of a chance encounter with anyone from his circle here in the Yee Fow enclave.

Dutton Dandridge set his sites on the Ah Loy cigar store—a more respectable location than where he now stood. He walked briskly through the horde of sons of Guangdong Province, assailed by smells of exotic spice and the sudden heavy scent of opium. He passed the chatter of gambling houses and the singsong of vegetable peddlers hawking their wares amidst the rambling hodgepodge of restaurants, laundrymen, butchers, and drugstores. Reaching his destination, he stepped inside and made a quick purchase of Ah Loy's finest cigars, muttering his thanks in Cantonese. Leaving, he turned sharply on 4th Street.

He worked his way through the backstreets of Chinatown with the confidence of a tiger gliding through an open field, cowing to no one. The Dandridges conducted business in all parts of town; no echelon of society was overlooked. Contacts were everything; his father, Judge Walter Dandridge, was one of the first and foremost names in the state.

As one of the authors of California's constitution, Judge Dandridge assisted the push to statehood. His iron hand in the courtroom thrust a backwoods frontier to the forefront of civilization. His influence from the bench was key to elimination of the Sydney Ducks and the Hounds, as well as the restraint of vigilance committees, governors of varying degrees of competence and sobriety, and the unruly Legislature of a 1000 Drinks.

Dutton's father cultivated alliances with tough, like-minded pioneers such as Garth Collier and political paragons like Leland Stanford to regain control of a ruffian terrain besotted with gold lust. When necessary, he negotiated in the shadows with powerful, sometimes less popular men—his unseen ties to Sam Brannan going back some fifteen years. Diplomacy and discretion advanced California to a more legitimate government, less dependent on brute force. Tolliver, a former Hound in his father's employ, was one of the few throwbacks to that more chaotic time.

As a gang member, Tolliver served as the judge's informant, scavenging tidbits and snitching on perpetrators of violent crimes. An ex-thief, his crime was distinctly marked for all to see—his earlobes cut up as a warning to others. Early vigilante justice decreed first offense robbers were whipped, second offenders had their earlobes cut like a bad horse, and third offenders were simply hung. A reformed man such as Tolliver proved useful.

Since his retirement as a magistrate, the judge handled unresolved issues with a more delicate pressure, a finesse backed more or less by law. His father had watched every noteworthy businessman and politician rise . . . knew their humble beginnings, their promise, and their weaknesses. Knowledge commanded allegiance. Dutton had a unique way of pulling tandem with strengths so long as the direction suited him. His schooling in such tactics began at an early age.

With the B. F. Hastings building on J Street now clearly in

view, and the populace surrounding him dressed in a more stylishly cosmopolitan fashion, Dutton slowed his pace. His thoughts volleyed from the sophisticated pleasures of Madame Mei Mei's that he left behind as he began to focus on business. He believed his particular penchant for all things Asian, celestial cravings so to speak, stimulated his mind. He allowed himself one last sardonic smile as he transitioned to contemplation of weightier matters.

Stepping under the corner awning of the Dandridge offices, he straightened, then tipped his hat as he recognized the Honorable Stephen Johnson Field. The prestigious Hastings building also housed the members of the Supreme Court and Wells Fargo & Company. He entered, taking the stairs to the second floor two at a time.

He nodded curtly to the secretary, Sadie, in the visitors' area of their lavishly appointed suites, removing his hat and frock coat as he passed through the corridor to his office. Across the hall, the judge's quarters were open, but empty. Expansion in investments, and a keen eye on the stock exchange, had required his father to remain in their San Francisco domain, a development not entirely disappointing to Dutton.

He hung his discarded attire on the coatrack and filled the handsome mahogany humidor on his desk with Ah Loy's finest. With a tug on his waistcoat, he settled in the tall leather chair to dive into the stack of correspondence Sadie had delivered.

Before long, Dutton heard annoyingly cheerful whistling from the hallway, announcing Neil Collier's arrival. He glanced up from his desk to see that his friend's unusual attire belied his status. Wearing a week's growth of beard and worn-out overalls, Neil had probably earned countless stares when he entered the architecturally elegant building. Neil rapped on the frame of his open door, much to the disdain of the secretary.

"Nice outfit," Dutton commented drily. "Remind me to send

over a wardrobe consultant for all public appearances. Is there a point to this?"

"There is, indeed. I return from a reconnaissance mission," he stated with flourish. "And thank you, I will have a seat."

Dutton fanned his arm towards the chair Neil already sat in. "Do tell."

"Nevada City, my friend. Just sat in on the first meeting of the Nevada City Miners Union."

Dutton leaned forward with interest. "A spy in their midst. Neil. You have skills I never dreamed of."

Neil laughed. "Oh, nothing as sinister as all that. As long as we have interests in Empire mines, I want to know what their thinking is on the local level."

"Hmm. Generally I'm not in favor of unions. However, I don't care for angry mobs, either. I suppose it is the civilized way to keep a pot from boiling over." He sighed. "So let's have the bad news."

Neil considered his response. "I must say, overall, I found it encouraging. I think miners organizing themselves leads to better communication and efficiency."

"Neil, seriously . . ." Dutton began in a snide tone. "What value is communication with men barely able to think beyond what they're having for dinner? These men don't ponder the future. They plod along, they work like mules with blinders on, and they live out their meager existence. They have no place in a decision-making process. They work; we pay them—that's it."

"Those are my future constituents, you're speaking of," Neil responded, frowning. "I think you've been behind a desk too long. These men have families. They *do* think of the future. They worry about it. You don't give them near enough credit for their experience, when at the same time we pay *experts* to come up with theories. I heard a number of men speak yesterday, and I was impressed. We'd do well to have our management listen to their ideas."

Dutton tried to respond in a conciliatory manner. "Isn't it better to move in and set up our framework as we see fit from the beginning, with no interference?"

"Many of them adjusted to a new order of life here. Some are just now coming out of the hills and giving up on their old claims." Neil uttered a wary chuckle. "You well know, Royce is still uncomfortable with how hastily Coleridge Sierra acquired those independent mines. Frankly, we need the manpower. If we dictate absolutely everything, as if they *are* only mules, there *will be* fights and delays. So far, they're looking to be fair. We can work with these ideas. Without opposition."

Dutton hesitated. "They won't be our people in place."

"They will *become* our people. And, politically, that's gold, don't you see? We'll *save* jobs, save communities. We'll take a failing mining operation and make it a success. Dutton, we need this as a shining example of a *promise kept*—of the kind of leadership we can bring. I've got a lot of stumping to do next week along San Juan Ridge. This is my platform."

Dutton's smile grew slowly at the potential of Neil's idea. "The intangibles could be worth as much as the mining project itself."

"Yes!"

"All right, you've sold me. Political capital like that is hard to manufacture. How do they want to proceed?"

"They've elected a union chief. From what I hear, the man's a hell of a blaster, a resident expert of sorts—made a decent enough claim a few years back but is more engaged with his horse farm these days."

"So what's he doing as union chief?"

"Popular choice—doesn't have a personal stake at the moment and knows what it's like to be in the trenches. Fair minded chap, looks after his neighbors, member of the Odd Fellows

Lodge—they trust him. He's organizing them in teams so their leaders meet with our management."

"Sounds reasonable." Dutton shrugged.

Neil relaxed. "I'm telling you—the union chief is impressive. This guy can move those people and save us a bundle in the end. Where we encounter opposition—he motivates. He's showing them a compromise we could not hope to create."

"Then, he's the man we want to be *our* people."

CHAPTER 6

The Collier Ranch

On the slow trek back from Lincoln, Royce schooled Justin on
operations at the sprawling Collier ranch. On approach, they
rode past lush and well-tended Collier orchards showcasing the
road to the main house. In addition, the Colliers owned
timberland, a sawmill, and promoted a valley dam project. The
family's largest enterprise, and Royce's biggest passion, was
cattle.

Other than irritating the black bull in Ella Louise's barn,
Justin knew little about handling cattle. Royce hired him as a
wrangler. As he settled in to his bovine surroundings, his skill
set in the saddle prompted his new boss's confidence in him to
surge. Demand for trained stock fed all aspects of ranch work,
and Royce intended to put him in charge of remuda on the
drive to market.

Justin's frustrating first attempts at roundup amused his new
bunkmates. He amiably succumbed to their ribbing for his lack
of prowess. Studying their cutting horses in action educated
him to the demands of their mounts. He tendered suggestions
to alter bad habits or offered to school the animals himself. He
developed an easy rapport with the crew, seeking to learn as
much as he coached, making his adjustment into their midst an
easy one.

His peers eagerly lined the corral fence to watch Justin's
proficiency in breaking stock. His awareness of each animal's

distinct characteristics of movement convinced some of the superstitious hands that he possessed mystic qualities. His mastery on a bucking bronc proved an arresting spectacle.

Justin's dependability captured Royce's regard. His imperturbable manner complemented Royce's volatile demeanor, and they became friendly. Justin admired his boss's decisiveness—Royce commanded respect and earned it. Wary of pushing boundaries, he attended Royce as a subordinate at all times, remembering James's admonishment to heed the wealthy with skepticism.

Royce's carriage was proud. Justin noted the long, deliberate strides of a man born with assurance and advantage. Royce may have fought the impression that ascendancy was handed to him, but he couldn't hide his noble air; the tilt of his head and the jut of his jaw displayed strength. His intense gaze appeared haughty.

Justin remained mindful of his own humble place. Where James advised caution with powerful men, Justin's steady, sensible way invited their trust. He knew loyalty was required; of fellowship he remained guarded. Still, he honestly *liked* the man.

Occasionally, he approached the main house to relay messages. The elegant home boasted prestige. The enormous, ten-foot, oak door was flanked by a set of double Corinthian pillars, their massively carved acanthus leaves rolled lushly over the tops. A deep, lead-glass transom was set over the front door. The entrance seemed to reflect the permanence of the family within.

Though Royce controlled the running of the estate, it hardly seemed the type of house that fit his persona. Garth and Eugenia built the home as their social status had risen. Since their deaths, Royce lived there with his older brother, Neil, and younger sister, Celeste.

Justin met Neil only once, a pleasant enough fellow. He dressed elegantly but put on no discernable airs. Justin understood him to be a businessman, running the estate's financial holdings, as well as an up and coming politician. He recently became engaged to Beth Payne, the daughter of a local railroad tycoon.

The younger sister, Celeste, he often saw flouncing around the stables appearing just as silly as Charlotte's friends at the same age. He had survived this ridiculous stage with girls before. He addressed her politely and chose to ignore her antics. Ranch hands reported she looked down her perky nose at those she deemed beneath her class, describing her as pampered, spoiled, and overprotected by her brothers. In contrast the oldest sister, Adele, was viewed as caring and compassionate. She had married a respected doctor and lived nearby.

Justin related his new life in great detail in letters to Charlotte, demonstrating contentment with his circumstances. She responded that she envied his freedom to test his mettle.

Today's tasks included breaking new stock. Royce had procured a few prizes in this bunch and was eager to oversee the process. Breaking from his usual pounding in the saddle, Justin manned the corral, helping a ranch hand to get set. Out of the corner of his eye, he saw Celeste approaching.

Royce and crew leaned on the fence, watching. Justin stepped back, and the black horse Wily sat took off. The young mare stamped, plunged, and bucked in frustration at the weight on her back.

"Hang with her, Wily!" shouted Royce.

Celeste waited patiently during the few short turns around the ring until the rider was felled.

"Oohhh." Royce pulled a face as Wily landed with a thud, and Justin grabbed control of the agitated mare.

"What's up, Little Bit?" Royce turned to her.

"I didn't think you saw me," she said pulling a telegraph message out of her belt. "It's for Justin. It came to the house a little while ago."

"Justin!" he bellowed.

Justin handed the mare off to the next rider, dabbing at the sweat on his face with his neckerchief as he walked over. Royce handed him the envelope. "Came a few minutes ago."

"Obliged." He nodded to Celeste. She looked particularly jaunty today. The sun glinted off her hair, giving her a warm glow; her mass of red-gold curls rested on her right shoulder. The light blue of her blouse accentuated the brightness of her eyes. His admiration of Celeste, however slight, came abruptly to a halt as he read the contents of the telegraph wire.

Royce and Celeste chatted mindlessly until Justin felt her eyes upon him.

"What's wrong?" she queried.

Justin looked up at Royce.

"It's from my mother."

"Bad news?" asked Royce.

"Trouble in Nevada City. My . . . sister." He hesitated, unaccustomed to explaining his family relationships. "I need to help my sister settle in Sacramento for a while until the danger blows over."

The stage was half an hour late. Justin stood on the platform holding his hat by the brim, mindlessly rotating it in his hands. The California Stage Company's office on the corner of K and Front Streets offered him the distraction of a pleasant view of boats on the opposite landing at the Steam Navigation Company. An agreeable breeze wafted off the water, alleviating the dry afternoon heat.

He turned, hearing the rumble and thunder of the team of six approaching. He craned his neck for a look at the passengers, but the oiled leather curtains remained rolled down to keep out the dust. The stagecoach rocked to a halt as the driver slammed the brake lever with his foot.

Justin stepped up to open the carriage door and offered his hand to an unfamiliar woman as she emerged. He grinned as he recognized the white-blonde head appearing next in the doorway. Lodie chuckled. "Ah, the greeting committee is here!" He stepped down and vigorously pumped Justin's hand. "Good to see you, lad. You look well!"

Lodie turned to assist Charlotte, but the second her foot hit the railing she sprang out to embrace Justin. She laughed in his ear and exclaimed, "It seems like ages!"

Justin hugged her, glancing up at the last passenger to descend. As he set Charlotte down, he looked at them both. "I suppose there was no convincing Mother to come after all?"

Lodie shook his head. "Of course not; she's a stubborn woman. As much as the thought of seeing you tempted her, she refused to leave the business after missing so much work while she recovered."

Justin frowned. "Is she safe?"

"It appears so." He lowered his voice. "She doesn't believe the current threat pertains to her. Sean and James will keep close. Ah . . ."

Lodie turned to catch Charlotte's bags as the driver tossed them over the roof railings of the coach. "Where are we taking these?"

Justin pointed away from the waterfront. "A few blocks, at Mrs. White's boardinghouse. I borrowed a carriage. My boss's sister arranged for Charlotte to stay there—it's only for women and apparently difficult to get a placement there."

Charlotte stood shielding her eyes from the sun as she scanned the activity on the streets. The small, fashionable hat she had chosen to travel in offered little in the way of shade.

"Well, I'm very grateful for that. I hope to thank her in person."

"You'll get the chance; they've invited us to Sunday dinner after church tomorrow."

"Wonderful! I'll get to see where you work!"

"Lodie, you're invited as well . . .'"

"I'm afraid this is a quick turnabout for me. I have a meeting with a supplier this afternoon, and I'm heading back on the evening stage. I'm just glad it worked out to accompany Charlotte." He picked up a small leather valise and tucked a silver-headed cane under his arm.

"Da will make a trip to check on me soon when he visits the horse market. Perhaps by then I can go home with him."

Lodie smiled fondly at the pair. "My dear, I leave you in the best of hands. I must be off."

Charlotte gave him a quick good-bye peck on the cheek. As they watched him walk away Justin asked, "When did he start carrying a cane?"

"I asked him about that myself. It belonged to his father—an interesting piece. Did you see the beautifully detailed wolf's head on it? He says now that he's at an age to be considered distinguished, he likes to carry it to important meetings and such."

Justin shrugged. "Are you tired? We can go straight to the boardinghouse if you like."

"No, this is a marvelous adventure!" Charlotte turned around from the waterfront to look down both ends of Front Street. "Give me a tour!"

Justin placed her two bags in the back of the carriage, and they strolled the waterfront, the train and freight depots, and toured the massive hardware store of Huntington and Hopkins. They gazed at storefront windows as they wandered and talked of events in Nevada City. Justin filled her in on ranch life. Exiting John Bruener's furniture warerooms, Justin listened to her prattle on—amazed at the colossal variety of household goods. He caught sight of a pair of men standing a short distance away and realized at once it was Royce Collier and his friend Carl Budleigh.

When Charlotte stepped out from under the shade of the building, he saw Carl remove his boot from its resting place on the rail and straighten up. He heard him exclaim, "Whoa, new looker in town!" The man nudged Royce and pointed in their direction, "Hey—ain't he your hand? That's some girl he's got there."

Justin glanced back at Charlotte and realized, thankfully, she had not overheard. He looked at her, seeing how the light hit her dark hair, highlighting glints of copper and gold running through it like finely polished mahogany. Her eyes were large and so bright—their color the same greenish gray as river water just under a sheet of ice on a sunny day. A thick fringe of dark lashes contrasted sharply with her porcelain skin. And, lastly, her slender, graceful form showed enough curves to catch a man's eye. He realized the burden that was upon him.

He saw Royce turn and study them before saying, "Yeah, we're sort of expecting her. I'll see ya, Carl." Royce walked away without a backward glance and waved at Justin, calling out, "Hey, Justin! Hold up a minute!"

Justin muttered, "Well, brace yourself."

Charlotte followed his gaze, again raising her hand as a shield from the sun. "For what? Who is that man?"

"That's the boss. Probably just wants to say hello."

"Boss, huh? That explains the swagger."

"Shush; you'll get my pay docked. Be nice." He spoke softly, as Royce's long legged strides closed the gap.

"Justin!" He smiled at Charlotte while speaking to Justin. "I'm glad to see your guest arrived safely."

Justin decided to play it lightly. "The stage was late. I would have blamed it on her packing, but she's usually pretty efficient."

"Oh?" said Royce joking, "Maybe she could teach that trick to my sisters. We can't get anywhere in any kind of time."

"I would appreciate it," Charlotte said, feigning annoyance, "if you two gentlemen would stop talking above my head."

"Oh . . . did I forget to introduce you?" her brother teased. Charlotte rolled her eyes.

"Royce Collier, may I present Miss Charlotte MacLaren."

Royce took her hand with a little bow. "My apologies, dear lady." As he raised his head, he looked full into her face. Justin saw him pause, unsettled. Recovering, he continued, "I hope you'll find our city to your liking, Miss MacLaren."

"It's wonderful, and so big! We've only seen a portion of it so far." She regarded him politely. "I understand your sister graciously arranged for my lodging. I'm very grateful."

"She was glad to do it. We think pretty highly of Justin, here." He eyed Justin. "I should leave the two of you to catch up. We look forward to seeing you tomorrow after church?"

"Absolutely. I'm staying at a hotel tonight to help her get settled, and I'll drive us out right after church."

"We'll probably see you at the service," said Royce. "Good day, Miss MacLaren. See you tomorrow, Justin."

"Sure thing, Boss."

Royce tipped his hat as he left. Charlotte nodded and watched him cross the street. "Likes to be charming, doesn't he?"

"When he's not giving orders," laughed Justin. "What, you didn't like him?"

"Oh, no . . . I don't know him well enough to say. Seems to like being important though, pretty 'full of his own'," she said plainly.

"Now how can you say that?"

"Intuition. Things you've said in your letters." She gave him a playful push. "Don't worry. If you buy me a nice dinner, I won't

59

cost you your job."

"Thanks," he said flatly. "Let's get you settled at Mrs. White's, then we'll find dinner."

CHAPTER 7

The Empire Mine

Sean rolled the handle of the huge cylinder with both hands until he reached the chart section displaying the tunnel he searched for. The metal axis screeched to a halt. Smoothing the heavy parchment and anchoring it into place over the flat map table, he pushed his sleeves up over his burly forearms and leaned against the table's edge to study it.

"There's a wonder ta behold. He *looks* like he's working!"

"Eh . . ." Vicente wavered his hand in a so-so gesture. "You know peoples say . . . busiest chicken in the barnyard . . . the one with his head cut off."

He scowled with his good eye at the mismatched pair. The tall, rusty-haired Scot stood in the doorway of the stone map room with the short, mustached Mexican.

"And you're late, MacLaren! Don't speak well of a man looking for work," Sean jibed.

James grinned. "I believe 'twas you asking for my help."

"Vicente, you ol' son-of-a-gun . . . haven't seen you in ages. You don't poke your head outta that saddle shop often enough."

"Is why I come! Has been since French Corral that we work together, no?"

Sean punched Vicente's arm affectionately. "Yeah, our days working hydraulics. The drought slowed that action down for a while. Now all the talk's about building bigger heads. Forget hoses and nozzles; giant monitors is what they're making—look

61

like cannons, with about the same amount of force. Seems like every new-fangled idea requires fewer men to run an operation. Even you eventually ran off and left me to my lonesome. Couldn't make real miners of none of you."

Vicente shrugged. "Lodie stop selling leather goods at his emporium . . . he make people try *my* shop. They learn to trust Mexican. The business grows, the children grow . . . But I like to learn, see new things with big mine here. We all still partners . . . many ways."

James glanced around the stone walls and up at the tin-roofed rafters. "Awhile since I've been up here. Then 'twas only a lonely office shanty with a hole of a shaft in the ground across the way. Ye look like a proper village. We saw Judd Olmstead outside. He had ta tell us which building ta find ye in."

"Come have a look at this map section—it'll give you an idea of where I'm taking you for the blasting. You'll get your bearings, then we'll tour around a bit."

Vicente stood slightly back, his thumbs hooked on his belt loops, observing while Sean and James huddled at the center of the map table. Sean traced their destination on the chart with his fingertip.

"Got a winze, about fifty feet deep, leading from a productive level to one we hope to get to. Had some problems with water at the end of the shaft that we've taken care of with the help of Cornish pumps—no problem as the passage starts the incline at the crosscut. What I need here"—Sean dragged his finger to a less defined area where the pathway ended and appeared to pick up again in a fork some distance away—"is a series of smaller charges requiring a delicate hand—which is why we've called you. Any bloke can blow stuff to holy hell. I'd like to send a coupla men with you, to learn the precision of such an operation. Some of 'em know basic drill patterns for black powder."

"Should na be a problem. I can teach how ta modify for intricate work, both the amount of powder and the number and pattern changes of the holes. Though drilling in *that* particular rock face, it's more important ta get the blasting holes in the correct order for firing."

Vicente stepped closer. "I help." He grinned. "I fit better to drill the *bottom* holes."

"You that eager to turn your fingernails black again? Besides, I'll be around if James needs me."

"Tunnels are dark. Better for me."

Sean flipped up his eye patch. "You sayin' I got a problem?"

"Your memory as big as your huevos, but you still have only one eye. You no need to lose a hand, too."

Sean smirked. "I'm joshin' you. I 'spect my bride-to-be would appreciate it if I don't lose no more body parts."

"Is all I am saying. She a patient woman, but . . . you not get any prettier."

"That's a fact!" He stroked his long horseshoe mustache and wriggled his brow. "Still got my charms, though."

James chuckled. "Feels like old times. Vicente, I accept. Will keep me on task while I teach the lads. The timing of this job could na be better, Sean. I'll get ta know more of the men, and it keeps me in touch with yer day ta day operations for union concerns."

"My thoughts, exactly. Let me give you the tour so's you don't look lost when you come up here."

The threesome exited the map room, the only single-story quarters in a long line of connecting stone structures. In the courtyard, a dozen or so men wearing variations of mining garb—cotton duck trousers, stagged off a little above the ankle to avoid the accumulation of mud, and heavy brogans—bustled about their business. Several made their way towards the mill building across the way. One fellow fed a steady supply of wood to a tall structure resembling the smokestack of a train, anchored to the ground and connected to wheels and belts.

"Most of the men are in the tunnels this time of day," Sean began. "That's our steam 'donkey'—powers most everything, including your bigger drills." He pointed clockwise around the quadrangle. "There's where the ore skips get hoisted outta the mine and up through the headframe . . ."

Vicente whistled. "How tall is the headframe?"

" 'Bout ninety-four feet. Lets gravity do the work getting the ore through the crushers. The ore gets dumped near the top through a grate we call a *grizzly* to sort and size it. Larger pieces slide down a chute to a gyratory crusher we got behind the smithy; the rest drops into ore bins. Then we load both batches into ore carts to haul 'em to the stamp mill over yonder. You're familiar with *that* constant pounding sound. Gets so's I don't even notice anymore, just background noise."

James agreed. "I notice more when I'm in town in Grass Valley; seems out of place there."

Sean rotated as he explained the line of production. "Once the stamp mill pummels the ore to sand, we add the water to the mortar box until it turns thin enough ooze to spread onto the long copper amalgamation tables. We coat the copper plates with mercury to attract the gold and separate it from plain sand. Once enough of the combination of gold and mercury clumps up—we call that the amalgam—we send it to the amalgamation room for cleaning. Basically, that's just more fine-tune crushing in a Berdan pan to separate out the mercury and whatever iron sulphurets are still clinging to the amalgam. After we wash out the impurities"—Sean pointed back behind them where they started and smiled—"that's when it gets interesting."

They faced the queue of buildings they had just departed—a row of impressive, neat stone edifices built from the slag heap of rock brought up from the tunnels, giving their presence a weight and a feeling of permanence. Stately parapets separated each structure, along with chimneys; the windows were surrounded on all sides by red-brick soldier rows. Doors, window frames, and the double-decked porches of the main office building displayed coats of spruce-green paint.

"So . . . from left to right—main offices there with the porches, map room, assay office, strong room, and medical-rescue office. Now, what you can't see from here is what's behind—the gold refinery and bullion room. Limited access to those buildings, as you can imagine. But, the boss has seen fit to let me show you the refinery . . . we'll step through the main office here . . ."

James and Vicente followed closely behind as Sean knocked at the refinery entrance. At the sound of a heavy iron bar being drawn from the inside, James recognized Judd Olmstead peering through the partially open door.

Judd smiled. "Desperados, as I live and breathe. 'Course, the worst one of you works for me. Come in, gents."

James loosened his collar upon entry. His breath felt forced from his chest. Even with the steel barred windows at the back wall fully open, the suffocating heat drew beads of sweat almost instantly.

"Bit warm, hey? See that little unit that looks like a still? That's the retort—they're heating it to what, Judd? Eight hundred degrees?"

"True enough, Sean. The mercury what's left is vaporized and condensed in the cooling tubes over there where we collect it, clean it, and reuse it. You see the gold that's left on those trays? We call that *sponge* because of all the holes the evaporated mercury leaves. We weigh that and put it in the bullion furnace and melt it again. We pour that into ingots; see those racks behind the glass in the back room?"

Vicente stood on his toes, straining to catch a glimpse of the liquid gold bars behind the secure wall. James gazed out over the top of his head.

"Hard to see from here, but the ingots cooling over there weigh a thousand Troy ounces each. The last step after they cool is to weigh them, assay them for purity, and label them. Then we ship them off to their new home at the U.S. Mint in San Francisco."

" 'Tis a wonder," breathed James. "I never thought much about what happens once we handed our ore over the counter ta cash it in."

Sean ribbed him. "You think every dang thing is a wonder."

He shrugged. "I'm a man with many interests."

"Maybe now I can interest you in that long walk into a dark hole where work needs to happen?"

James chuckled. "Of course. We'd best go, Vicente—so Sean can boss us around whilst he still has a chance. Judd, I thank ye for letting us see the operation here. Remarkable."

Judd nodded. "Anytime. And I'll just say again how glad I am you've taken on this union. I feel better knowing the man I'm dealing with is one of the old sports I can depend on. Let me know if I can answer questions, or be of help—we really have the same goals at heart here."

James shook Judd's hand. "Aye, that we do."

CHAPTER 8

Sacramento

"Governor Burke! I'm pleased you could see me on such short notice."

Dutton trailed behind his father, the Honorable Judge Walter Dandridge, as the portly man strolled into the governor's office as one accustomed to being the most important dignitary in the room. Perhaps more notable than the chap he put into the governor's mansion, Dutton mused.

Governor Burke rose from his stately upholstered chair and walked around the front of the massive walnut desk, greeting the judge warmly and shaking Dutton's hand.

"How could I not? It seems a minor miracle to find you away from San Francisco, Judge. And, Dutton, I hear you're doing great things here in the capital."

The tall, distinguished man motioned to plump leather chairs in front of his impressively carved desk. "Please, please be seated. What brings you to town? Although, I'd guess it has something to do with your new offices?"

Judge Dandridge eased his heavy bulk into the chair. As Dutton took his seat, he noted a flash of displeasure in his father's eyes. The governor sat back on the edge of the desk in front of them, suggesting he meant their meeting to be quick. Mistake.

"All part of the family business. Dutton is putting my Harvard investment to use by saving much wear and tear on me as he handles operations here. How are Maisie and the children?"

67

"Splendid, thank you. Maisie has her hands full with the boys—ten and twelve years old now. And little Elizabeth is six."

"Wonderful to hear. Tell Maisie they grow up too darn fast. Mary can hardly believe Dutton is a grown man." He winked at Dutton. "She's a little too eager for grandchildren if you ask me. Now . . ." The judge clapped his hands together to change the subject. "I know you're a busy man, so I shan't tarry. I may be in need of a favor, Tom."

"I certainly hope I can help, Judge. You've been my biggest supporter over the years."

"And rightly so. You're doing a marvelous job for the state thus far. In fact, what I've come to call to your attention will be helpful in a second term bid."

Governor Burke sat forward with interest, "Oh? An early jump on the competition?"

"Exactly. Interim elections are coming up. Changes could be a help or a hindrance for you in another two years. I'm here to suggest help."

"Really?"

"I'm looking for two things: primarily, support for a senatorial candidate. He'll make a fine junior officer for your command."

"Do I know the man?"

"You know his family. I'm speaking of Neil Collier—Garth and Eugenia's boy. A Harvard friend of Dutton's, so I've had opportunity to know him intimately over the years."

Governor Burke shrugged. "Impressive family."

"He's sharp, innovative, has a real touch with the people. It's no secret his family's been vigorously active in charitable movements across the state. Neil was instrumental in clearing legal hurdles to begin construction of the Sacramento orphanage. His sister and her husband, Dr. Hensley, serve on its board of trustees. He's been a huge asset crusading for the Central

Pacific—he's a man whose ideals very much mirror your own. You would find him a valuable resource."

"Now that you mention it, I do recall his name in association with a number of civic causes. He does have the pedigree . . . sounds promising—he's a little young, perhaps. Judge, I'll certainly give this some thought. As you know, it's still in the hands of the voters."

Dutton looked down, quietly smoothing his deerskin gloves across his lap, smiling internally at the man's utter lack of recognition of his true position.

His father's demeanor stiffened. He leaned forward menacingly, his dark, bushy brow contracted sharply into a frown. He spoke in a low, intimidating tone. "I think we *both* know it is simpler to run for U.S. Senate than local office. I remind you, it's cheaper to *encourage* a limited group of legislators to secure an election to the Senate than to run a statewide race before voters."

"Er, yes. Of course. I'll certainly promote him amongst my colleagues. I *see* the importance of supporting such a man."

It amused Dutton to watch the governor attempt to look away from his father's stern face. The judge continued his bulldog stare a few more moments before relaxing back into his chair.

"Good. I knew I could count on you." He added pointedly, "I also expect results. While we're at it, I have a man from Nevada County needing an appointment in the state legislature. I sense someone is due to retire early for . . . illness, shall we say?"

The governor's face visibly twitched. "I . . . don't understand."

His father's lips drew back in a snarl. "We *missed* you at the Empire mine meeting."

Dutton waited until the albatross of understanding rested

heavily on the governor before he chimed in. "Nevada County's gold production reaches a crucial turning point as it becomes commercialized. It requires knowledgeable supervision for the state to reap the benefits of growth. California's future depends on this industry to thrive . . . thus local representation is key. Your man's name is Lodie Glenn."

"Begin the transition immediately," stated the judge.

Governor Burke stuttered. "Who am I to replace?"

Judge Dandridge rose to leave. "I leave that entirely up to you. I have a board meeting to attend. Pleasure to see you, Tom. We'll talk soon."

He left the room with the same measured air of supremacy that he entered it. Dutton fell in behind him. They walked in silence until they reached the mid-day noise of the streets.

"Now that he's actually been in office, the man's too confident in *his* ability. Extremely proud." He walked at an aggravated pace, quick for a stout man.

Dutton replied, "As you suspected."

"Yes. A good thing we're hedging our bets. Speaking of which, any news in that other matter?"

Dutton smirked. "Measureable progress."

"Good. A fox in every henhouse."

"Shall I give you a rundown of my presentation? See if I've missed anything?"

"Excellent. Proceed."

As they progressed through the crowds down the long blocks to the B. F. Hastings building, Dutton rattled off his major points. Upon arrival, he opened the heavy door to the office and held it for his father. Upstairs, they cruised down the long corridor, and, nearing their destination, the judge abandoned his irritation and put on a welcoming smile. Dutton heard the resonating sound of men in conversation. His secretary, Sadie, handed him a message as they entered the conference room full of guests representing the very epitome of prosperity.

"It appears everyone is accounted for, but me." The judge's voice boomed above the discussion. "I must throw myself on the mercy of the court."

Good-natured chuckles resounded at the judge's attempt at humor.

"I'm sorry for the delay, gentlemen. I hope you enjoyed the refreshments during your wait. If you'll be seated, we can begin."

Dutton glanced hastily at the note, frowned, and stuffed it in his coat pocket. Pleased to see their venture capitalists display a jovial mood, he sought to build on that momentum. Earnings were on their way up and plans for advancement in the offing.

Dutton stood next to his seat near the head of the table, where the judge presided.

"I have a brief summary as to where we stand to date. Then, we'll hear a report from each department about issues, developments, or concerns. Neil, would you be so kind as to record the minutes? Some topics may be too sensitive to engage a secretary at this point."

"Of course."

Dutton proceeded around the table. "Neil Collier—Collier Ranch and Enterprises, Conrad Fitz—Bank of Sacramento, Martin Payne—Shortline Railroads, Jess Summerville—Summerville Freight, Bart Risney—Nevada City Foundry, Lucius Weeks—Nevada City Stamp Mill, Ben Alexander—Chief Engineer, Caleb Redmond—Empire mines, Judge Walter Dandridge—president of our board, and, of course, myself, Dutton Dandridge."

He took a dramatic pause to look around the table, nodding and smiling. "Gentlemen. This is an illustrious gathering—a quorum with experience developing great achievements. Coleridge Sierra is a financial investment group, begun and backed by a deeply rooted Sacramento family, the Colliers, and a long-standing San Francisco family, the Dandridges. Both well established, enduring testaments to their belief in the potential of California. Our company cannot fail to be likewise.

"We hold the utmost respect for each man at this table. Your success brings value and knowledge to our company. On the East Coast, greater financial minds than my own employ a system of self-sufficiency—an assemblage of resources to control all aspects of one business . . . a system we hope to emulate."

He smiled at Conrad Fitz.

"Our expertise in banking led to the successful acquisition of all the mines now enveloped by the Empire Mining Company."

Dutton paused for the anticipated applause around the table. He nodded at each man as he spoke of individual contributions.

"We own interests in railroads and freight companies—decreasing our transportation costs. Our engineering team plans to reconstruct the framework of our mining group with square-set timbering, allowing access to ore previously believed unreachable. This *greatly* increases our output. Collier Timber supplies our need for lumber, again lowering costs.

"The Nevada City Foundry. How can we forget the ceremony to dedicate the largest mortar casting yet installed at the stamp mill—fifty-six hundred pounds of power! Even now, the foundry is working in tandem with our engineers to develop the biggest swing nozzle head ever produced! Their effort revitalizes the stalled hydraulic mining industry. Progress—by leaps and bounds!

"The Stamp Mill, in a coordinated effort with our freight and railroad, spells efficiency! Efficiency means profit!"

Dutton paused for effect. "In other words, we own companies in a supply chain. Each link in our chain produces a specific product or supplies a service that satisfies a common need. This way, we control timing . . . and eliminate delays, because we are not at the mercy of someone else's business. If we own the company, we own the schedule, and we own the priority. We look to acquire other companies suiting our needs and advancing profit."

Dutton held up a finger to emphasize each point. "Again: lower transaction costs. Synchronization of supply and demand. We lower uncertainty and enable higher investment. We possess a strategic independence, thus, saving us on taxes and regulations on transactions. Our future, gentlemen, is bright indeed."

Applause broke out around the table.

Dutton waved his arms downward to signal quiet.

"Now. We are busy men, eager to get on with the jobs that brought us here. Let's hear from our department heads. Caleb Redmond, tell us what's happening at the Empire."

Caleb stood as Dutton ceded the floor. "As Dutton stated, we are hard at it, refurbishing the mines. Hiring is at an all-time high. We are enlisting seasoned, experienced men and expect increases in productivity because of it. Our recent hires formed a Nevada City Miners' Union, to which we assigned a company supervisor, Jim Schuester, to keep tabs on them. For the time being, we see this as a positive development. They are proceeding in an orderly fashion, and the workers seem content and more confident with representation . . ."

Dutton left his father to entertain the board after the meeting. He weaved a snaking trek through smaller side streets until he found *The Pig and Whistle*. He didn't like demands from anyone and certainly not a subordinate requesting favors. The dingy bar reeked of stale ale and tobacco. He wondered how much of the odor would follow him home on his clothing. Annoyed, he pushed his way through the crowded room until he spotted Lodie hovered over a shot of whiskey at the end of the bar.

"This had better be important. I have a board dinner to attend . . ."

"And I have a late stage to catch." Lodie glared at him with what he could only interpret as malice. Dutton stopped short in surprise.

"Have you any idea what your shaggy cretin has been up to?" Lodie began.

"Tolliver?"

"Two months ago, he nearly killed a woman. A prominent woman, and a dear friend."

Dutton's eyes narrowed as he recalled his conversation with Tolliver. He replied blandly, "Must not have bothered you but so much, if you're only coming to me now."

"I didn't know it was him! I *thought* it was an accident."

"Yes, he's good at accidents; it's one of the things he's paid for. As I remember, you were the one upset she had glimpsed the two of you together."

"Well, that's just lovely. Is he paid to get seen doing it? A witness came forward! Described him to the smallest detail. If he shows his face, *anywhere* near Nevada City, he'll be arrested immediately. She saw *him*! Not me. It was a stupid, risky, meaningless thing to do!"

Dutton stood, silently fuming. "Well, this is a problem . . . I'll have my father curb him in San Francisco." He looked up, studying Lodie. "Now we decide what's to be done to fix this."

Lodie finished his drink and sighed. "I took care of it myself. Probably not the best plan, but the situation had to be dealt with."

Dutton frowned.

"I had to divert attention from Althea." Lodie looked up at him sharply. "I don't want her touched again; she knows nothing! I had to say it was a broader threat. After the sheriff got involved, I'm afraid I cast aspersions on Empire, shifted the threat to others. I put a note on her door warning the new union chief not to stir up trouble."

Dutton relaxed. "If necessary, we may be able to blame the rumor on William Bourn. We'd like to force him to sell his stock." Dutton nodded slowly. "At least, it shows you think on your feet."

Lodie clenched his fists. "I did not sign on for this! I won't be part of people getting hurt."

Dutton sneered. "Like most people with lofty goals, you don't care about details as long as you get your payoff." He held up a finger to the bartender. "Whiskey!" He looked back at Lodie. "What can you tell me about the union chief?"

"I put him there. He's a good friend. He and I, along with an Empire foreman, are former business partners. I hear about everything that happens—which is fortunate, since my contact in the assay office spooked after Tolliver's *accident* and left town for good."

Dutton smirked. "Do your former partners know about your 'aspirations'?"

Lodie grew silent.

"Ah, not so good of friends after all, eh?"

"Some things, they don't need to know. They aren't . . . big-picture men. Their concern is for the individual—the small, the insignificant."

"And you?"

"You know my thinking. Certain niceties in life must be sacrificed in the name of progress. No different than failing independent miners—so engrossed with rights, they're willing for the whole town to collapse. I protect the town. No sense in the whole ship going down. I look after everyone's best interest."

"Sensible approach." Dutton nodded, smiling. "You continue to surprise me . . . you're incredibly . . . enterprising. Your appointment is coming through very soon, by the way."

Lodie looked astonished. "How soon?"

"Congratulations are forthcoming. My father spoke with the governor this morning."

CHAPTER 9

Sacramento

Justin considered himself a man at peace with God. Not since he was a small boy caught filching the last piece of pie off his mother's counter had he felt nervous in church. And yet today, watching over Charlotte unnerved him.

When he picked her up at the boarding house, she stepped out to greet the day wearing a belted dress in robin's-egg blue and a matching coat. He felt proud to escort her to church. She described in great detail how she had embroidered the edges of her paletot jacket with the pagoda sleeves, a creation she made popular in his mother's shop. Impressed, he acknowledged her skills.

Now, he was distracted from the pastor's sermon—though he was no more inattentive than Royce. The Collier clan sat a row behind them on the opposite side of the aisle. Charlotte sat in perfect profile for Royce to indiscriminately gaze upon her while appearing to focus on the pulpit. He felt somehow he should block Royce's view.

As if her feminine presence were not enough, she soon drew attention as only Charlotte could. They stood to sing. At first the hymn played softly, but as the chorus rose so did Justin's angst. He lost all sense of the control he never possessed to begin with when her head tilted back, and the music hit its crescendo. A note higher, sweeter, and stronger than any from the congregation ascended all the way to the choir loft.

Justin glanced back swiftly. Not only did Royce stare; the entire row of Colliers looked on in awe. People all around them shuffled to find the source. He looked over and saw her eyes close and her head cant slightly to the side. Her voice soared to a point that Elvin Sweetwater nearly fell off his director's block trying to turn about and identify the owner of the spectacular sound.

He stepped down on her foot. Hard. Startled, she stopped abruptly. She looked up at him questioningly as he released the pressure and muttered, "Rein it in." Her cheeks colored as she realized people watched them. From then on, her gaze remained steadfastly on the hymnal, and she kept the glory of her voice in check.

After the service, she stood next to him in the churchyard. Justin noticed a number of men looking her way, and a few sidled close enough for an introduction. Celeste caught sight of them and bounded over; he felt grateful for her buoyant and intrusive personality.

"Hi! You must be Charlotte. I'm Celeste. I wasn't sure if you had arrived yet until I heard you in front of us . . . then I saw Justin, so I figured it must be you!"

Charlotte smiled weakly as Justin shot her an "I told you so" look. Adele and her husband, Stan, Neil and his fiancée, Beth Payne, and Royce gathered around. Before Justin could present her to the family, a thin little man broke into their group.

The man adjusted his wire spectacles as he studied her. Justin recognized him as the choir director.

"Young lady . . ." he began, "I'm Elvin Sweetwater. Your voice caught my attention during the service . . ."

"I'm terribly sorry. I get carried away sometimes," she offered.

"Well, I wish you'd consider doing that from my choir loft."

"Oh . . ."

The Colliers waited. Royce looked amused.

"Of course, I'd like that very much. For as long as I'm visiting."

"Splendid!" Mr. Sweetwater clapped his hands in delight. "We'll see you at choir practice." He turned to catch the pastor's attention as he dashed off. "I do believe I've found my new soloist."

"Wait!" Charlotte looked alarmed. "Was there an old soloist?" But the skinny man had already disappeared. She looked up, speaking to herself more than anyone, "Oh, I don't like starting out making anybody mad."

Neil stepped forward extending his hand. "I hardly see that as a possibility. You sing magnificently." He smiled kindly. "I'm Neil Collier, and this is my fiancée, Beth. You've met Royce and Celeste." The Hensleys stepped forward. "My sister Adele and her husband, Stan Hensley. Welcome to Sacramento."

"Thank you." Charlotte looked demurely at the surrounding family. "It's lovely to meet you all and so kind of you to invite us to your home." She glanced from one blue-eyed Collier to the next. "I've heard so many nice things about you from Justin."

Adele broke in. "We look forward to getting to know you. Right now, I'm rather anxious to get back to the roast in the oven. Justin, you'll follow us back?"

"Of course."

Justin relaxed on the long drive out to the ranch as Charlotte marveled at the countryside. She surveyed the panorama of rolling hills covered with long, golden grasses; the sun's rays set the tawny knolls aglow. Clusters of trees garbed in soft greens dotted the landscape, stretching their branches like parasols to shade huddling groups of cattle. On approach to the house, the scent of ripening fruit drifted on the breeze from the peach orchards lining both sides of the dirt road. Turning into the bend, the house came into view through the enormous arched gate bearing the Collier name. Charlotte gasped.

He pulled the buggy to a stop. She stared.

"I've never seen anything so grand."

"It's something, isn't it? Past the gate you'll see enough barns and outbuildings to make it feel like a small town." He glanced over at her. "Try not to let your mouth hang open when we get inside the house."

Once indoors, Justin found it equally challenging to focus on his hosts and not let his eye be seduced by splendor. Lavish rugs and furniture surrounded them, and a massive chandelier loomed overhead in the foyer. As Stan took Charlotte's wrap, Adele inquired, "Charlotte, I've been admiring your coat—it's beautiful. Wherever did you find it?"

"I made it myself," she said lightly.

Adele, Beth, and Celeste swarmed around her.

"What?!" exclaimed Beth. "It's exquisite. It matches your dress perfectly. You *didn't* make that as well?"

"Yes, actually." She glanced up at Justin. "Justin's mother owns a dress shop in Nevada City. I work with her there; she's incredibly talented."

"I should say!" said Beth.

"Neil, why don't you and Royce take our guests into the drawing room while I check on the cook. Dinner should be ready shortly."

Justin escorted Charlotte into the sprawling room filled with curvaceous Victorian furniture. He selected a long sofa by the fireplace. Most of the family settled onto the opposing sofa and favorite overstuffed chairs as they became acquainted, while Royce positioned himself by the hearth. Charlotte asked questions about the orchards, cattle, and Justin's role as a wrangler. Royce expounded on their cattle operations, as well as timber. Justin learned of Neil's interests in the senate, his upcoming marriage to Beth, and Dr. Hensley's practice and support of a new orphanage near Sacramento.

"I thank you for your hospitality," said Justin. "Our family's had trying times lately, and your kindness is most appreciated." He smiled. "Though you're putting me in a tough place with the other hands."

"I'm not aware any of them have charming sisters," said Royce.

Neil laughed. "Well, that is a deciding factor, isn't it?"

"Oh, you two!" said Beth. "Don't embarrass her. Charlotte, I hope Mr. Sweetwater didn't put you on the spot."

"On the contrary, I'm grateful for something to do. I'm only now realizing how much time I'll have on my hands. I'm used to working in the shop, or training horses with my father. Justin will obviously be busy here, and I'm not sure how long I'll be staying."

"You work with the horses?" asked Celeste.

Justin nodded, "She's very good with them. Thistle Dew is a small farm, so we all pitch in."

Adele entered the room and sat next to Stan, "Dinner will be a few more minutes." She looked at Charlotte and mused aloud, "I may have a solution for you. I have a friend, Mrs. Van Oss, who owns a dress shop in town. She's quite overwhelmed for help. You're obviously skilled; I could inquire if you like?"

Charlotte looked startled. "That would . . . be wonderful. Thank you." She looked at Adele with eyes brimming with gratitude. "You've done so much already."

"Nonsense. You're quite welcome."

"It would certainly be a relief to me," added Justin. "I wouldn't worry about you being alone."

"Me, too," chimed in Royce. "I need him focused so he doesn't land on his head."

Charlotte laughed. "He's pretty good at landings. He's been trained by the best."

"I can attest to that," said Royce. "And you? Certainly you're not breaking broncs?"

"Oh, no. I do some schooling work in the ring, grooming, feeding, general care."

"She runs their feed off," teased Justin.

"Oh, you like to race?" Royce's question was posed with a hint of challenge.

Charlotte opened her mouth to answer, but Justin jumped in. "Constantly. She scares my mother to death."

"Really? I'd like to see that."

Justin shook his head. "No, you wouldn't. Can't tell you how many times she's beaten me."

"Sounds like a dare, Justin." Royce wore a wicked grin. "How about a race?"

Charlotte cocked her head. "Perhaps, you should race Justin first. Then, you'll be ready to take me on."

Celeste squealed with delight. Neil and Stan chuckled at her banter.

"How do I know you're not exaggerating?" Royce probed.

She gave a silly toss of her head. "I never exaggerate."

"Oh, come on," he boomed, "the Irish are known for . . ."

He stopped short as he saw her eyes widen with surprise. Her soft, full mouth fell open as if she'd been struck.

Adele exclaimed sharply, "Royce! This is not a bar room."

Justin felt stuck in the middle of two indomitable personalities. If his boss sometimes displayed a short fuse, Charlotte would know how to spark it. He watched her face as she recovered. Her mouth was now a line of determination, and her chin raised to square off with Royce. One brow was arched as she looked at him with a steady, steely gaze. Justin knew that unsettling look.

Apparently, it rattled Royce. "I'm . . . sorry." He cleared his throat. "I didn't mean . . . I shouldn't have said . . ."

"Do you have a particular dislike for the Irish, or do you merely assume any touch of Gaelic lilt to a voice belongs to one that should be suspect? I, myself, have heard the *Irish* are known for judging good whiskey and good horseflesh. Now, I am told we *Scots* are too stingy to indulge heartily in draught, so, under your definition, I guess that leaves horses." She leaned towards him. "If you're bold enough to test the talents from across the Atlantic, then we've got ourselves a friendly race. If not, I guess you'll have to indulge your summations of the Irish and Scottish in saloons." She slowed her rapid-fire retort and added, "But I hear you're a man bent on expanding your horizons beyond the thinking of others."

Justin groaned inwardly. Royce stood stung, and Justin could see he felt the weight of his blunder. He took a step towards Charlotte, while the rest of his family looked on.

"I owe you a tremendous apology. I don't know why . . ."

Justin watched Charlotte frown as she sized Royce up. He held his breath as she stated, "I think maybe you surprised yourself with that one." She waited.

Royce nodded gratefully. "I'm really sorry, I . . ."

She held up her hand and shook her head. "Heat of the battle?"

"Yes." He gave her a sheepish smile.

Her eyes twinkled. "Then we have a race?"

He laughed. "I don't see how I can refuse a lady gracious enough not to hand me my head on a platter. Next week?"

"I'll be there." She nodded.

To Justin's relief, Adele announced dinner. Neil led the way to the dining room, escorting Beth. Justin and Charlotte followed closely, as he was eager to leave the conversation behind. Celeste walked with Stan, while Adele turned on her brother. "She was gracious, indeed. Really, Royce!"

CHAPTER 10

Nevada City

James rubbed his head wearily. He slept poorly in the months since Althea's accident; too much baring of the soul had dredged up ghosts once laid to rest. Sold, but untrained horses filled his barns. Routine farm work piled up with both Justin and Charlotte gone, and a procurement trip to Sacramento was urgently needed to expand his business.

His role in the miners' union consumed time like a greedy hog at a trough, though he found it rewarding. He had inspired a strong infrastructure of committees and, with their elected leaders, generated a gratifying fraternalism amongst the men. Miners knew their jobs and took confidence. Committee heads brought valuable suggestions and concerns to light, issues largely undetected by Empire management. Regardless of advancements, James sensed the grace period of trust from Empire beginning to fade. Problems waited too long to be addressed. The men invested themselves in their new roles, and they expected action.

Empire management's unavailable and inaccessible executives frustrated him. Schuester remained a nervous joke of a man, his input a total waste of time, in Sean's opinion. Schuester solved nothing and knew even less. Too cowardly to approach anyone above him, questions went unanswered; plans foundered; concerns were left dangling. James needed a high-ranking source to voice their issues to.

84

He awaited Lodie at the Silver Moon. The Nevada City mayor had garnered enormous support from the Merchants Bureau. James felt grateful for Lodie, a like-minded friend who believed sweat and ingenuity built futures and who willingly took the role of community servant.

Entering the bar, Lodie called out, "Whiskey!" As he caught Rob's eye, he pointed to the table where James sat.

"That bad?" asked James.

Lodie appeared distracted. "Ah, no. Helps me separate today's business from tomorrow's." He glanced at James. "You look terrible."

"Wearing too many hats at the moment. Na sleeping, either."

"I know that one. Wake up, and thoughts race willy nilly through your mind."

"Something like that."

"Did you speak with Sean?"

"Yes; I have a list from his point of view."

Lodie sipped from a shot glass. "Much better—would help you sleep, you know." He swirled the dark-golden liquid, gazing into its depths as if looking for respite. He cleared his throat and stated flatly, "Sean's being watched. His bosses want to discourage his pipeline of information to the miners—or to you, for that matter—so they're reluctant to tell him much." He looked up. "You've spoken to the union committee heads?"

James nodded. "Well, on the positive side—some improvements. The hoisting cages for one—they've developed a brilliant new cable. Sean says it beats anything he's seen. The old hemp ropes broke under the weight pulling from deeper shafts—too much strain. They've invented a flat, woven wire rope. Much, much safer. Strong as Atlas."

"That's one for the engineers."

"Allows them ta transport more ore as well. In addition, re-timbering projects are well under way; they've revamped a

85

number of tunnels. The foundry is on the brink of perfecting the largest hydraulic nozzle ta date. That'll put men back ta work on ridges near French Corral, North San Juan Ridge, Malakoff diggings. On the down side—they need ta increase the Cornish pumps. Sean's concerned over water issues in deeper shafts. On the whole, the men are fairly positive . . ."

James hesitated, drumming his fingers on the table, mulling things over.

Lodie studied him. "I sense a 'however' coming."

He shook his head. " 'Howevers' trouble me. Trends I do na like continue with no response—that does na bode well for the future. The men are patient now, but they need ta believe they have a voice. They do with us, but bloody good it does if their grievances never leave the schoolhouse meeting. Then our union becomes a club of gripes and complaints. Unanswered concerns can grow inta something ugly. That breeds strikes and worse."

"Empire's happy with the progress. They intend making more improvements."

"They're happy 'cause nothing's gone wrong, yet. Yes, timbering's reset at a good rate. But they still send teams ahead ta treacherous areas before timbering crews get there. It's more than just a wee bit of water down there. There's rotting, old timber supports—that leads ta poisonous gas. Got ta get water out faster. Deeper shafts ha gone below the water table. If they do na solve water issues now, what happens at the next spring thaw? When hydraulics start up again?"

Lodie raised his brow. "That's not all of it, either, as far as the hydraulics. I've spoken with Mayor Hammond Creed. There's a lot of noise coming out of Marysville *and* Yuba City. They're afraid of more flooding, and they intend to make a fight out of it."

"As well they should. We know first hand what they deal with." James reflected. "No, I need ta get the attention of someone who matters. If the only one I can talk ta is this Judge Dandridge, then so be it. I'll dog the man until I find him."

Lodie frowned. "Why him?"

"Might as well go straight ta the top. We'll see how far it trickles down after. I leave for Sacramento shortly. I've business at the horse market, and I need ta check on Charlotte. I'll scour the city while there." He pushed back his chair to leave.

"I'll be interested to hear what you find out."

"Ye'll be my first stop when I return."

CHAPTER 11

Sacramento

He waited, enjoying the catbird seat.

Judge Dandridge barreled down the hallway like an oversized cannonball.

"Sadie! Bring me the file on Conrad Fitz."

Sadie stood and bolted from around her desk, waving her hands at the judge, who paid her no heed.

"Sir? Sir, please . . . ? Sir, wait . . . There is a man in your office."

Judge Dandridge stopped abruptly. "What man?"

"Well, sir, he did not give his name."

"Is that not your job to find out *before* you admit someone to my office?" His tone suggested extreme irritation.

Sadie looked at the floor. "Yes, sir," she stammered. "I tried everything. I told him I had no idea when you would return. He said he didn't care, that he would wait."

"Well, what the devil does he want?"

"He said he had business with you concerning the Empire mine."

Judge Dandridge scowled. "Anything else?"

"No, sir."

The judge turned and stalked towards his office with no further discourse. He halted in the doorframe and scrutinized his unauthorized visitor. James sat in an upholstered office chair facing him, one long leg crossed with his heavy work boot resting on his knee. His fingers were interlaced, and his hands rested comfortably in his lap. His fierce, pale-green eyes fixed on the judge, reflecting an equal level of inspection. He waited for Dandridge to speak.

"I don't believe we've met." The judge walked to his desk and dropped his valise with a thud. He turned towards James. "Nor do we have an appointment."

James rose slowly, gazing steadily at him. "Appointments with anyone in yer organization prove ta be a difficult thing ta come by."

James towered over him. This alone seemed to pique the man's aggravation. The judge closed his eyes and shook his head as if trying to rid himself of an inferior position. "I'm sorry," he said sarcastically. "And you are?"

"James MacLaren. Union chief for the Empire mine."

"And what can I do for you, Mr. MacLaren?"

"Two ears would be a start."

"Mr. MacLaren, I am not in the habit of receiving people who storm past my secretary; but, given your position with the union, let's say for argument's sake you have at least provoked my curiosity." The judge walked behind his desk and plopped down in his high-backed leather chair. He leaned back with his arms crossed in front of him, resting on his paunch. "What is it that you want to say?"

The rusty-haired Scot remained standing. "There seems ta be a broken line of communication. I have a list of grievances. At the moment they are merely concerns. I would like ta hear some feedback from management before they become grievances.

"Judge Dandridge, the whole point of bringing problems ta the attention of management is ta make them aware. I realize everything can na be tackled at once. The men bring forth issues na just for themselves, but because they want ta take pride in their company. They bring them up because it should be of some concern ta ye. They should be commended for looking after *yer* mine and *yer* interests. They realize misfortune can be avoided if caught early. They catch it, report it, and it goes nowhere. They bring it ta me, and I can na get past Schuester, who must have some function in life, but I'll be buggered if I can figure out what it is."

The judge raised his bushy brows, looking irritated.

James pursed his lips, then quipped, "Ah, so ye do know Schuester."

The judge sighed. "Please sit, Mr. MacLaren."

James reclaimed his chair and continued. "I truly believe the man meets with me and then walks in circles talking ta himself until he gets a grip on his nerves. Then he waits until I call ta meet with him again. There are no answers. I'm na certain he's even posed the questions."

James paused. "It would appear . . . that he has been told not ta. If the man is only window dressing then best tell me now, because believe me: in order not ta waste yer time with matters ye see as unimportant, ye're wasting a hell of a lot of my time. Passing concerns *will* build inta problems, and beyond that inta problems that cu ha been fixed but no longer can without great cost ta the company. Then ye'll want ta know why no one brought it ta yer attention. So, I'm here ta jump the line and tell ye myself."

"We have engineers to inform us of these things."

"And have they?"

"So far they've had nothing of significance to report."

"Really? That *they* cu find, ye mean. They aren't in those mines every day; they aren't familiar with our mountains, our rivers. They're giving ye a best guess on what they've seen *elsewhere*. Here: let me give ye an example of a problem looming ahead with potentially disastrous results. Yer *experts* versus our local knowledge."

James leaned forward in his chair, his words tumbling forth passionately,

"I recently discovered the biggest setback attributed ta the failed fixes of the flood patterns here in Sacramento, Marysville, Yuba City, the whole area was . . . what do ye think? Experts! They cu see the results of flooding but had no basis ta judge our mountains, the snows, the driving winter rains, the lack of change in elevation from the Yuba all the way ta the coast . . . any of it. They gave advice proposing an aggressive assault on our lands all along the Sacramento River.

"Their recommendation on the size and stature of levees *they said* would fix our problem was based on calculations of the biggest river they had knowledge of—the Mississippi! They gathered no observational data on stream flow on which ta base this conclusion. The Mississippi's a huge body of water ta be sure—wider, but far slower than what we have here. The flooding reports on the lower Mississippi River basin were commissioned by Congress nearly twenty years prior. There was all sorts of la-di-da promotions amongst the corps of engineers over this huge pile of data—data that was useless ta the California landscape.

"*Experts* demanded action with calamitous results. They called for levees *only*—no bypasses, no upstream dams, no controlled release points for floodwaters ta spread." James counted off the issues on his fingers. "They wanted higher and higher levees keeping control within a single channel. Why? They believed this increase in the propulsion of flow would force the river ta dig out its own bed; the force of the flow would plow away the tailings and debris that kept cargo ships from safe passage. They hoped ta provide the needed channel ta prevent overflow and increase flood-bearing capacity. And, even now, the Empire mines are creating the biggest nozzle yet, ta restart hydraulic mining and send more rubble and dregs down-river."

The judge squinted hard as he followed James's logic. "How do you know all this?"

"Besides living it for fifteen years? I've done my research. We've our own crusader, our Mr. Will Green, who's observed and analyzed the cause and effect on our rivers for the last ten years. He's read this damn tedious corps of engineers' report and fears that it's disastrously wrong. The theory assumes the floods of a huge lowland river will respond identically ta our longer, more narrow version—which is fed from melting snow caps and gains velocity ta a point it barrels out of the mountains like Neptune furiously out ta capture sea nymphs in flight.

"Our valley's simply too close ta the mountains producing the floods. We do na have hundreds of miles of channels as does the Mississippi. It all stops here, swiftly and furiously. What we end up with is more silt, more debris. A bigger problem than what we started with. Green's been screaming for years there's too much water for the Sacramento ta carry all of its own floodwater in one channel . . . so far, he's been right."

Judge Dandridge threw up his hand and began dismissively, "This is all very enlightening, Mr. MacLaren, but . . ."

James leaned in closer, his eyes narrowing. "My point being, yer *local* knowledge needs ta be tapped when ye make the decision ta go forward with new hydraulic methods. The union men won't oppose ye; they want the work. But the towns will. There's enough knowledge between the two, and they're willing ta work with yer management. *That* will make this project succeed for ye. Don't shut us out."

"Again, all very interesting . . ."

James felt his temper edging up on him. "Which part did ye find interesting? History of floods in the region? Or the fact that we're not all ignorant brutes?"

"There is no need to be insolent."

"That is where ye're wrong; there's every need. Hydraulics is a problem that has na arrived yet. We can help with that. There are current problems ye have ta address. Methane gases build up where rotten timbers need ta be removed. We need more Cornish pumps ta get rid of the water and flooding issues. There are improved methods of blasting that need ta be taught and implemented."

James squared off in his chair. "I've patiently worked through yer channels. This boob, Schuester, that ye've pawned off on us has no facts, no queries, no answers, no results, no interest, and, largely, no backbone. But he keeps telling me politely that he will take these things under advisement. It appears his only function is ta be a buffer of complete ignorance. Surely, this is na what ye had in mind?"

"We are still in an adjustment period, Mr. MacLaren. I hear your concerns, but it will yet take some time to settle out and see what the most pressing problems are."

"All I'm trying ta do is bring ye what the men see day in and day out, as just that. Surely we can agree it's in everyone's best interest ta fix something broken before it causes damage? Or physical harm? Profits don't stem from disasters. The men are doing their jobs by telling ye what they know ta be true. Why is there no one ta hear them?"

"It's why we sent Schuester."

"Whom as far as I can tell is deaf, dumb, and blind. I'd do as well with three blind mice."

"Oh, for God's sake, I'll have Schuester moved aside if he's such a problem. Whom do *you* suggest?"

James's heart leapt with inspiration. "Give me Sean Miller."

"He works for the mines?"

"He's a foreman for ye, yes, sir."

"Done."

Chapter 12

The Collier Ranch

Justin saddled Baron and was headed back to the barn to scout out possible mounts for Charlotte when he heard Royce's indignant shout.

"What are you doing here? It's race day. Shouldn't you be on your way back from picking up Charlotte?"

"Nope. She sent word yesterday she'd be coming in from someplace near Buckeye. Her father came to Sacramento for the horse market, and she's traveling with him. They made stops at two ranches yesterday on business."

Royce gave him a dubious look. "Whose ranches?"

"James calls on the Ely ranch and the Briggs place . . . bound to be them."

"Huh." Royce crossed his arms in a rigid stance while he mulled this over.

"You know them?" asked Justin.

"Yeah, for years. Good outfits, good neighbors. He selling them ranch stock?"

"They've both been increasing business with him over the years. Both started with bigger animals for hauling in alfalfa and hay. They're starting to pay attention to his saddle horses now. Why?"

"Hmm. No, I was just thinking. Ben and John both have a sharp eye for horseflesh. Maybe I ought to take a look myself."

Justin shrugged. "I'd recommend it."

Royce chuckled. "Guess you would. What's Charlotte's interest in traipsing around horse markets?"

"You forget—we both cut our teeth on this stuff. She's always taken a keen interest in the business. As talented as she is at dress making, it's hard for my mother to compete with her love for horses." Justin nodded towards the house. "So, Adele and Stan came to watch today?"

Royce turned to see them making their way to the barn, Celeste trailing behind. "Why not?" he smiled. "They want to see how close she comes to backing up her bold talk. You pick out a mount for her yet?"

"I've got a couple of suggestions. She'll make the final pick."

"Good morning, all!" called Stan on approach. "A fine day for a race." He looked down the road to see Charlotte riding in with James. "Looks like our other contestant is on her way in."

"Who's that with her?" asked Celeste.

"That would be her father."

Justin turned to peer down the road. Startled, he straightened up and squinted hard at the distant pair. As they progressed just a bit farther, he burst out laughing.

Royce frowned. "What's so funny?"

Justin grinned. "This just got a whole lot more interesting."

Royce moved next to him and whistled as he stared. "That is *some* stallion!"

Banshee's phantom form moved with precision and pride, his head and tail erect, and ears perked inquisitively forward. Sunlight shimmered on his silvery coat as well-developed muscle rippled beneath. His finely groomed mane, the color of pale slate, crowned his arched neck like a royal robe.

"Looks like quicksilver," Royce breathed.

Justin nodded. "She pretty much hand raised him. He was a sorry sight when James found him."

Royce turned to the barn and bellowed, "Antonio!"

95

His stable man hurried out into the doorway. "Yes, patron?"

"Saddle up Buckshot."

The man looked confused. "I thought you say Midnight?"

"Changed my mind." He shook his head at Justin. "Ante's going up if that's what I'm up against."

"Smart move."

Banshee pranced a high stepping trot in rhythm with Rusty until the MacLarens pulled up in front of their waiting audience.

Royce looked up at Charlotte with a smirk. "Certainly brought the big guns, didn't you?"

Charlotte smiled. "Royce, I'd like you to meet my father, James MacLaren."

James dismounted and extended his hand. "Good ta meet ye, lad. Heard good things about yer ranch from Justin." He looked around, "Magnificent does na begin ta cover it."

"Da, this is Celeste Collier and Adele Hensley, Royce's sisters—and Dr. Stan Hensley, Adele's husband."

James greeted each one earnestly. "I appreciate ye looking after my family; ye've been very kind."

Stan quipped, "Well, Justin works for Royce, so I don't know how kind that is."

Royce muttered, "I'd be admiring that blood bay of yours if he wasn't standing next to this guy." Royce circled Banshee, looking over every inch of him.

James chuckled. "Rusty's smooth as silk, he is. But I see yer dilemma. Banshee's been missing Charlotte, so I brought him along for a surprise. I did na know about yer race."

"He's got spooky eyes." Celeste wrinkled her nose.

"Yes, my mother says he looks like a ghost. Hence the name," said Justin giving him a pat.

"Why has he got that big, ugly scar?"

Charlotte stroked his neck. "Someone beat him when he was

96

a colt. We nursed him back to health."

"Justin's talked a lot about your farm. It appears I'll have to pay you a visit," said Royce.

"Happy ta show ye 'round the place, anytime. Ye tell me what ye're looking for, I'll find it for ye," said McLaren. He cocked his head as commotion from the back of the barn caused them all to look at the buckskin gelding, who was yanking the lead from Antonio's hand. "Well, he's a handsome fella. I see ye like strength—he looks ta be built for stamina."

Royce folded his arms and gave a smug nod. "Modoc."

"Really?" James walked towards the buckskin. "Always been fascinated by these Indian ponies."

"Can't get my hands on them often, but, when I do, I grab 'em. Buckshot's quick on the turns working cattle and solid as a rock on a drive. He's long on endurance, all right."

"I'd be interested in a couple mares if ye come across some yer not taking yerself."

Royce looked pleased that James was impressed. "I'll keep an eye out."

"Ahem," Charlotte called from her seat in the saddle. "Are we going to race or admire the animals?"

"Nervous?" Royce teased.

"Stalling?" she countered.

"Oh, ho, ho . . ." Royce chortled. "Let's go!"

Royce and James talked business while waiting for the rest of the group to saddle up, Royce calculating out loud his needs for the ranch. Justin sidled up to Charlotte as she spoke quietly.

"You have any idea where we're going?" she asked.

"We picked out a course while out on the range the other day." He jerked his head towards Buckshot. "He'll be a pretty even-money challenger. Plenty of spirit, likes to bolt at the start, so don't let his first burst of speed rattle you. He settles in to stride after that."

"Good to know."

"Royce will go for the hard drive to the finish. He doesn't have quite your uh . . . imagination for taking a course."

Charlotte smiled and patted Banshee.

Celeste came alongside riding a small, black mare. "I hope you beat him, Charlotte. I don't think he really thinks you can."

"I'll do my best."

"Ready all?" shouted Stan. "Lead the way, Royce."

Justin watched the interactions of the group with amusement, feeling he might be the only one with a clue to everyone's thinking. He kept waiting for James to catch on to Royce's interest in Charlotte, but his boss was so infatuated with the horse it certainly didn't show. James appeared to be focused on picking up a new client and was eager for Banshee to show well. Just as well, he thought. He'd hate to see those two square off. As for Charlotte, he couldn't decide if Royce appealed to her, or she just enjoyed needling him. He looked ahead at his boss giving James the nickel tour on the way.

Celeste and Adele rode behind him, chatting together. Stan pulled his horse up beside them and said to Charlotte, "You be careful, young lady. There's a lot of quick hills through here, easy for your horse to stumble or come up lame."

Charlotte had been eyeing the terrain as they rode. "Thank you. I can see what you mean."

They followed the fence line along the wagon-worn road until they came to a gate leading to a sizeable hay shed. Royce pulled up the rope latch and gave the gate a shove with his boot. They rode up to the shed and stopped.

Long, yellow grass covered the hillsides, rippling one after the other. Justin watched Charlotte study the view in front of her. A large shade tree not far from the shed seemed to have rooted at the bottom of the divide between two steep and nearly treeless hills. Its foliage fanned out such that the dark-green leaves nearly touched the ground on the left side. Upon closer inspection, it was in fact two trees a few feet apart with a shared canopy making it appear from a distance as one lush, green oasis in a sea of gold.

Past this shady haven lay a substantial gulley up ahead on the left—a winding channel, dry this time of year, forcing the racecourse to the right. If not careful of her position, she could be pushed up on uneven ground. The slope on the right ascended such that a solitary oak seemed to grow sideways off the bank. Beyond this, a cleft between the two hills formed a straightaway running for several hundred yards.

Charlotte turned to Royce and asked, "Do you mind if I ride ahead to look at the course?"

He smiled magnanimously. "By all means." He pointed and motioned. "We'll begin at the double-tree, head through the valley way, over the first two ridges through the trees, to a dead spruce up on the third ridge—you'll see it when you get close—then back. First one past the starting point wins."

She nodded and took a slow canter towards the series of wooded dells, the mounds appearing in staggered waves, as if a huge rolling pin had come down from the sky and pounded them into closely formed loaves. Justin scanned the course as Charlotte picked her way across it, looking carefully at the ground on both sides as she rode. He decided he had no additional advice for her. He glanced at Royce busily scrutinizing Banshee's movements and negotiating with James for the stallion's future offspring. Charlotte wheeled about and headed back to the starting point.

"Ready!" she called.

James, Stan, Adele, and Celeste took refuge under the double-tree, and Justin dismounted to stand between the two riders and their stamping, pawing mounts. He drew a red neckerchief from his back pocket and held it skyward as Charlotte and

Royce focused on the course ahead; both leaned forward in anticipation.

"Ready . . . Set . . . GO!" He swiped the bandana down.

Shouts and cheering sang out at the cue. The horses lurched forward to take the field, kicking up clods of grass. They barreled neck and neck through the straightaway, their lead positions shifting from one to the other, depending on ruts and rocks to be avoided in their path. Justin noted Charlotte settle comfortably into stride, pressing close to Banshee's neck.

As they crested the first sharp peak, they swiftly disappeared on the other side of it. The buckskin was the first to emerge and drove powerfully up the second slope, weaving expertly between the trees. Banshee followed close, threading the wooded path as smoothly as waxed string through a needle. Buckshot remained in front through the dense cover on the second ridge, leaving the spectators only glimpsing quick bursts of silver or buckskin flashing amongst the foliage.

"Oh, I can't see them!" yelled Celeste.

Cheering died down as they waited, guesses and musings aloud taking its place. James peered hard to catch the first hint. The buckskin again was first into view, headed for the dead spruce at the top of the last summit, Banshee a good two lengths behind.

"Take him, darlin'!" he growled. "Ha!"

As Royce rounded the craggy, broken spruce, Charlotte swung in the opposite direction to make her turn, circling past him before returning to their common path. Justin began to smile. Royce, distracted by her maneuver, broke his stride, faltering as his eye followed her instead of the course. Again they thundered over hill and dale, topping the crowns and then vanishing from sight.

The sound of driving hoofbeats intensified as they topped the last ridge before the straightaway. They appeared side by side, pounding the turf for home. The squeals from Adele and Celeste rose above the booming shouts of the men as the riders advanced at breakneck speed. Charlotte lay nearly flat against Banshee's neck, her hair streaming like a banner behind her. As Justin predicted, Royce drove hard for the finish, slapping his reins furiously across Buckshot's withers. As they drew closer, the shouting was deafening. Justin saw that Royce crowded Charlotte toward the gulley in his bid for the finish, pushing her into a position of having to fall behind and go around to avoid it.

Charlotte fanned out abruptly—towards the gulley. She gave a long, sharp whistle, and Justin began to chuckle, knowing all too well it was meant to signal Banshee and rattle Royce. She headed the silver stallion straight for the gulch, lifting slightly from her saddle, and the two sailed as one over the divide. Banshee landed with sure-footed agility and continued fleetly past the double-tree, a full two lengths ahead of Buckshot.

"*Yes!*" James pumped his fists above his head and shouted, "Beautiful! Well done!"

The family crowded around, laughing and all talking at once. Royce circled Buckshot around and pulled him up beside Charlotte, shaking his head.

"Well . . ." he gave her a cockeyed grin. "That monster you're sitting aside . . . that had to be the most brazen piece of riding I've seen in a long while." He extended his hand. "Congratulations."

"Thank you," she said, smiling prettily. "I guess you know now, I don't exaggerate."

"No, ma'am, you do not!" He laughed.

CHAPTER 13

Nevada City

Althea concluded men were never *just* busy. Work either consumed them entirely, or they piddled about whatever little thing appeared right in front of them. She stood, hands on hips, surveying parcels of new inventory to be unwrapped and sorted. The throbbing in her leg suggested too much time spent on her feet. Customers flocked to her shop all day, creating a gathering Sean would rightly call a big hen party. Good for business, though. And it filled the lonely time. Lately, she found all the men in her life devoured by monstrous tasks.

Admittedly, she was no better. Professional determination helped her fight past injury and the aftermath of unburdened secrets. At that reflection, her mind flew to James as a bird takes wing to the trees for shelter. For every crisis in her life, no matter how determined to soldier through obstacles on her own—he watched over her.

Cast out from her position, a child on her own, beginning a business—he supported her as much as dear Emma did. When they lost Emma, somehow they forged a makeshift family for Justin and Charlotte. Sean's struggles, and indeed when it seemed he had disappeared from her life forever . . .

A fleeting memory of the Nevada City Ball. The sudden flutter in her chest surprised her. Mercy! She had let her thinking wander into a maudlin place.

She decided the unpacked boxes would wait. She hobbled to

a chair and plopped into it, debating whether to spend the night at Lodie and Matilda's or go home. Thoughts of the farm's deserted quiet saddened her. She missed Justin terribly, and, without the distraction of Charlotte's vivacious chatter, she gave in to a blue mood. Surely, James returned today from Sacramento. She realized he would worry and come looking for her if she stayed.

With effort, she pushed herself up from her resting place and gathered her wrap and reticule. On a peg in the back room hung the skirt to her wedding ensemble. She stroked it lightly and murmured, "Soon enough, I'll be living in town."

A knock startled her. She peeked out from the storeroom to see James peering through the glass. She rushed to open the door, forgetting the pain in her hip.

"There ye are!" he exclaimed, entering. "I settled three new horses, the rest fed and watered, and not a soul ta talk to."

She smiled sadly. "Depressing, isn't it?"

He bobbed his head right to left as if deciding. "A bit, but I'll deny I said as much if ye tell either of them. I thought I'd drive ye home."

"What a welcome treat. Do you mind if we sit a minute? I'm quite weary."

"Sure, sure." He pulled out a chair for her.

She looked up at him wistfully. "How are they?"

"Cu na be better. Both of them." He cocked his head. "I'm afraid we've got ta prepare for this, Thea. It's the natural way of things. Although it's unfair for me ta say since Charlotte will come home when this union mess is settled."

She looked down. "I know. How does Justin look?"

"Stop yer worrying; he's good. Loves his job . . . and I gotta tell ye, it's some spread he works for . . . spectacular place."

"You went all the way out there to see him?"

"Ah, yes. How cu I na? I knew ye'd ask a million questions.

Besides, the trip was a tale in itself."

"And Charlotte?"

He chuckled. "Still a sprite. Not certain I'm keen for her new found love of independence. She's keeping busy, even has a job. Working as an apprentice in a ladies shop." He swept his hand in gesture to Althea, bestowing credit for Charlotte's success. "Impressed with her training, they were. I think yer lad's grateful she's out of his hair during the week."

Althea's spirits lifted. "Was she excited you brought Banshee?"

"Over the moon. And that plays inta the tale I spoke of. Appears she and Justin wagered with his boss that she cu beat the man in a horserace . . ."

"James, no!"

He laughed. "I know, it sets yer teeth on edge. She would ha picked a horse from their lot, but when she saw Banshee, neither of us cu resist."

"She won?"

"Of course! She rides that animal like they were one being. The Collier fella was so impressed with the stallion he hardly paid attention ta Charlotte. I suppose he thought she'd just mince along." He poked his thumb into his chest. "He did na know about *my* training. She shocked the sugar out of him. Arrogant bugger he was, too."

"Oh, dear." Althea felt a jolt of warning.

"No, no. Not ta worry. Nice enough man. Really appreciates Justin, thinks very highly of him. Justin will do well there— though I'm hoping he'll come back here someday. I talked a bit of business for Thistle Dew—there's interest in my breeding program. Will give us good reason ta keep tabs on Justin." He winked.

"No, I meant . . ." Althea hesitated. From what she remembered of Justin's letters, his boss was only a few years his senior.

She scanned James's face for signs of unrest. She decided against voicing intuitions that could ignite a protective father. "Never mind. Tell me about union concerns . . . did you find answers?"

"A few. Discovered as many new questions as answers. I found Judge Dandridge anyway." He inadvertently frowned. "One piece of good news: he's agreed ta move Schuester out. He'll name Sean as union liaison."

"James, that's wonderful! Sean will be thrilled!"

"We'll see. I do na trust the man, but a small victory it is." He stood. "If ye've got a second wind, I'll tell ye about it on the way home."

"Yes." She stood decisively. "We could both use the rest. I feel better knowing you've seen the children and they're well."

She picked up her wrap and her walking stick, looking again at the boxes. "I should come in early tomorrow," she said sighing.

James offered his arm. She smiled. "That's nice. The less I use this stick, the better." Nagging thoughts plagued her. "James, how long do you think Charlotte need stay away?"

"I'm na sure. I wonder if I didn't act too impulsively at the threat in the note, but I sense much unrest in the wind. My attention is so divided lately; I have na had any for her. I'd never forgive myself if I overlooked her safety. Let's get through a few union meetings ta see where Empire's response is headed."

James bolted upright in bed, his face washed with sweat. He fought to clear his vision beyond the encroaching pool of blood. He shivered there in the dark, panting, heart pounding. Slowly the room came into focus, the light of the moon finding a sliver between the curtains. He looked at his trembling hands. He fought the urge to run. Again.

He sat alone in the shadows of night until his breathing

returned to normal. He remembered they arrived at the farm late that evening. He got up, went to the kitchen, and put the kettle on.

The meeting with Judge Dandridge left him feeling nettled and skeptical. He disliked the man; he distrusted him. Experience taught him once the rich are rich, they elevate themselves one level closer to gods and farther from every man. Dandridge was MacFie in a different skin. When James witnessed honorable men pitted against tyrants, the dream that chronicled his fateful past returned. How could he make it stop?

His visit with Charlotte filled him with hope and promise. Somehow, she seemed older in a setting on her own. Working, of all things. He felt old. The children, no longer children any more. And Emma . . . so far away. His mind struggled to bring the details of her lovely face into focus anymore, though he never stopped trying. He looked out at Althea's cottage. He knew his oldest, dearest friend was lonely for Justin. A familiar, prodding catch gripped his chest. He envied Sean. More than he should.

He ventured out into the night air with his cup of tea. He sat in the rocker, gazed at the stars, and let his thoughts retrace the steps leading him out of Scotland.

The huddle of MacLaren brothers and uncles had been somber and quick. Only one answer presented itself, and James must be gone. Certainly, he'd not gone unnoticed entering the refinery. The charge would be murder, and he'd be hung. Rumors circulated that he'd signed on to a ship bound for the Americas, a tale he sorely wished true but served its purpose. Cropped curls and blackened hair were necessary changes along with a swift departure as they smuggled him aboard a colliery rail from Greenock. He found work in the mines of Northumberland where daylight rarely illuminated his face or features. He worked a few months to sustain himself and stake his travels to the next mine, as he moved across the English countryside.

When he had his fill of darkness and dust in his lungs, he decided it was safe enough to travel in the open. He knew to stay just long enough to keep the past from catching up and then move on. He could never go home again, nor contact his family for fear of incriminating them. He abandoned his youth the day he left.

He became a man always on his guard, leery of the entitled and wary of his own temper. He learned the fates of others could impact a way of life for all. Bullies and tyrants could not be tolerated on any level but must be dealt with in a clear and levelheaded frame of mind. Their type of malice spread like a plague, and the innocent always suffered.

James observed a lonely cloud as it passed in front of the moon. He made a decision. This time . . . the MacFies of the world would not chase him away. He would not allow them power over him again. He would stand. And he would help the others to stand with him.

CHAPTER 14

Nevada City

James held a hasty conference with Lodie the next day. Ridding themselves of Schuester they counted a victory, but Lodie agreed: growing enmity with the upper echelons of management existed. James sought to avoid these sentiments with the men for now. He needed to position them for positive momentum. They decided to call in the committee heads. It took two days to bring them in from various locations.

The schoolhouse became an official gathering place. Sean arrived early, greeting James with a broad grin. "I don't know how you did it, my friend." Sean punched him on the arm.

"By making myself a bigger pain in the arse than Schuester. I'm hoping ye already know more than he did."

"There's a few things in the hopper," he acknowledged. "First off, somebody's stumping for public office through the camps. Wants to know our concerns and such. Seems honest . . ."

"Don't they all, in the beginning?"

"True enough. On a serious note—you heard what's happened at the Yellow Jacket Mine?"

"Can na say that I have."

"Fire. Bad one—thirty-five men dead at last count. The same issues we're complaining about. They're unable to put the fire out even yet. Timbers collapse, feeding the fire, and poison gases expand with the flames to fill their tunnels. Our men hear this, and they're concerned. This event only helps our case . . ."

108

proving what can go wrong."

James frowned as he mulled this over.

"There's something else," Sean continued. "I overheard a rumor, some of the bosses talking." He lowered his voice. "Someone in the mines is feeding information to this Coleridge Sierra."

"What type of information?"

"The kind leading to loans and takeovers of smaller mines. Somebody that knew the output from each one—and which ones needed loans the worst. Who knows what else? Did you find out who Coleridge Sierra is?"

"Not yet. I found they're listed on the stock exchange. I'm pretty sure our friend the judge is tied in, but I did na pin him down on it." James furrowed his brow. "Keep that information ta yerself for now. And keep yer ear ta the ground."

"It's what I'm here for." Sean glanced outside. "The fellas are arriving. Best open the doors."

James nodded. He welcomed each of the committee heads as they entered the schoolhouse, chatting with them informally about their concerns. He focused on giving them a strong, encouraging message. They cheered Sean Miller's appointment as the company representative. Sean accepted their good wishes and directed them to benches pulled to the front of the room. James faced them, leaning against the teacher's desk.

"Welcome, gents. I imagine ye all have new information for the group from last we met. Ye may have heard: I reached one of the investors in Sacramento. Ta sum that visit up, I say it gave us a foot in the door. However, we've a ways ta go in convincing them we have a voice that needs hearing."

James folded his arms across his chest. "After that meeting, I experienced an encounter with my youth. I thought about the town where I grew up. My father and brothers were shipbuilders. Good, honest trade. Ships were important—to our port city. Sugar cane was brought in from faraway islands in the West Indies. The family owning the refinery controlled the town, drove the commerce. They owned the ships, the cane, and the refinery. *Everyone* dependent upon them in one fashion or another, and they became tyrants."

James wagged a finger and posed the question. "When one group or family company overpowers an area, how do ye fight back? How do ye get control?" He looked at their faces. "By bits and pieces. Where ye can."

He straightened and slowly walked the schoolroom floor as he spoke. "Some amount of conformity and public good has ta happen first. *We* need ta be involved. *All* of us. It's a company mine, but its na a company town unless we allow it," he said defiantly. "How do we gain influence? By working harder."

Groans arose from the men on the schoolhouse benches.

"But . . ." James looked at them pointedly. "*Not* in the mines."

He had their attention.

"We volunteer. We get involved. It's na so different than when we had each other's back in those early days of mining—protecting each other from lawless outsiders. We had trust, dedication ta each other, and hard work."

He began to pace again. "Now. We need men from the union ta volunteer in law enforcement . . . in fire protection. Ye that have returned from battle, join the militia. Offer yerselves up in local government. The wealthy run things now because it is in their best interest ta run things—not for any great love of us. *We*—in these meetings—we nominate from amongst our own for positions. We nominate and we put *one* man forward and we agree ta stand, all of us, one hundred percent behind *that man* in town meetings, local elections. We take control!"

The men began nodding and murmuring their assent.

"We'll have ta start small, take logical steps, grow inta these jobs—many of which the mine owners don't want anyways."

Clancy called out, "How does that help if they don't want those jobs?"

James spun towards him and pointed. "Because they're still jobs that *need* ta be done. When they stop getting involved on the lower levels, they'll be more vulnerable at the middle levels. They'll be busy running after business pursuits, and they'll let go. They'll become dependent on us, rather than the other way 'round. The more of us bound together in this effort the stronger we'll be—the more likely we are ta be heard. We're not a faceless bunch of nobodies asking for favors as though we're beggars. We are the teachers of their children, protectors of their wives and families in town, the ones providing the services ta all their daily needs.

"We already have a foothold—our merchants. If we take care of our merchants and their needs they will make certain we hold offices."

Lodie stood to the side, nodding in agreement.

"*This is na* about making demands from an unreachable, unreasonable tyrant, or begging scraps from their table. This is about empowering ourselves ta meet them at the table as men!"

The men jumped up from their seats, roaring their approval.

"Take this message back ta yer men. Get organized. Today, we take hold of our future."

CHAPTER 15

Sacramento

"When do you return?"

Dutton carried his father's bags to the end of the stage platform.

"I imagine at least a couple of weeks. Issues are piling up at the office in San Francisco and heating up on the stock exchange. I have a slew of cables to answer; everyone's screaming for answers." He sighed. "I don't see leaving San Francisco for a while. At least, not without bringing your mother with me." He winked at Dutton.

"She misses you. One can only attend so many ladies' teas without more exciting events to be escorted to. Besides, there isn't anything here I can't handle."

Judge Dandridge looked up at him, beaming a father's pride. "Of that, I am certain. That being said, you have a great deal to execute in my absence. Keep me posted on Neil's progress. I intend to speak to our backers while I'm home. So far, the feedback on him is remarkably favorable." He shot Dutton a warning look. "Keep an eye on the miners' union. After we implement the new policies, I expect you'll hear from them."

Dutton bestowed his best Cheshire grin. "I'm rather looking forward to meeting this Scottish rogue."

"Be careful. He's shrewd and sharp witted."

"Well, he's wrong about one thing," Dutton replied smugly.

"Profits *can* stem from disasters."

"It's what we're counting on."

"Charlotte, you're a wonder!" Mrs. Van Oss marveled as she inspected the storeroom. She turned from one rack of open shelving to the next, noting all boxes labeled, cut fabrics stacked neatly according to type and color, spools of trim and lace lined up as if showing off and begging to be selected. "This room was a disaster, and look at it!" She patted Charlotte's shoulder. "I know this isn't the most exciting work to ask of you."

Charlotte shrugged. "It's important. I've cleared and organized many a tack room for my father—he insists on order. And Althea's as neat as an English garden."

In truth, she did not mind. Mrs. Van Oss displayed a regimented, no-nonsense way about her, but she requested tasks politely. Charlotte respected her, though she missed her chummy working relationship with Althea.

Mrs. Van Oss spun around at the sound of someone calling out, "Hello?" "Never a quiet moment . . ." She walked briskly to the front of the store. Charlotte followed.

"Ah, Celeste . . ."

"Good day," said Celeste brightly. "Adele asked me to pick up a blouse you finished for her? Hi, Charlotte. Justin said to tell you, he'll stop by after he finishes loading our wagon."

Her employer looked at Charlotte over the tops of wire-rimmed spectacles she usually wore only when sewing. "Why don't you take a lunch break now, dear? I've hemming work for you this afternoon." Mrs. Van Oss disliked men in her shop. As it was, Justin usually waved from outside or popped his head in briefly. "Celeste, I'll wrap the blouse for you, if you'd like to stop in before you leave town?"

"Lovely. Thank you." Celeste turned to Charlotte. "I'm meeting a friend for lunch shortly, but I'll walk out with you." She began fluffing her skirts. "I'm all wrinkly from the long ride."

Charlotte reached behind the counter for her bag while Celeste prattled on. "I'd ask you to join us, but my friend Laura is having *such* a time with her beau . . ." She widened her blue eyes with an expression Charlotte could only assume she meant as worldly. "So . . . I'm afraid the conversation will be of a personal nature."

"Quite all right," she assured her. "I'm going to grab a quick bite and see Justin." She looked up to observe Mrs. Van Oss biting the inside of her cheek and shaking her head. The shop owner was a widow with two married daughters and overheard the antics of women of every age, all day long. Charlotte smiled as she joined Celeste. "Where did you say Justin was?"

They stepped outside on the wide plank sidewalk. Celeste pointed to the Collier wagon in front of the harness shop, on the opposite side of the street, nearly thirty yards away. The heat of the Sacramento sun bore down from its midday height on the bustling commercial street. Even with no breeze, the passing wagons, horses, and foot traffic stirred up small clouds of dust. Charlotte found the capital city summer much hotter than Nevada City, even here near the edge of the Sacramento and American Rivers.

She saw Justin walk out of the feed store to fling a heavy, burlap sack of grain into the flat bed of the wagon. She was somewhat surprised to see Royce walk out behind him, also carrying a sack across his shoulder. He cut a strong figure, she admitted. Broad shouldered and tall, obviously used to demanding physical work, accustomed to giving orders—and very, very sure of himself, she noted. Lately, Royce's initially irksome traits now held some amount of intrigue.

Vaguely aware that Celeste jabbered on not requiring response, she watched him toss the weighty sack effortlessly into the wagon. As he turned back for another load, their eyes met. He smiled, catching her gaze. She looked away as if she hadn't seen him at all.

Charlotte refocused her attention on Celeste's conversation, full of fluff and adolescent notions. Celeste looked at Justin as she spoke, interrupting her own tales by blurting out, "You know, your brother is quite handsome."

Charlotte nodded, stealing furtive glances as the men continued loading. She found it curious that with each trip Royce seemed to take a little longer than the last. She heard Celeste say his name, provoking her into probing. "I'm sorry?"

"I said: if you're trying to get Royce's goat, you're doing a great job. Nobody ever stands up to him." Celeste cocked her head. "I think he likes that you don't flirt with him, though. All the girls do that."

Charlotte smirked. "I'm not much for flirting."

"Well, you have to practice, silly!" Celeste fluttered her eyelashes, and Charlotte laughed.

"Celeste, you're too much."

The girl put on a wicked grin and said, "I *know*." She gave an exaggerated sigh. "Must be off for my lunch date."

"Have a nice afternoon."

Charlotte chuckled as she viewed the wagon. Justin headed in for another round, but Royce must be settling the bill, as she hadn't noticed him on the last three of Justin's trips. She took a few hesitant steps toward the street, watching. She subconsciously leaned to see where he'd gone. There sat the wagon, and he did not reappear. She decided to run a quick errand in the other direction and catch Justin when he finished. She turned and all but plowed into Royce, planted there with his arms crossed over his chest.

"Looking for me?" He grinned.

"Of course not!" she sputtered. "Why on earth, would I be looking for someone bad mannered enough to startle the daylights out of a lady?" Flustered, she tried to pass him. "Excuse me."

He laughed and caught her arm.

"Now, hold on, hold on," He gestured surrender with an upright hand. "I was thinking, and this is just a suggestion mind you . . ."

She raised an eyebrow and watched impatiently, mortified that he caught her.

"I thought maybe it might be time you and I stop pretending we annoy each other so and . . ."

Her hands flew to her hips. "Who's pretending?"

"Now, now. I'm trying to call a truce. Miss MacLaren, I would be deeply honored if you would allow me to express my deepest apologies for bad behavior by taking you out for supper."

She searched his face for signs of teasing.

"I'm asking genuinely," he coaxed. "Would you perhaps be free on Saturday?"

"Well . . ." She hesitated. "If we weren't out too late . . . I have to be at church early for choir."

"I'll stop by Mrs. White's about six o'clock?"

She smiled slightly, bobbing her head.

"All right, then. I look forward to seeing you." He glanced up. "Here comes big brother. I suppose I'll have to clear my good intent with him on the drive back. Until Saturday."

Charlotte watched him saunter back to the wagon, nodding as he passed Justin.

Justin greeted her with, "What did he want?"

She shrugged. "Dinner."

CHAPTER 16

An Empire Mine

Clancy greeted him warmly. "Good to see you, James."

Four men stood a few hundred yards away from the opening of Old Lucky Seven. James made his way up the hill and shook hands with each man at the mine's entrance.

"Good ta see ye. Is this all the committee that cu get in today? Where's Sean?"

"It's possible a few more may come. These boys talked with leaders closest to their location, so we've more input than it looks."

James glanced around at the operation teeming with men and carts of ore moving rapidly in and out of the mouth.

"One of the bosses called Sean in. He said he would catch up with you later."

James nodded. "Looks as though the company is keeping busy."

"That it is. And on a union note, members wholeheartedly signed up for their civic duties." Clancy inclined his head to the other miners with him. "Martin, Joe, and Cirrus all report it's a real bonding experience for the men. Builds their confidence seeing each other in these jobs. It's a fine thing to realize one of your own has your back."

"Very unifying," added Martin. "Our progress gives us some sense of control."

James was pleased. "Very good. Authority's essential ta influence elections in local government. Volunteerism leads ta the ballot box and garners community support during disputes. I'm proud of the way ye're all pulling together."

Joe spoke. "Just a matter of a plan and organization. I'm most encouraged."

"What about improvements from Empire management? How is that going?"

"Slow. But, we see movement," said Clancy. "They sent engineers to work on the Cornish plunging pump. We're pulling about eighteen thousand gallons of water out per hour. Now that we've dropped shafts below the water table, we need to move it at twice the rate." He grew serious. "But, we're taking canaries down. Old Lucky Seven's putting out methane. We carried three unconscious men outta there a week ago." Clancy nodded at the others. "We're taking a stand. We've waited long enough. Until it's fixed, nobody goes deep in any operation. The bosses don't like it."

"They've little choice now that we're a united front," said Martin.

James concurred. "Ye've done exactly what ye had ta for the situation. If they confront ye, it calls for a sit down with their management and ours. Working conditions are a large part of what the union is about."

Cirrus added, "We're hoping to encourage solutions. I will say, in my area the timbering goes well, and management isn't pushing me to send men ahead of the timber crews."

"Sean's brought in a schedule from Empire to train men in new blasting techniques. Should cut down on mishaps," Martin said.

James gave a quick nod of approval. "All right, then. Moving forward. What else do ye need from me?"

"Keep pushing 'em, James."

"I'll be the burr under their saddle. Keep me posted. Ye know where ta find me."

James left, especially pleased the committee heads worked together without his involvement on every level. He looked forward to refocusing his attention on the farm. He rode down the sloping hillside, careful to avoid potholes in his path. Rusty was showing some age and not as sure footed. The thought of putting his favorite steed out to pasture disheartened him. He was nearly halfway home when he noticed another rider in the distance. He continued to watch the progress of the man headed in his direction when he recognized Sean. He dismounted to give Rusty a rest and waited.

Sean pulled alongside and hopped off his horse.

"Missed ye at the meeting," quipped James.

"Yeah, well I was attending one of my own," he replied sullenly.

James's brow knit into a frown. "With management?"

"It's not good." Sean fought for control. "They're going to tear apart any progress that we've made."

"I don't understand. Clancy says progress is slow, but they're fixing problems."

"Oh, yeah. Proud of it, too. But, they said they need ways to pay for improvements because investors are unhappy. Said profits are falling, because we *allow* shafts to flood, costing manpower to fix and needing more pumps—which we've begged for from the beginning! That ain't nothing new!"

"Pay for it how?"

"I'm to inform the committee heads: they're cutting wages. From four dollars a day to three fifty. And that's just for now; it could get worse."

James stared at him. "The men will never stand for it. It's a set wage. Always has been."

"Not anymore. James,"—Sean looked at him anxiously— "they *will* strike."

"Empire's trying ta throw us off balance. They don't like na having ultimate control, so they want ta throw us inta chaos. We can na let the men react. How soon do ye have ta tell them?"

"Now."

"Can ye buy me any time?"

"What are you going to do?"

"I'm going ta dig. I'm going back ta Sacramento."

"I'll do what I can."

CHAPTER 17

Sacramento

Sadie stood in alarm. She opened her mouth to speak as James charged past her desk.

"It's all right, love. I know my way."

The office at the end of the hall was empty. James heard movement in the next room and stuck his head in the doorway. Dutton looked up, startled.

"Well, Mr. MacLaren." Dutton rose from his chair.

James scowled. "I'm looking for Judge Dandridge."

"My father is back home in San Francisco for the foreseeable future. I'm Dutton Dandridge. I handle the office here. What can I do for you?"

"I'm here for the big dog, not the whelp."

Dutton studied him. "I can assure you that *I* . . . . control all the decisions concerning the mines from this office. I assume you're here to discuss . . . . oh, recent changes?"

James glared at him. "So this is how it's going ta go? Ye have their strength, their loyalty, their hard work. And this is how ye repay them?"

"Please sit, Mr. MacLaren." Dutton motioned to the chair in front of him.

James took the chair slowly, eyeing him as he sat on its edge, ready to leap up at any second.

"Thank you." Dutton sat down behind his desk. "See now, it's the repayment part that's a problem. Our shareholders are

121

upset. There are rumors the mines are flooding, and production has come to a standstill."

James's eyes narrowed. "Given the recent nature of this event, that's a pretty fast moving rumor ta run from mines ta general public. And, like most rumors, it bears only a sliver of truth."

"If the business isn't profitable, there is no pay out. It *has* cost us a pretty penny to fix these problems you've so adamantly laid at our feet. We're doing our part to share in the men's future safety. It's only reasonable they should share the cost of protection."

"Whose payout concerns ye? Any company takes time ta build business up. Safety's a foundation. Shareholders are in this thing for the long haul."

"It's funny how the word 'gold' seems to be exempt from all the normal rules. Investors expect to see something as weighty as the word. When they see substantial earnings, *then* they put in more money; it's how these things work." Dutton reached into a humidor on his desk and pulled out a cigar.

"Isn't that the cart before the horse? Somebody has ta get the gold out of the ground before it has value."

"No work for the horse, if someone doesn't invest in the cart for him to pull," Dutton snapped. "The mines were dead to them. We pay for equipment to do the job. If there's no financial gain, then there's no work. I'm working for the best interest of all—no profits, no jobs."

James sat back in his chair, glowering. "Really? It might surprise ye ta know that I've done a bit of checking on that."

Dutton hesitated.

"What I found is this: not only did the company take more profit last year than ever before, it was sixty-one percent more. Not a bad start. But then, I'm not telling ye anything ye don't know, am I, Dutton? Perhaps ye'd like ta tell the men about yer cut of the increase. Ye can see our problem—ye're not wanting ta take cash from earnings; it's coming from our pockets."

"That's ridiculous."

"A publicly traded company has published reports available, I did my research. You, and a handful of others, made a tidy sum when ye went public, and yet ye dip inta the communal pot as well. What I have na checked yet . . . is how far up the line does yer mismanagement go? Who knows and approves? If ye provoke a strike . . . why, productivity goes down, and so do profits."

Dutton grit his teeth.

"Don't look so surprised, man. We aren't all ignorant brutes, no matter what ye'd like ta think, or how much ye'd like ta keep us down. Ye're not dealing with a faceless kind. Ye're dealing with men, men with families. Perhaps yer stockholders need ta see a face. Well, they can start with mine."

"You're out of your element, MacLaren. Your people need to get a grip on who's in control here."

"My people? You people? *Those* people. Ye say that with more than a touch of distaste. Those people . . ." He paused to swallow down his rising temper. "Those people ha been the bloodstock of the settlement of these lands."

Dutton interrupted coldly, "What is it you want from us, MacLaren?"

"I'm wanting ta see they don't become the livestock of yer movement ta conquer the almighty dollar. We left our feudal lords and came here as free men. But it seems the rich always pull some card out of the deck and play it out of turn. It's not so much they want. We're na asking ta take a thing from yer table, and nothing we have na earned. Do ye have so much money ye just like ta see those ye consider inferiors squirm? Ta see them grovel at yer feet as if that's what'll make them admire the likes of ye?"

"Don't be so sanctimonious in your cause, MacLaren. It isn't about the miserable drunken species that you are. It's about money. It's all about money. There are cheaper ways of running a mine. Ways that don't include a bunch of whining, no-goods looking for handouts." Dutton struggled for control. He took a deep breath and paused to caress and undress his cigar. He smirked a calculated smile. "There are . . . shall we say . . . humbler . . . more subservient peoples than yourselves, you know. Ones who know the value of what they're being offered . . . and are grateful for it."

"Strikebreakers! Ye would dare ta bring Chinese in here?"

"Been known to happen." He lit the cigar and puffed it with an air of superiority as he dropped his secret. "Of course, these decisions are made at levels much higher up than myself." He circled the cigar in the air so that its trail of smoke spiraled upward. He watched it and recited smugly, "Life is a Valley of Tears . . . and we are here to suffer . . ."

James growled, "Ye don't appear ta be suffering too badly."

Dutton blew out a cloud of smoke. "I suppose some of us are better at it than others."

James stood, leaning with his knuckles bearing on the desk. "You coward. Ye'll bring on riots the likes of which are only in nightmares."

"I'd advise your people to pack up. We'll need the space soon."

James straightened to his full height, fixing his glacial, green-gray eyes on Dutton until he blinked. "This tilt has just begun."

He stalked from the room, brushing roughly by a man in the hallway and breezed past without a glance.

Neil turned and stared as James threw open the door and disappeared from view. He peeked inside Dutton's office.

Dutton glanced up. "Ah, Neil, my boy. I knew my day had to get better. Cigar?"

Neil looked at him quizzically. "Wasn't that . . . ?"

"The union chief, yes."

Neil sat in the abandoned chair. "He didn't look very happy."

"Are they ever? Nothing but complaints, no matter what we try and do for them." He sighed. "Improvements take time. What more can I tell the man?"

Neil looked posed to ask another question.

Dutton waved his arm in dismissal. "Forget him; I've got more important things to discuss." He sat forward at his desk and shuffled through paperwork. "Here's the thing. Father is monitoring the Coleridge Sierra stock closely—it's why he returned to San Francisco. He feels we're at a peak. We're getting hit with substantially rising costs over the improvements we're making to the mines. With flooding problems as well, we'll have to shut some locations down, and our profitability suffers. Don't ask me how, but word is getting out—shareholders are nervous. He's advising us to sell a significant block of our holdings. I intend to inform the board immediately. I'm advising you to get out now."

"When did all this happen?"

"Neil, you've been busy—out campaigning with the little folk . . . we need to catch up. Let's discuss over dinner, shall we?"

Neil looked concerned.

"Don't worry. These things have their ebbs and flows. The stock will take a temporary hit. When we think it's at the low point, we'll buy back with gusto. It's all about watching the signs." He looked over Neil's head and shouted, "Sadie! Get in here."

Clicking sounds from Sadie's shoes rang out as she hurried down the hallway. "Yes, Mr. Dandridge?"

"Get me a courier. I have a confidential correspondence to send to my father tonight."

"Yes, sir."

He glanced up at Neil as he reached for a pen. "Can you give me a few minutes? Then I promise you a big steak and a long conversation. Good enough?"

Charlotte dabbed the cool, damp cloth on the back of her neck as she washed up for supper. The Sacramento sun displayed summer's sultry heat during her evening walk back to Mrs. White's boardinghouse from work. She looked up, studying her reflection in the washstand mirror, chiding herself that she so recently stood here and fretted over how to arrange her hair.

She wondered whether or not it was wise to have accepted dinner with Royce the other night. The man certainly appeared cocksure and proud, so she expected nothing but boast and bluster. She felt confident she was in for an evening's worth of his recitation of accomplishments and connections. He surprised her. The slightest of smiles escaped her lips. She still faced the mirror but dreamed in front of it, no longer seeing her own image.

He had arrived at the boardinghouse somewhat subdued for the boss man of the Collier ranch. Meticulously polite and aware of her every comfort, he escorted her to a popular restaurant—the clientele not too fussily upscale, but respectable. While the food was exemplary, she hardly noticed what she ate, except for the pastry chef's famous chocolate confection at the end. She liked that he chose the venue for that exceptional detail.

Royce spoke very little about himself unless she inquired, though he talked a great deal about Justin. It impressed her that he noticed Justin's best traits, recognizing his value as a trusted friend, as well as the skills he had been hired for. He asked a lot of questions about her, Nevada City, and Thistle Dew. Normally talking about herself made her uncomfortable, but their repartee tumbled forth effortlessly, and she sensed he held the same devotion to family as she.

In the soft glow of the floral painted lamp on their table, Charlotte probed about the things he cared about. She delighted in watching his blue eyes sparkle when he talked about land, cattle, horses, and building a legacy beyond himself. She told him the story of Banshee, at which point he admitted how impressed he was by her horsemanship, and they laughed about their race. It amused her to watch him continually sweep back one errant shock of hair that fell across his brow from its slicked-back position.

She found him articulate and engaging when allowed to see behind his tough façade. By the end of the meal she felt completely at ease. After driving back to her residence in his carriage, they were sitting on the front porch, enjoying the cool evening air, when he asked if she might accompany him to a barn dance in a few weeks.

A sharp knock on the door brought her back to the present. She opened it to find Miriam, a nice girl who lived across the hall and worked as a cook at one of the hotels.

"Mrs. White says you have a guest downstairs."

"Who is it?"

"She didn't say."

"Thanks. I'll be right down."

Charlotte hurried down the hallway to the front parlor, the only room where boarders were allowed to receive guests. She immediately recognized the towering figure looking out the front window. "Da?"

James turned, giving her a tired smile. "Ah, darling. I'm sorry ta interrupt yer supper."

She rushed to give him a hug, exclaiming, "You look exhausted."

"Aye."

He squeezed her hard and kissed her forehead. He held her in such a prolonged embrace she grew concerned.

127

"Da, is something wrong?"

"Only that my girl is too far away. Here I am and have ta leave immediately. Can we sit for a minute?"

"Of course. I didn't know you were coming." She motioned towards the large divan flanked by wrought-iron plant stands bearing bright-pink begonias. She saw him glance around at his feminine surroundings, lace doilies and antimacassars covering every piece of furniture.

"Neither did I. I'm afraid there's going ta be more trouble at the mines." He frowned. "I hate that ye have ta stay away."

"It's very nice here, Da. I'm fine. But what about Althea? Is she safe?"

"She should be fine. It's the men I'm worried about. Empire management is pulling all kinds of shenanigans, shutting down shafts instead of making them safe, cutting pay and the like. There will likely be a strike."

"A strike! Sean's in management; can't he stop it?"

He shook his head. "He's trying ta hold the men together until they hear from me. Pay decisions are far above him—even above the Empire management he answers ta. That's why I came. They say the cuts are coming from the investors. Up ta now, it's been unclear exactly who they are—an entity called Coleridge Sierra. I cu na find the information I needed here, so I rode ta San Francisco ta search records at the stock exchange. Then I rode back ta confront one of the buggers here."

His jaw tightened; his tone grew sharp. "He threatened worse than pay cuts—arrogant, insolent fool. Spoke hatred for men he did na even know. Clearly, he thinks anyone na wearing a fancy suit no better than animals, and that's how he intends ta treat them. If he makes good on his threats, they'll have ta strike."

"That's awful. How can people be so cruel?"

"Seems if ye give a man enough gold, it turns a heart stone cold." He took her hands. "Sean'll be waiting on me. I've got ta head back right now. I need ye ta talk ta Justin for me—soon. Ye need ta warn him ta keep his eyes open."

She looked at him blankly. "Why?"

"Because I found the names of the investors squeezing the livelihoods out of our miners. Leading this bunch of thieves are the namesakes of the company. Coleridge Sierra stands for Collier and Dandridge."

Charlotte felt a sudden jolt. "I don't understand . . ."

"Those two families started this nightmare—they've swindled the independents of their lands, and now they're beating down their livelihoods." Too agitated to sit any longer, he stood. "I've got ta go, darling." He pulled her to her feet and kissed her cheek good-bye.

She mumbled, "Be careful, Da."

He winked. "Always. We'll get ye home soon. As soon as this mess is over."

Charlotte nodded as she watched him leave, thoughts tumbling through her mind like river over rock. She did not know the Dandridges, but she only saw kindness from the Colliers. She wondered if her instincts could be so wrong. Then she remembered Justin—always a solid judge of character, not easily swayed or fooled. No, some element of truth had to be missing or distorted. She must get to Justin.

Nevada City
At the end of the business day, Althea drew the shades on her shop windows. Dejected, Sean sat at her worktable—his head in his hands, his fingers raking furrows through his chestnut hair. James sat opposite him, drumming the table, contemplating next moves. His thoughts came sluggishly as fatigue set in. He had briefed Sean late last evening after a long ride from Sacramento. They spent the day tracking down union committee heads, agreeing to meet after closing in the shop; informa-

tion at this point was too incendiary to risk being overheard at the Silver Moon.

"I put on a fresh pot of coffee." Althea swept her wrap over her shoulders and picked up a large marketing basket. "I'm going to pick up a light supper. You'll both feel better after you've had something to eat."

James nodded. "Thanks, Thea." He tried to remember when he'd last eaten.

"I called the men in. Believe me, they'll *all* be here tomorrow. They've heard speculation about the wage cut, and they're hoppin' mad. Why'd Redmond tell *me* to give them the news if Empire intended to leak it?"

"Management's testing reaction without putting themselves on the firing line," James said flatly.

"Those milksops only work with us when it suits them. Don't know why I ever thought their intentions were good."

James shot him a look. "That's the type of thinking we have ta get ahead of. I agree, but we've got ta try ta control emotions. Besides, we have na had problems with middle management. It's that weasel scat at the top."

"James, bringin' in Chinese'll throw the men over the edge."

"*That* only happens if we strike."

"We lose control of wages—there's no going back. Especially knowing they got plenty profit without taking it from the men. Of course they'll strike! A lot of these guys lost claims on bad loans and still trusted Empire for the steady job *I* promised them."

"Och. Righteous anger is easily ignited. It's no justification for blindly rushing inta a fight. Ye can na let yer heart carry ye further than yer head allows. It's na worth the price if violence breaks out. Believe me, there's many an old man wishing he'd done something different when the terrible memory of another man's death brands his soul."

Sean chewed on the sentiment before answering. "Sometimes a cause is just. I ain't wearing this eye patch for decoration." He sighed. "You're right; we've gotta go at them with determination and cool heads. But this fight is gonna escalate."

"Let's na start at the point of no return. We work within the law as much as possible. If the men riot, or destroy property, it justifies management's ability ta rain on our heads with impunity," warned James.

"Then together we present the facts and call an organized vote to strike or not. I'll talk to Lodie first thing in the morning and make sure he's present. He adds stability to a situation."

"Agreed. After the vote I'll work ta find out who *else* is on that board and when's the next meeting. There's got ta be more reasonable people at the top. *Life is a valley of tears,* indeed! Arrogant pup!"

James and Sean spoke as two sides of the same coin—one preached reason and the other restraint. The struggle to control the outrage of the miners proved more than the equable calm of Lodie Glenn could repress. Anger simmered, then boiled over at suggestions of compromise. The vote went as expected. Refusing to back down, union members decided a week henceforth to enforce a public notice demanding a closed shop in all Empire mines and the four-dollar-a-day wage upheld. If ignored, they planned to march in mass on the headquarters of the Empire mines.

Afterwards, James stalked up into the hills for nearly an hour before he gave thought to where he might be going. It dawned on him that outrunning his temper was no easier than outrunning injustice. Involvement in this brawl seemed unbearable; his peaceful dreams lay waiting for him at Thistle Dew. He wanted to believe this was not his fight—no reason for him to be dragged into the muck and the mire.

131

Exertion's sweat dripped down his face as he sat in a heap on a boulder. Nearly twilight, the sky was smeared with lilac and the moody clouds above as heavy blue as a field of heather. The wind whipped warning of coming storms. "Och, let them pull themselves out of it. I'm done," he thought. But he wasn't.

He reflected on the vote. He stood sternly as Sean read the results. He said resignedly to Lodie,

> *"Whom are we trying ta fool? This whole business illustrates an unspoken class system in a country that insists one does na exist."*
>
> *Lodie had said gently, "That's our whole goal here, James. For it not to exist."*
>
> *"By pretending it doesn't? I can pretend I'm King of Scots but it doesn't make it so."*
>
> *"You've counseled peaceful ways—always, James. That's what they need to hear, especially now, going forward."*
>
> *"It was na my peaceful countenance ye were seeking when ye pushed me inta this job. In this case it's better ta lose than na fight at all."*
>
> *Lodie gave him a rueful smile. "I pushed you to the front. We're all in this job."*
>
> *Reading the unhidden angst on his face, Lodie had offered, "Let me play a hunch or two. I'll see if I can get you some names of board members. Perhaps we can find someone sensible yet. You gotta have faith."*
>
> *"Faith is still the ability ta see correctly—when others can na see at all. Either ye walk on the water or ye sink. Faith is a victory, not a forfeit," he had said.*

The gusty evening air tousled his sandy, auburn locks. A fine mist spritzed his face as he peered out of the hills seeing lights blink on in town like so many fireflies. His thoughts began to manifest in unyielding truths. The indifference of the Dandridges was clear. Their attitude of superiority struck an old, but hard chord within him. A smoldering began in the back of his eyes. He straightened his shoulders as if adjusting for the mantle he took on at that moment.

James felt a strange, calm sigh of resignation come deep from within. Clan histories arose in his mind, stories of indomitable men held under by those in power until they could no longer breathe—until they forced their way to the surface.

It was time to come down out of the hills and prepare to lead them.

Thistle Dew

James threw his saddle on Rusty's back, ignoring Althea's worried tirade. He shot a concerned glance at Sean as he stood in the courtyard, adjusting his stirrups.

Althea fretted. "You're taking them on your shoulders because you think they can't survive on their own. James, you're exhausted. Please wait until the march. It might work itself out."

"There's no response from decision makers, and the men grow restless. Work slows as they look for answers that are na coming. Every day I worry a fight will break out—we have ta give them something ta focus on. We march in five days; that's the message."

"But they *know* that."

"Thea, we last spoke ta them in a mass meeting at the vote. Anger grows and feeds off itself in large numbers. If Sean and I talk ta them in smaller groups we can reach them—so we don't turn inta a mob but approach as men with a rightful cause. Empire is far more likely ta listen ta reason—that's what we need for the now.

"The men have ta keep working as loyal employees until

133

then, give management every chance ta answer before we march. I want a peaceful demonstration, a united front ta bring grievances ta the table; it's na a strike yet. We want ta talk, that's all. The power in our numbers only works if we're cool headed. Ye can ignore a man waiting ta have a chat, but can ye ignore a couple hundred staring ye in the face waiting for an answer? Negotiations, that's all we want. I've got ta try and talk ta the hotheads on our end and ta get ta someone reasonable with authority on theirs. Perhaps after a day or two the need ta strike will seem less urgent."

Sean kissed Althea on the cheek and mounted his horse. "He's right. A strike isn't good for anyone. This may be a last ditch effort, but we've got to try."

She wrung her hands and looked from James to Sean like a schoolteacher admonishing her pupils. "I hope you're right. Godspeed." She turned and retreated to the house, her struggle with her limp personifying distress.

Sean sidled his horse up to Rusty. "There's someplace I need to go first," he said lowly. "I found out who was feeding information to Coleridge Sierra during the takeovers of the independent mines."

James stared keenly.

"It came from the assay office. Old man Hollister."

"Och. I'm agog. Why? Money? But he's retired and gone now."

"He's got a cabin about eighteen miles from here—near Washington. I thought as long as he gave information, he might've gotten some. Could give us some answers."

"That's a hell of a ride up Harmony Ridge. Three times the distance on flat land would be a quicker trip. But, I'd say it's worth checking. All right. If I don't see ye before, God willing, I'll see ye on the front row of the march. We'll meet at the upper end of Main Street in Grass Valley."

CHAPTER 18

Sacramento

Dutton grew fatigued with the underlings. Encouragement not his strong suit, his methods of motivation vacillated wildly from dangling carrots to threats. This business of reassuring people in their weaknesses proved tiresome.

He strode back and forth on the rich carpets outside the governor's office. It paid to place people in the know everywhere—a fox in every henhouse, as his father said. He recently endured listening to his protege drone on endlessly about the mining wage reduction. Lodie Glenn was an asset torn between helping his town and his need for prestige. His political future in exchange for local information had produced an equitable arrangement.

Dutton assured him no Chinese would be brought in. The board even agreed to a closed shop though, for reasons he would not explain, a strike might be a good thing—to settle the dust. He explained with a sense of irritation that a show of strength, however staged, was necessary to set things forward between owners and management. Dutton loathed handholding. He informed Lodie that, if he expected to see the inside of Congress, he'd better drop his attempts to reconcile board members with the miners' union.

The door to the governor's office swung open, and Dutton gave a polite nod to a railroad executive as he left. Governor Burke smiled warmly at him. "Dutton, please come in!"

Dutton shook his hand upon entering. "Governor Burke, it is a pleasure."

"How's your father?"

"Incredibly busy, as always."

"Well, that's good news for the State of California, so it's good news for me as well. What can I do for you? Would you like a drink?" He motioned towards a decanter of brandy.

"No, thank you. I know you have a tight schedule, as do I, so I'll get right to it. Tom, we're going to require help with some matters concerning the Empire mines. We've moved posthaste to bring the mines up to par with safety and organization issues. The men have unionized—not altogether a bad thing, but it seems they elected a fanatical hothead of a leader, who is stirring them up to strike. We must suppress this strike for the good of all. Communication has broken down, and they intend to storm the Empire mining offices any day now. I need a show of force to stop it. I need you to send in state militia."

Governor Burke retreated behind his massive desk. He sat slowly and offered a disapproving look. He began cautiously, spreading his hands in a conciliatory gesture. "Now, Dutton, I would like to help, but that's a pretty demonstrative step. We're not in the habit of sending out troops just for show. Surely, you don't intend for them to actually fire upon these men?"

"Of course not," Dutton snapped, "but they have to see we're serious. And they have to *know* we have leadership behind us." His look hardened. "I'm not asking, Tom."

Governor Burke squared his shoulders. "Your father has backed me in my every endeavor. I'll go to him directly."

"Whom do you think sent me?" he sneered. "It is at his pleasure that you're sitting in that chair. It seems you may have outlived your usefulness."

"It's excessive force. I won't be a part of it."

A nasty smile crept across Dutton's face. "It would help,

Governor, if your tastes did not run so far to the peculiar. Your opium habits, were they known . . . would be enough to put you in the condemning glare of the public eye."

Dutton reached inside his coat and pulled out an envelope. He tossed it across the desk. "But under the influence of such, your judgment's impaired. Chinese prostitutes? I'm not sure these are images the public—or your wife—will likely forget."

The governor grew pale. "You . . . you introduced those girls to me."

"Yes. Well, they're not to my liking, but you've embraced them as quite a habit. Now. I think we're entering a more logical state of negotiation. You see my point as to the importance of squashing a rebellion of anarchists. I want the strike stopped."

"It's political suicide," the governor protested shrilly.

"No, what's in that envelope is political suicide. But the miners' union—Well, you never know which way the public is going to lean on an issue like that. Always a chance they'll commend you . . . for restoring law and order. Do we have an understanding?"

137

CHAPTER 19

The Collier Ranch

Charlotte waited by the corral fence near the main barn, the sky alight with soft, pink-bottomed clouds as the day dawned and shadows fled away. She looked anxiously at the bunkhouses and the mess hall, anticipating Justin's appearance any second. In the few minutes that had passed since she hopped off the rented mare and hailed the Colliers' stable man, she had managed to dig trenches in the dirt with her boots for all her twisting, turning, and nervous pacing. Sleeping little after James's visit, she arose to track down Justin rather than spend the remainder of a restless night worrying.

She turned to see Justin duck his head around the triangle hanging in front of the mess hall as he approached. He hurried towards her.

"Criminy, what time did you get up to get out here at this hour?"

"I wanted to catch you before you went off working someplace where I couldn't find you."

"Any earlier and you'd've only had hoot owls to talk to. You found me. What's wrong?"

"Oh, Justin . . . I don't know what to think. Da came to see me last night. There's more trouble at the mines . . . he thinks there will be a strike . . . the investors are telling management to cut wages."

"Wait, James was here?"

138

"He came to find the investors, to try to reason with them. He went to talk to that judge again but found his son. The man made threats. Da rushed back to Nevada City to help Sean control things there. The men that lost their claims to Empire feel cheated; the others won't take less pay. It's a powder keg." She looked down at her dusty boots and took a deep breath, "It gets worse. The investors that started all this—it's a company called Coleridge Sierra."

"Yeah, I heard him mention that."

"Justin—it stands for Collier and Dandridge."

Charlotte took a small measure of comfort from the confused expression on his face. She gave him a look pleading for an answer she knew he didn't have. "Dandridge is the judge. But . . ." She glanced over her shoulder towards the residence. "You don't think . . . how can this be true?"

"I'm as stunned as you. It doesn't fit, somehow."

"Da seemed pretty sure."

He looked up at the house. "Neil is in the best position to know what's going on. He got in last night."

She grabbed Justin's arm. "Then we should ask him! There's no reason to speculate or wonder or worry; we should just ask."

"Charlotte, he's still my boss. I can't go accusing them of anything."

"I don't want to blame. I don't want to believe it's true! But if it is . . . I want someone to understand what the miners are going through. We have to find out!"

Justin said little as she prodded him up to the front door. He mulled things over, but she knew he'd have his thoughts together by the time they got inside. They waited in the foyer displaying a sheepishly contrite manner for rousing Neil. He greeted them curiously as he came downstairs dressed, sweeping his bed-tousled hair into place.

Neil showed them to the study; they sat facing him at his

desk as Justin apologized for the intrusion and the hour. Charlotte felt awful for the questions posed, seeing how openly cordial he seemed at their concerns. Justin asked the hard questions politely, stressing they merely sought to understand the situation in the best interests of all concerned. Then he allowed Charlotte to repeat all of what James had confided in her.

Fully awake after her recitation, Neil gave her an awestruck stare. "Our union chief is *your* father? I've not had the pleasure of meeting him, but I have heard him speak." He looked at Justin and chuckled. "The man's incredibly charismatic . . . he had me eating out of his hand. I snuck into a miners meeting to hear what's going on up there . . ."

Charlotte realized suspicion showed on her face. Neil caught her meaning. "I *am* running for office. In order to know how to help, I have to know the people's needs, who I'm going to represent—see?"

She relaxed. "Of course. I'm sorry. This is all very confusing to me."

He frowned. "I admit this wage cut business is news to me. Several issues you bring to light I held a different understanding of. Are you certain this information is correct?"

"Absolutely. He'd just come from talking with Dutton Dandridge."

"Ah. I remember now; I brushed past him in the hallway. He looked in a bit of a rage."

"He's very passionate about the subsistence of the men."

"I understand. I could tell that from his speech to the miners. But . . ." Neil seemed to weigh his words. "Look . . . from what Dutton said, your father is rather set in his ways."

Charlotte squared her shoulders, and her eyes glinted as she said in measured tones, "As he would tell you—any man who stands for anything *is* set in his ways."

Royce's voice boomed unexpectedly from behind her. "She's right."

Neil looked up. Charlotte and Justin turned around.

"What's this about, Neil?" Royce demanded.

Justin began urgently. "James came last night. There's big trouble at the mines. Coleridge Sierra is pushing the miners to strike. James met with your partners—twice—both the judge and his son. He says they're out to start a fight—men have been swindled of land; now they're cutting wages, ignoring safety issues."

Royce's jaw tightened. "Neil?"

"What do you want me to say, Royce? I've been out campaigning, and I'm just hearing this myself."

"*You* were uncomfortable with how we acquired those mines . . ."

"Dutton assured me . . ."

"Dutton!" He spat the name. "I've never trusted that polecat—he's always been a little too slick . . ."

"Royce—not the time to discuss family business." Neil looked pointedly at Justin and Charlotte.

"Regardless . . . we need answers on this!" Royce fumed. "This is the last thing Father would ever have wanted."

Neil stood up, thinking aloud. "There's a board meeting in a couple days. I'm going up there."

"Why weren't you anyway?"

"Campaigning, Royce. Dutton felt . . ." He stopped talking.

Royce threw his hands up, chuckling angrily. "He sure knows how to pull your strings."

Justin stood swiftly. "Okay, I think we have a sense of what's going on here. At this point, we'll leave you to tend to your business. Charlotte, we should go." He put his hand lightly on her arm.

She got up to leave, then stopped hesitantly. "Is it too much to ask . . . that you tell us what you find out when you get back?"

"Since you brought this to our attention . . . I'll tell you what I can," Neil answered.

"Thank you," she said softly. She avoided Royce's eyes as she walked past.

He followed saying, "I'll walk you out."

She turned and looked at him, knowing where her first loyalty lay. "Justin can see me back to my horse." She gave a slight nod towards Neil. "You should stay and talk to your brother."

CHAPTER 20

In winter, the drowsy mountain hamlet of Washington was kept in isolation from the rest of the world by the tortuous four-mile stretch of highway Sean now traveled. James told him, if not for the steady patronage from the Washington-Nevada City stage, no reason existed to lure him to negotiate this treacherous path. In these four miles, the road dropped nearly two thousand feet from Harmony Ridge to the bottom of the Yuba River canyon. Sean swore he'd never hurtle around the corners of this rutted, narrow, winding route in a stagecoach.

Sean cursed, realizing he rode in circles. Twice, he misread the under-utilized trail leading to Hollister's cabin. Finally finding the house, he marveled to see it squeezed tightly between enormous ponderosa pines. He dismounted and banged loudly on the door. No answer. He tried looking in the windows, but the absence of light in the shade of the trees hindered his limited vision. He heard movement from inside, so he returned to the door and resumed his pounding.

The door opened a crack. A short, elderly man squinted and asked, "What do you want?"

"Mr. Hollister?"

"Yes?"

"My name is Sean Miller. I work for the Empire mines."

The door opened a bit more, and Mr. Hollister stepped outside. He looked Sean up and down. "Yes . . . yes, I think I remember you from the old days."

"Yes, sir. I have some important questions for you. Do you mind if I come in?"

"Come in, come in." The old man beckoned as he moved slowly back into the house. "I don't get many visitors up this way. But the fishing is mighty fine, so I like it. Forgive me, I don't move quite as well as I once did." He turned and squinted at Sean. "Yep, yep, I do remember you. The eye patch threw me for a second. Was the war, was it?"

"Yes, sir. Mr. Hollister, I need some information about the assay office."

"Please sit, son. I'll do my best." He eased himself into a rocking chair. "What is it you need to know?"

Sean took a deep breath. "Mr. Hollister, it's come to my attention that a great deal of information concerning the output and grade of ore from some of the smaller outfits was given to an investment group that in the end bought up those mines for the Empire Mining Company."

The old man frowned. "Yes?"

"I was told the information came from the assay office."

Mr. Hollister shook his head vehemently. "No, sir. Not on your life. I took an oath."

Sean pressed on. "Perhaps your memory ain't as good as before. There's a huge strike hanging in the balance. Men's livelihoods are at stake. I need to know whom you gave the information to and what you got in return. I want to know what you know about these men—starting with their names."

Mr. Hollister looked bewildered. "I told you . . . no one, I swear. The bones may be failing, but there's nothing wrong with my memory. Do I look like I got something in return? Look around you."

Sean saw he was upset. Mr. Hollister shook his head. "I would never talk to outsiders like that. No, sir. The only person I ever talked to about anything was Lodie Glenn 'cos he was always

144

interested, you know, in the work. And maybe I shoun'ta talked to him neither, but it was harmless curiosity . . . bar talk, you know."

Sean stopped breathing. He blinked hard, trying to clear his thoughts. "When? For how long?"

"Oh, for years. Lodie's always been fascinated with these things. He wasn't in mining anymore, so it was harmless. Guess he couldn't quite give up the glory of it when all you boys went your separate ways."

Sean struggled for his voice. "Thank you . . . Mr. Hollister. I've got to go now." Sean got up, shook his hand, and bolted for the door. He scrambled onto his horse and rode hard for Nevada City.

145

CHAPTER 21

Sacramento

Dutton stuffed the relevant folders into his leather bag, preparing to head for the Empire mining office. Necessary revisions to the model in the secret war room were in process.

He still cursed Governor Burke for not showing up to extend his support to the board at the unveiling of the secret room. Only a handful of people knew of its existence, and necessarily so. The entry room, its windows now blackened, had once been a work station leading to the assay office and refinery. In this area used to sort ore, the observation windows allowed management to prevent the practice of "high-grading"—ore that traveled home in a pocket rather than its intended course to the assay office.

Connected to this meeting room, the war room lay behind a massive locked door, descending farther below ground since it occupied a long, played-out tunnel whose vein had ended abruptly. With walls some eighteen feet tall, the cavernous space lent itself well to secrecy. It housed a library of land parcel maps, legends of mines and tunnels, and engineering reports on every mining practice and problem known to the civilized world. Mammoth oak conference tables topped with enormous iron candelabras stood in the center of the room on which to spread and study the amassed intelligence kept here.

But the little alcove at the end of the war room displayed Empire's magnum opus: a colossal scale model portraying a labyrinth of levels, tunnels, and rooms—Empire's as well as every competitive mine in proximity. It had taken Caleb Redmond, a stolen employee from the Brunswick mine in Grass Valley and now their chief engineer and head of operations months to convert the tunnel maps into the complex network of working riches displayed here. Judge Dandridge had strategically hired away at least one prominent employee from each profitable company to add to this exhibit showing many mines, many miles apart.

The tin model illustrated the twisted and intertwined connections of horizontal and vertical underground passages. Metal strips colored in black represented existing Empire shafts. The red ones indicated the path to expansion. The red tunnels of the independent mines Coleridge Sierra had bought out of foreclosure were repainted black, feeding their network with untapped resources. In this intricate spider's web of wealth, Empire looked to gobble up unclaimed land or claims they could dispute—who was to say where a vein began and ended? Many a courtroom battle raged over a vein on one property and the owner's right to follow it where it went—to a neighboring mine or not. Encroach, infringe, trespass . . . possession.

Dutton sighed as he changed his focus to the tasks ahead. The unpleasantness with the governor might have been avoided if the man had not fallen victim to believing he *was* the persona the Dandridges created for him. A shame to outlive usefulness so soon, but Dutton felt vindicated involving Burke with the Chinese. If one paid careful attention, an opponent nearly always told you how to hang him before he realized you were adversaries.

He tugged at the heavy gold watch chain crossing his waistcoat, clicking the stem of the Swiss watch to check the time. He needed a closer look at the model to reference the proximity of flooded shafts to his intended expansion before the board meeting. He expected input from middle management on manpower and how to best deploy it. And, of course . . . he did not want to miss the show provided by the governor's office.

The courier he awaited finally arrived. Dutton snatched the correspondence from him and ripped it open. He scanned the missive from his father. ". . . *show of strength only. Absolutely no violence. The uncertainty of the strike alone is enough to drive down prices. We need to put men to work immediately, once we've demonstrated control.*"

He glanced up at the courier.

"Any return message, Mr. Dandridge?"

"No, not at this time. Did you find Tolliver?"

"Yes, sir. He's waiting in the lobby."

"Good. Send him in. That's all." Dutton crumpled the message into a ball, feeling irritated. He piled more papers into his valise.

The scruffy man entered his office, looking about furtively.

Dutton glanced up as he fastened the leather case, "Ah, Tolliver." He reached in his pocket with his right hand, picked up the satchel with the left, and strode towards the door where his minion stood. He glanced up to see Sadie looking in their direction. He leaned in and spoke lowly. Then Dutton put the gold coins in Tolliver's hand and said firmly, "I want MacLaren kept away from my board meeting. Understood?"

Tolliver's eyes glistened through the unkempt hanks of hair hanging in his face, and his lips curled into a wolfish grin. "My specialty, sir."

CHAPTER 22

Nevada City

Lodie fidgeted in the storeroom of his emporium. He arranged and re-arranged the shelves, but no amount of order soothed his spirit. He stared blankly at his ledgers for a while, then decided he needed physical labor to take his mind off his troubles.

He glanced at his father's silver-headed cane leaning in the corner. The first day he brandished the cane, this symbol of his new identity carried him into the inner circles of influence. Nervously, he had followed Dutton's guard down two ill-lit levels of stairs and a maze of dingy, narrow hallways to a secret underground room beneath the main offices of the Empire mine. After Sean's tour, James and Vicente yammered on and on about the precision and sophistication of the map room. Little did they realize theirs was a mere glimpse at the inner-workings of Empire. His inclusion, however small, in the secret consortium left him awestruck, igniting dreams he never imagined possible.

Startled, he sensed another presence in the room. He turned sharply to find Sean, his face stricken, watching him.

"For the love of God, Lodie . . . what have you done?"

Lodie stood silent.

"Why?" Sean demanded.

Lodie's mind scrambled for logic. "I tried to do better by us all. To bring us a peaceful town, a profitable town, with no

149

fights is all—the men need help to see where their future *is*.
They ignored the obvious; they ignored the warnings, they . . .
they . . ."

"All this time. You've been nudging us along. Pointing us in
the direction *they* wanted us to go."

"No, it wasn't like that. I needed to be in a position to help
the greatest number of people, the town. I did it for us."

"You've played both sides! It's a jot and a tittle, man! You
can't divide the two! What did they promise you?"

"I thought I could *help*," Lodie said stubbornly. "The men
could not survive without intervention."

"Are you daft? You thought of yourself. I asked you a question: what did you get out of it?" Sean yelled.

"Only an opportunity to represent us. I did it for us," he
repeated. "Who, better than I, can represent our needs to
Congress? I'll stand for all of *us*." He faltered seeing Sean's eye
grow wide. "Sean . . . towns founder when they depend only on
independent mines. We've managed to thrive. As the Empire
mines grow, Nevada City grows in its shadow."

"You've been spending too much time in the shadows, *Congressman*. You sold us to elevate yourself."

"A lot of ghost towns exist where thriving communities used
to be; did you want to see that happen to us?"

Sean glared at him. "Politics suits you better than I thought.
At what point were you going to keep our confidence instead of
theirs? It's no different than when you got it in your head to go
your own way—and left me and James and Vicente. All of a
sudden, the friends that supposedly matter to you got thrown
over for your ambition—without word, without warning. And so
it goes again now. The miners are a hair's breadth away from a
strike. Strikebreakers are being sent in! Men will be hurt. You're
responsible for this fight . . ."

"There *are no* strikebreakers!" Lodie bellowed.

"What?" Sean's eyes narrowed. "Are you sure?"

"They're bluffing." Lodie fought a panic rising within. "Sean, there isn't time for this. Listen to me. I don't know why, exactly—control . . . I guess, a show of power against the union . . . They intend to send militia to make a statement."

"You *knew* this?" Sean shook his head in disbelief. "What happened to you? You're caught in a devil's knot of trying to decide which way to jump. For us or for them? You jumped wrong, Lodie! You've jumped your soul straight to hell. Look at you . . . eyes blazing at me! I can only guess it's the flames lapping you up that're feeding that look." He turned away in disgust.

"Where are you going?"

"Where I belong." Sean gave him an ugly look. "To the side of my friends."

CHAPTER 23

Grass Valley

They gathered at the intersection of Main and Auburn. As he passed the popular Exchange Hotel, James pictured himself, beer in hand at the bar, with Sean and Lodie at day's end. From where he stood on Main he pivoted slowly, viewing the deep-green hills upon hills surrounding the village as if providing no way out—an island of a town encircled by a sea of pine and fir covered ridges. He took a deep breath and stretched, leaning back to gaze up at a bright-blue sky. High clouds wisped by in loose puffs, seemingly pulled apart in tatters by the breeze. A fine day for a march, he reckoned.

He could only imagine the eerily quiet mines. All work stopped. No activity, save for the water level rising in deep shafts where no one remained to feed the steam operated pumps. He surveyed groupings of men clad in baggy canvas pants, congregated in batches according to company. Word of Empire mine events hastened through bars, neighborhoods, and worksites of many operations. Men weary of remote mine owners and suspicious of distant job altering resolutions sought representation in their union. They came in droves from nearby North Star, Union Hill, Idaho-Maryland, and Pennsylvania mines, having watched with a wary eye the clashes at Empire.

An awe-inspiring assembly of men, James estimated their numbers at something over three hundred. They cleaned up for this encounter, shaved and bathed, wearing hosed-off heavy brogans, an array of cotton and woolen shirts tucked neatly or anchored with suspenders. Wool felt hats with rounded crowns and narrow brims had been beaten and dusted. He watched them milling about and studied stalwart faces deep in discussion. Resolutely, they waited to make this empowered stand.

As they flocked together, James walked amongst them, encouraging individual men about their hopes, concerns, and accomplishments. He turned to see Clancy standing in mock salute.

"Chief! Reporting for duty, sir!"

"Och, none of that." James chuckled. "Good ta see ye, old friend."

"Grand turn out! I hope management's expecting this many of us for tea."

He laughed. "I'm glad spirits are high. It'll be the best approach, ta be sure. Have ye seen Sean?"

"Not yet . . . was gonna ask you the same. It's getting late; we ought to be getting started."

James looked up at the sun's position in the sky. Perhaps Sean was busy ushering more men towards them. From here it was only a mile and half to the Empire mining offices. He gazed down Auburn Street, a fairly flat walk until they reached Empire Street and began the steep, mile-long hike up the hill. Sean would catch up. He called them to huddle in closely. James nodded at Clancy. "Want to address the troops?"

Clancy grinned. "Certainly." He turned towards the crowd and called out loudly, "I see you brought your Cousin Jack."

A ripple of laughter rolled through the multitude.

Hand over his brow, Clancy playfully scanned the crowd. "Jack, Jack, where are you?"

A roar went up as the Cornish contingency, over two thirds of the assemblage, yelled, "Aye!"

James felt uplifted by their spirited display. Despite the threat of the wage cut they appeared heartened by unity, emboldened by brotherhood.

"Well, I suppose it's time now ta march up the hill and have a wee chat . . ." James announced. Laughter again moved through their ranks. He smiled at them warmly.

"I cu na be more proud. We welcome our new brothers in arms." He paused as the crowd broke for applause. "This is a grand step we take today. This is a march ta set standards in motion—a closed shop . . . fair wage for fair work . . . safe working conditions. We will define our fortunes for a long time ta come. We walk towards stronger communication with management . . . towards authority over our own lives. Be proud of yerselves; be proud of each other, for facing adversity head on. We go before management today from a position of strength and truth and community. We go as a united voice ta march up that hill ta meet them as equals. C'mon, lads! It's time ta have our say!"

Deafening shouts sounded out. Men pumped their fists in the air and slapped one another on the back. It was a crowd carried by the inspiration of hope.

CHAPTER 24

The Empire Mining Company Office

At the top of the hill, Dutton prepared for the onslaught of miners on a myriad of levels. He hurried from the flat-tabled map room adjoining the offices back to his more centralized command post in the large first-floor main office. He spent the last hour with his engineers as they unfurled extensive maps, cross-sectioning the location of shaft intersections, bolstering his knowledge for his upcoming event in the lower-level, secret war room. He found that far-flung tunnels followed veins of dubious ownership between Empire and North Star. Where order began a lattice-like descent of seams embraced with ore, chaos left open a door of doubt as veins flowed off on a spidery course.

Dutton paid lip service to a half-dozen area managers, from which his union representative was conspicuously absent. He readied them to face the miners they supervised daily and the indisputable aftermath to come. Ben Alexander, his chief engineer, stood talking quietly in a corner of the room with Bart Risney from the Nevada City Foundry. Dutton required the presence of a few noteworthy board members today. He wanted plenty of witnesses.

Managers and engineers occupied themselves during the wait by sorting through employee rosters and securing each of the buildings on their row. In the quiet hum of tense conversations and shuffled papers, he realized Empire's chief operating officer, Caleb Redmond, was unaccounted for. He strolled outside onto the lower porch of the two-story main office to survey the wide, functional courtyard of the Empire realm.

He moved to an outside corner of the decking to gaze through the enormous redwood gates, swung wide in welcome from massive stone columns crowned with rustic pyramids of rock. The long stone wall fronting the road led the way through the entrance into the working quadrangle. Beginning with the rear of the double-decked mining office, all buildings to the left side stood as a continuous line of stone structures butted against each other like a quaint village row. Constructed of waste rock dredged up from the mines, each structure featured parapets separating varied roof heights, and each building flaunted windows and doorways enhanced by bricked surrounds. This stretch of headquarters contained the map room, strong room, and assay office, which adjoined the bullion room and gold refinery, with the medical-rescue office tacked on the end.

Dutton inspected the sequence of larger, tin-roofed warehouse structures opposite where he stood—the machine shop, head frame, and the mill building. He squinted momentarily over the tree line behind the mill-building roof before shifting his attention to the company of heavily armed militia standing guard in the courtyard. Their ranks filled the breach in the empty work-yard between office row and the industrial shops.

He heard Caleb Redmond's voice from inside behind him. Remembering his mental agenda to discuss before the miners arrived, Dutton hustled inside. As his eyes adjusted to the change in light, he stopped short. Caleb walked in from the strong room with a tall, sandy-haired man. Dutton looked sharply from Caleb to Neil Collier, surprised and rattled. He analyzed Neil's authoritative attire of frock coat and string tie. He swiftly choked down rising concern and called out, "Neil, old man! I wasn't expecting you. I thought you'd head home to

Sacramento from the campaign trail."

Neil looked up, nodding cordially. "I did." He pointed to his attire. "I'm a bit rumpled, as I didn't have time to change out my suitcase."

Dutton chuckled. "No need for that kind of rush. You'll wear out before election day."

Neil hesitated. "The family felt it was important that I be here. They've been catching a few whiffs of discontent concerning operations."

Dutton studied his face. "Of course! The mining district is a huge portion of the state's growing economy." He answered coolly, all the while thinking, *something's off*.

"True. Issues here could well spread to other outfits. The better I understand our own investment, the better I can answer questions elsewhere. I'll be available for the board meeting tomorrow. I've missed a great deal of activity in the last few weeks."

Dutton told himself that Neil was only educating himself on the process. Up to now, he'd been content to rely on Dutton's advisements. He decided his old familial friend warranted some attention.

"Well—since you're here, I can fill you in on union demands."

"No need," Neil replied lightly. "I bumped into Caleb on my way in, and he brought me up to speed. Will our San Francisco partners be joining us tomorrow?"

"Father sent me their proxy. It's largely a housekeeping meeting." He looked away. Addressing the room full of Empire managers and board members he continued, "If that's all then, I'd like everyone to head outside for a brief word?"

They filed out onto the porch facing the open courtyard. Feeling guarded with Neil's presence, Dutton crafted his words carefully. He cautioned, "I remind you all—this is strictly a peace-keeping measure. We don't know the union's intentions.

We will not assume the worst, but this *is* a strike." He swept his hand confidently towards the company of soldiers.

"I'm proud we have the support of Governor Burke, who recognizes the value of our contribution to the growth of the state of California and our willingness to work through this conflict to swift resolution. It is in *all* of our best interests for employees to feel secure in their jobs and get back to work as soon as possible. Let's prepare to hear them out." He acknowledged the troops loudly. "Carry on, Captain."

Dutton pivoted to speak to the group on the porch. "Our board meeting will take place here tomorrow as scheduled. If pockets of unrest remain, we shall keep military support until confident this siege is over. Neil, you and the other members may want to join me upstairs."

A sound in the distance caused his audience to look up over his shoulder. Dutton turned as they watched the main gate. It was the clamor of marching men.

The union men steadily climbed, following the snaking road as it ascended, with as many abreast as fit on the roadway. They kicked up dust along the broad, pebbled path bordered by a dense, fern-laden forest. They encountered scattered stretches of sunlight where trees drew back, exposing small grassy fields. Miners ducked as the boughs of evergreens dipped low on the sides of the road. Baritone rumblings of male voices resonated as they sang mining chants on their journey. The sound of marching feet fostered a feeling of power. The cadence of boots invigorated their resolve, and they felt the potency of their convictions.

Scotland's son looked up through the fretwork of leaves at the feathered clouds, deeming each one a thought, a memory adrift. He felt the coursing of clan blood through his veins, calling on kinship to lead him this day. Longing for peace, he understood the reality of having to defend it. Always it would be, as long as men drew breath.

James had walked this road a hundred times and only now noticed how much like the perimeter of a medieval fortress this stone wall appeared. Years of blasted by-product, chunks of waste rock, picked and chiseled, piled and stacked, formed the rampart surrounding Empire's stronghold. Rough, craggy boulders set along the wall's top created a haggard sentry, a picket of protection along the border. Now as the men approached the crest, they fell silent.

James turned at the hush. At his farthest line of sight behind the last rows of marchers, Sean pushed his horse to catch up. James walked backwards, watching his friend urge his mount up the road, then duck off the pathway between entwined trees. Seeing Sean hop off and lash the reins to a fallen log, he turned to face the final bend.

James inhaled deeply. His mind tuned to the rhythm of their steps, and the men crowded on all sides of him. He felt part of a living, breathing machine. As they rounded the turn, his eye searched through the pyramid capped columns of the open gate. Inside the courtyard he spied rows of soldiers. Alert and wary, his stride shortened as he took in the meaning. He stopped and held up his arm, signaling those following to stop. The men on the front lines buzzed with uneasiness.

James turned and stood tall. "Steady men. Pass the word back—troops are ahead. It's a good show they put on there. They mean ta intimidate us, but we're here ta talk. Let's not give them the satisfaction of seeing they've rattled us."

Echoes of agreement drifted down the lines. James waited, aware of a riffle through the parting crowd as men shuffled aside. Sean pushed his way to the front. He gave James a tired grin.

"I tried to get here in time to warn you that we'd have

company. Obviously, I need to see you later about a faster horse."

James smiled. "Anything else ta report?"

Sean looked at him darkly. "Nothing that won't keep until after we've handled the business at hand."

"Where's Lodie?"

"Lodie ain't no warrior."

James sparked a curious look, then threw his arm around Sean's shoulder.

"Glad ye're here." He looked down the lines at the men and waved ahead. "All right, lads! Forward we go."

A solemn mood descended as they marched towards the office. The noise of their stamping feet grew purposefully louder. James halted a comfortable distance from the troops standing stiffly in formation.

The union men filled in the space around him, crowding every side to hear. He saw Dutton's smug, swarthy face looking down from the upper balcony of the office building where he had positioned his group. An officer bawled a command, and the soldiers lifted their rifles at the ready. Not one union man flinched. Dutton stepped forward out of the shadow and leaned against the railing.

"That's quite an impressive welcome, Mr. Dandridge." James's voice boomed across the divide.

Dutton smirked. "Compliments of the governor, gentlemen. He felt it necessary to emphasize California is a law-abiding state. We don't tolerate mob mentality keeping legitimate business owners from prospering."

James spread his arms wide and low, demonstrating nothing to hide. "There's nary even a rock in one man's hand here, Dandridge. What is it ye fear, that ye would show up with this? We come as peaceful men, with grievances ta be discussed, face ta face with other men. We're here, in the open. We did na expect ye ta hide behind authority that is na even yers." James scowled at him. "It's a false picture ye're trying ta paint here."

Dutton dropped the smirk as James watched him simmer silently. Caleb Redmond stepped up beside Dutton at the railing.

"We're willing to hear you out, Mr. MacLaren. Now let's just pull this confrontation back a bit."

"What authority, have ye?"

"I'm chief operations officer for the Empire Mining Company." Redmond squinted and yelled out, "You, with the eye patch. Don't you work for me?"

"That I do, Mr. Redmond," called Sean. "Sean Miller, your representative to the union. I've attempted a number of appointments to bring these matters to you personally, but there are a great many managers between you and me that didn't see the importance of what I had to say to you, sir."

Caleb Redmond turned to look questioningly from face to face of his men gathered in the doorway, many of whom looked away. He looked up at Neil.

James could not hear but saw a heated conversation taking place on the veranda. He yelled out in an insistent tone, "I can see this information is startling for ye, Mr. Redmond. I find that particularly surprising since Mr. Dandridge and I had numerous conversations about the problems in yer mines."

Redmond whipped his head around to stare in open-mouthed astonishment at Dutton. Neil looked on grimly.

James added loudly, "Ye see, we weren't expecting troops here today—but the Chinese strikebreakers that Mr. Dandridge promised would be taking our jobs."

James watched in amusement as Dutton appeared to be seething. He gripped the railing, his shoulders hunched and tight as if ready to leap over. He hissed at Redmond, "Get them up here. Let's talk!" He avoided looking at Neil.

Redmond turned back to face the throng of miners. "All right, MacLaren. Let's get this thing out on the table. You, Miller, grab a handful of others if you like and come up to the offices. The rest of you men will have to wait outside. Apparently our communication suffered a serious breakdown. As a show of good faith, I can tell you this much: we've already voted on *and agreed to* a closed shop!"

Thunderous cheering went up from the men. James and Sean pointed at committee heads from the back-slapping horde to accompany them to the offices. Sean waited as chosen representatives pushed their way through a jubilant crowd. James turned and locked eyes with Dutton as he strode towards the office. Dutton slowly raised his right hand.

The noise and commotion from the miners all but muffled the crack of a single rifle shot. Sean twisted to look out over the roofline of the mill building, then whirled back around. James stood stock-still. His legs buckled, and he inexplicably fell to his knees. He heard Sean howling as if from a tunnel, "Nooo!" and saw Sean lunge at him. Another clap from the rifle echoed in his ears, and Sean collapsed on top of him as they hit the ground.

A stunned silence stilled those on the front rows as they stared in horror. Confused infantrymen looked at each other to determine the origin of the shots. Their captain ran up and down his lines searching for a culprit. Shock subsiding, rumbling cries of anger arose from the miners as some began storming the offices. Shouts came from every direction. Dutton held up his hands from the veranda, yelling at the troops, "Hold your fire! No shooting! Hold your fire!"

Clancy broke away from the pack and ran in front, waving his arms furiously at the men blinded by rage. He screamed at them, "*No!* No more violence. We have men *down!* Help *them!* Don't make this worse!" He momentarily broke their trance of fury. He grabbed the man closest to him. "Go and get a wagon. Now!"

Caleb Redmond and Neil Collier ran down the steps to hold a similar stance in front of the troops. Clancy turned and ran towards James and Sean, diving down to James's side. Neil pushed his way towards the circle of men that had formed around the fallen.

Sean's back was covered in blood. James struggled to push up on one elbow. He coughed, and the effort brought a fresh gush of blood from his chest. He fought to sit up, and he rolled Sean over. He grabbed Sean's face between his hands and began to shudder. James gazed deep into his friend's eye and growled hoarsely, "Hold on. Ye got ta hold on."

Sean's lips moved slightly. He seemed to know it was too much strain to talk. His eyelid closed for just a second. He opened his eye and gave James an almost imperceptible nod. "Told you . . . Lodie . . . ain't . . . like us . . . He ain't . . . no warrior."

James whispered, "Help is coming . . . by God, ye've got . . ." He slumped against Sean's shoulder as he succumbed to blackness.

Neil whipped around to the troops shouting, "Captain! Get over here and help them!"

CHAPTER 25

Nevada City

Lodie sat on a high stool behind a counter in his store, polishing the head of his cane. No amount of busy work made waiting for word go any faster.

He rubbed the silver top until the shine came through. He held the cherished possession, a reminder of his father, out in front of him. His father had been a great man with no higher ambition than his own family and farm. Lodie wondered if he'd be proud of how much his son had achieved. Everything seemed tainted now.

He frowned thinking of Sean. In his mind, his actions remained completely defensible. He'd make Sean and James see that he was right.

Matilda rushed through the doorway with her head down. He looked up, a question poised on his lips. Matilda stared at him with fear in her eyes.

"Something went terribly wrong," she whimpered. "There was shooting up there. They have James at Dr. Wyndem's. Lodie, he's been shot."

Lodie bolted from his chair, feeling a sudden tightness in his chest. "Is he going to be all right?"

Matilda looked uncertain. "He's lost a lot of blood."

"Is Sean with him?"

Matilda stood wide-eyed. Her lips began to tremble. "Yes . . . but . . ." Her eyes filled with tears. "Sean's dead."

Lodie blinked hard as understanding crept into his consciousness. A rushing sound filled his ears. Matilda's lips moved, but he could no longer hear. He felt his chest being crushed in. He put the cane in his hand to the floor and leaned heavily on it for support. His knees gave way, and he grasped the silver-headed cane desperately as he sank to the floor.

West of Sacramento

Royce flung open the front door and stalked inside. He stood in the middle of his sister's foyer and shouted, "Adele!" He glanced up the stairs, turned towards the kitchen, leaned towards the study looking for the first sign of movement. "Adele!" he bellowed again.

She came scurrying from the kitchen. "Royce, for heavens sakes . . ."

"Where's Stan?" he demanded.

She pointed at her startled husband now standing in the doorway of the study.

Royce jammed his fists on the back of his hips, taking an agitated stance. "We got big trouble."

Stan hurried over. "What's happened?"

"Oh, dear. Perhaps we should sit down," said Adele.

"No time. We've got to make some quick decisions."

"Royce, you have to explain what's going on." Adele tugged on his arm until he followed her to the parlor. He spilled details loudly as he walked behind her.

"I just put Justin and Charlotte on the stage to Nevada City." He took a deep breath. "Neil sent a wire. All hell broke loose up at Empire. The governor sent militia up there as a warning, and two people were shot."

"Shot!" exclaimed Stan.

"Yes. Our union representative is dead. Our union representative that Justin has known all his life and was due to marry his mother in a matter of weeks!" he spit furiously. "The other was the union chief, Charlotte's father."

"Oh, dear Lord." Adele covered her mouth with her hand, looking stricken. She slumped into a chair.

Royce pointed accusingly off in the distance. "Of all the people up there, you tell me they weren't targets."

Adele paled. "Thank heaven Neil wasn't hurt."

"This is a disaster. What can we do to help?" Stan looked up sharply and answered his own question. "Well, I'll tell you one thing. Whatever those men were striking for, we give it to them. Without question. This is unacceptable. Why on earth was the militia there in the first place?" He looked at Royce. "We have no business being involved with an operation like this when we have so little understanding."

"Agreed," he said fiercely. "Neil witnessed the whole thing, but it isn't clear who started the shooting or why. It's a miracle more weren't killed. The board meeting's been deferred until after an inquiry."

"We can't wait until then to act," said Adele. Stan nodded his assent.

"There is something . . . Neil mentioned it after Charlotte and Justin first brought the problem to us." Royce looked sharply from one to the other. "William Bourn is the largest shareholder of the Empire mine outside of Coleridge Sierra. He's approached Neil more than once about buying our shares. I vote yes. If you agree, I'll find Bourn and complete the transaction immediately."

Adele looked at Stan. He nodded. "What about Neil?"

Royce patted his vest pocket. "He's convinced. He doesn't like what he's heard from Caleb Redmond, either. He wired his proxy to be used as long as we're all in agreement."

Stan frowned. "What about the men? I don't feel right about

bailing out of our responsibility to the miners."

"Part of the deal. I'll make sure of it. Neil won't leave until he's certain their demands are met. I'll take him the papers as soon as the ink is dry."

Stan patted Royce's shoulder. "Go. Get it done."

Royce turned as if off to battle.

Adele called, "What about the Dandridges?"

He growled, "They're free to dance with any devil they choose. But they aren't dragging us onto the floor anymore."

167

CHAPTER 26

Nevada City

There remained the tiniest sliver of a chance. Lodie watched the crowd of miners jamming the front porch at Dr. Wyndem's. They murmured quietly amongst themselves, looking anxiously for the door to open. His shock subsided, fear followed, and reason returned, as Lodie tried to think his way out of this. He shoved aside guilt and regret. He prayed that, as long as Sean was gone, perhaps recriminations went with him. He gathered his nerve and bolted towards Dr. Wyndem's door deciding, no matter what, to continue pushing.

As the men at the back of the crowd moved aside, he heard his name shouted. His heart fluttered in his chest as he bulled through them, ignoring faces. When the crowd clustered and impeded his progress, he realized he heard friendly calls, hails of sympathy. He waved tersely, stopping momentarily on the steps, and stated, "Thank you all for your concern. I'll bring news as it's available." He reached the front door. It's all right, he breathed! He opened Dr. Wyndem's door and squeezed through.

Vicente sat on a bench holding Althea's hand, her face swollen from crying. Lodie stood transfixed. Vicente's mournful brown eyes sentenced him to the feeling of plunging into an abyss. Fear of looking at Althea made him willing to take the fall.

"James?" he choked out.

Althea stood, clutching a wrung-out handkerchief. The crystal fire flash in her eyes told him she knew it all. She raised her chin declaring, "They're both here."

He looked down, searching the floor for answers, and stammered, "Does that mean they're both . . ."

Vicente stood and studied him as he would a stranger, his voice ragged with sorrow. "He will live. The bullet, it goes through. He is not conscious."

"You don't belong here, Lodie," Althea said softly.

Lodie felt himself break, "Althea, I'm so . . ."

"*No.* You aren't. I saw Sean before he went up there. *You* put them in harm's way."

"I had no way of knowing . . ." he pleaded to Vicente.

"No, *they* had no way of knowing what *you* knew," she persisted.

"Althea . . ."

Vicente stepped forward. "You should go. She is right."

Stunned, Lodie replied, "You . . . huh . . . I paved the way for you in this town."

Vicente solemnly shook his head. "It is not the time."

Lodie deflected. "I . . . I made you successful."

Vicente stepped uncomfortably close to him, staring up into his face like a reflection of inescapable truth. Lodie felt the man's breath on his chin, and Vicente said lowly, "Who made who?" His mustache twitched above his tightly closed mouth as he sounded, "Hmm?"

Lodie shot Vicente a bitter look and turned on his heel, stopping as he heard Althea.

"Lodie . . . You did this. *Remember that.* I always will."

He left without another word.

In a quiet restaurant corner inside the Nevada City Hotel, Dutton parried Neil's endless questions. Always a wrestling match with Neil's conscience, Dutton played a patience game of re-assurance. Though merely a matter of managing expectations, some days he wearied of the task.

"What else can I say, Neil? It happened so fast it was all I could do to control troops with a couple hundred angry men ready to storm the offices. I don't mind telling you, I was terri-fied." Dutton pushed his dinner plate away. "You talked to Red-mond and the others . . . what did they tell you?"

Neil sat back from his half-eaten plate of food. "Not much different than you. I don't understand why they can't pinpoint who broke in that line of militia."

"Well, obviously they're covering their own rear ends."

"But *why* were they even there? MacLaren's not a violent man."

"Sending troops was our governor's idea—more on that in a minute." Dutton pointed at him excitedly. "For the life of me, I never understood your fascination with that man. He certainly has no love for me. Believe me, the way he charged into my of-fice—he has very aggressive tendencies."

Neil looked away. "You didn't see him in action. He's protec-tive of his men, and he fights for what he believes. If I can't do the same, I have no business running for senate," he challenged. "I'll tell you another thing: this tragedy happening on my watch . . . does not exemplify the leadership I expect. I won't let this rest, Dutton. I want answers!"

Dutton studied him. He decided to acquiesce. "You're right. It was tragic. Forgive me for trying to push past it, but, speak-ing as one who was present, it's a picture I'd rather not keep. Nothing to be done now other than to see the miners taken care of."

Neil appeared irritated.

Dutton pushed on. "We gave them the closed shop they wanted. Safety issues are being resolved. Their wages are intact.

It's all we can do."

"We should never have lowered the wage to begin with."

"All right, a mistake, but let's not lose sight of the fact the company suffers a substantial loss at the moment. Those shafts are deeply flooded, taking weeks, maybe months, to get them operational again. Our stock has plummeted."

Neil looked at him wryly. "Funny, how timing works that to our advantage. You said sell, and we did. Now we buy and ride it to the top again."

"Neil, I'm talking about cost of our improvements. I could never have foreseen anything like this." Dutton sighed as if trying to make sense of it all.

Neil said solemnly, "It's stock jobbing, Dutton."

"What are you saying?"

"I'm saying, we built a speculative bubble, and we got out before it burst. Now we stand to profit on the cycle back up."

"Mining is a speculative business."

Neil smacked the table with his hand. "At what point does self preservation take over another man's right to live?"

Dutton bit his tongue. His political pony proved more spirited than he anticipated.

Neil sighed. "Dutton. In view of the catastrophe and loss at the Empire mine, the family strongly feels we should no longer be involved with its operations."

Ah. *Now* he knew where to jump in. "I understand, Neil. You were instrumental in settling demands—it's a good note to back away on, and you needn't worry. I can take it from here."

"You'll have to. We've sold our shares to William Bourn."

Dutton stared. He leaned forward, putting his elbows on the table, and lowered his head until it rested in his hands. He looked blankly at the tablecloth, lost for words.

He began slowly. "You realize . . . this gives him a majority. Why . . . why didn't you come to me?"

"Frankly, I didn't think while running my campaign this was something you and the judge should be tied to either. I still believe I've something to offer in service to this state. If the judge no longer wishes to back me, I understand. The Colliers aren't willing to take another dime of profit from those mines. I can't ask you to do the same. The decision is up to you and your father."

Dutton sat back, giving a cynical laugh. "Oh, Neil. Your timing couldn't be more ironic." He leaned close in a conspiratorial manner. "Father's heard a great deal of criticism out of San Francisco concerning Governor Burke over this incident. It seems likely his only term in office. We just set your aim a little higher."

CHAPTER 27

Nevada City

"Matilda! I can't find the other trunk."

"Land sakes." Matilda bustled into the parlor carrying a stack of dishes. "Here—behind the chair in the corner." She scrutinized her husband's efforts. "Must you take all those books?"

"I want my constituents to see I'm an educated man. How's the rest of the packing?"

"The maid finished with the boys; they're making the rounds in town saying good-bye." She looked down at the plates. "I wish I could decide which set of china to take."

"Take them both."

"Lodie, we'll still come back on holidays and to visit."

"Don't count on that right away; we'll both be busy breaking into Sacramento society. I imagine we'll spend the first Christmas there."

Matilda's face fell. "Oh." She glanced around her home longingly, turning at the sound of a sharp knock at the front door. "Mercy, who could that be?"

"I asked the new manager of the Emporium, Mr. Collins, to come, but I'm not expecting him for at least another hour."

Lodie dragged the trunk over to the bookcase as Matilda hurried to the door. He grasped three volumes at a time, scanning titles on the spines, and separated them into piles.

He mumbled aloud, "I suppose there's not room for all of them." He glanced up seeing Matilda return wearing a pained

173

look. He straightened as a tall, russet-headed figure stepped into the doorframe behind her. Bereft of speech, Lodie stared into his hawk-eyed glare.

Unable to bear the silence, he muttered, "James."

"I'll leave you." Matilda retreated, pulling the parlor doors closed behind her.

Lodie noted James's right arm bound tightly to his chest. "I'm glad to see you're doing better."

James notched his chin higher. "Surprised this is the first I've seen of ye. Missed ye at the funeral."

He looked away. "I came to Doc Wyndem's. Althea made it pretty clear how she felt. I thought it best to wait until we could talk over . . . things. Under the circumstances, I wanted to preserve some sense of dignity."

"Many words would fit ye like the skin ye shed—dignity is na one of them."

"That isn't fair."

"Fair? Sean's dead. Ye left a string of betrayed friends in yer wake." James glanced around the room full of packed boxes. "Just on yer way over for that chat?"

Lodie's chest heaved. "I did *everything* for the survival of this town."

"Our first conversations at Silver Moon—when ye dragged me in by my civic conscience—ye were aware of 'new' financing. Ye put Sean in the middle. What of his survival?"

"I never wanted Sean to take that job! You *know* the independents should've listened and sold out sooner. They took bad loans and got foreclosed on—too proud to let go, too proud to take jobs. Refusing reasonable offers was just plain stupid. They were hurting us all, James! They were dragging the town down with them."

"Huh. Can barely acknowledge him, can ye? Can na admit the role ye played. All right then, let's look at the rest. Ye played

174

God. It was their lives, their claims, their choices, Lodie. Ye took their dreams, man. Ye harnessed yerself ta lousy politicians, so ye cu become one!"

"Part of any good business is good contacts. Building higher, you have to reach out to policy makers, bankers, even to the governor himself."

"Och. Ye're holding a wolf by the ears. Ye used people. Old man Hollister never knew ye picked his brain for yer own ambition."

"No. I thought it would give Nevada City inside information."

"It did. And how did ye go and use it? Against us! But then, ye talked ta everyone, knew everyone's financial status . . . ye steered the bad bankers straight for them. Rammed them and sunk them, ye did."

"They were offered a decent price. But, as in any business, if you wait too long, you miss the peak. Not my fault they waited." He balked. Lodie peeled off explanations by rote, the more twisted reasoning he threw at James, the more he justified his own belief in his actions.

"But ye knew the end game—details ye did na share with the rest of us. Ye knew yer friend the judge needed all the small properties ta follow the main veins without contest or court systems involved. Ye moved towards profit and left people behind."

"I'm all for a man going for the dream; if he wins or loses it's on him. Nobody cheered harder for their success than I—it brought business and prosperity to Nevada City." He grew agitated. "But once they failed, ran out of cash, or lacked the equipment to succeed, they selfishly put the reputation of the town at risk!"

"When did it become *yer* town?"

Lodie froze. He stammered, "I was afraid. If the small mines

175

gave out and folded . . . investors stop coming, the town vanishes, everything I worked for all these years is for naught."

"So ye traded your nothing for theirs? Ye're a bloody mercenary."

"Look at the way the world works, James! You need influence for leverage, for dominion over those that would take from us—you have to accumulate power, collect it and protect it. I'm not going to apologize for defending what's mine. I won't grovel because I was the one willing to go after the authority it takes to create a better life for all of us. Without the weight of government behind us, we languish here. You can't deny that! I stepped up to bring power to Nevada City."

James stood, silently shaking his head. He narrowed his eyes, holding Lodie's gaze captive in his sway, and stated, "Ye're a shadow of a man, Lodie. A shadow has no power because it no substance."

James maintained his formidable stance, staring as though taking stock of the bond of years between them and deciding to leave them behind. He turned and departed the room. Lodie heard the lonesome sound of the front door closing.

Lodie gaped at the empty doorway. His shoulders sagged, feeling the weight of an irredeemable hollow within.

CHAPTER 28

Thistle Dew

"Death is a dark night of the soul, and we are meant ta get through it. No one can show ye the way."

Charlotte nodded at her father's quiet assertion. The spirit of Sean's presence hovered with a lingering impression they could turn at any second and find him standing alongside, grinning. James struggled to pin down some proverb, something to ease the grief. No expression, no feeling, no reason justified his loss. Snatched from them as fast as powder flash, it seemed Sean should reappear on the other side of the smoke cloud.

Charlotte placed her hand on James's left arm as they sat together in the front porch rocking chairs. His right arm remained bound tightly to his injured chest, supporting mending muscle. Each day he looked physically stronger, a far cry from the frightening white visage drained of essence she had faced when she rushed into the sickroom. She shuddered at the incomprehensible image of this titan of a man lying in a foundering state. Weak from every form of exhaustion, he had opened his eyes and reached out for her. Instinctively, she had crawled onto the bed as she had as a little girl, ducking her head under his good arm, and eased onto his shoulder. His lips brushed against her forehead, and he succumbed to rest.

Althea retreated far within herself in her bereavement, reminding Charlotte of a little wounded bird, huddled as small as possible. Justin worried she appeared to slip away, listlessly

177

going through motions of time and empty space. Upon arrival, they witnessed Althea labor fiercely around the clock tending to James's care and then Sean's funeral arrangements. As James recouped strength, he fervently consoled her. They talked long hours into the night, clinging to each other like the last pair of a vanquished breed.

Charlotte gazed out at the corral, watching Justin put a mare through her paces. She worried over him also—so intent on supporting his mother he pushed his own grief aside. Stoic Justin, seeking tasks he claimed as "cleansing sweat." With Da unable to work stock for several weeks, there would be plenty of that for them both. She sought peace in spending time with the horses, finding a normal rhythm to life in the saddle. A steady stream of food coming from miners' wives in Grass Valley and Althea's friends in Nevada City limited their need of her in the kitchen.

She looked at Da. He stared off at the hillock overlooking her mother's garden. The sunset pink and yellow rose bushes they had planted around the little graveyard flourished into wildly flowering clouds. Sean kept her mother company up there now.

Union men had borne his casket up the hill. James led the procession, and Althea followed it wearing widow's black, her soft, blonde hair swathed in ebony lace. Hundreds of mining families had come. Friends from Marysville, Nevada City, and a dozen farms in between gathered to pay respects. Even Neil and Royce Collier came offering support, standing in the distance so as not to intrude. Everyone came. Everyone, but Lodie. In an odd twist of fate, Lodie slipped away from them, too. Da remarked only that Lodie had been lost long ago.

Charlotte stood as she saw riders approaching down the main road. She turned to her father. "They're here, Da."

Abandoning his reverie, James snapped to attention. Neil and Royce rode first to the corral to speak with Justin. They dismounted and tied off, Neil breaking away first and heading for the porch. He had traveled between Thistle Dew and the Empire offices many times in the last few days, playing union advocate and courier to assist James in hammering out an agreement with management.

"Mr. MacLaren, good day, sir."

James stood and offered his left hand. "I'm hoping there's finished business in that bag of yers. Come . . . sit." He nodded towards the rocking chairs.

Charlotte drifted down the porch steps as Royce sauntered up. He nodded his greeting to her father.

"Good to see you again, sir." He turned, scanning the landscape behind him. "Beautiful place you have here. Built it all yourself?"

"Aye. Justin's put a fair piece of his back inta it."

"I'd love to get a look at your stock while I'm here—especially anything sired by that silver stallion."

James chuckled. "I'll just bet ye would. Perhaps Charlotte can show ye around while I go over paperwork with yer brother. I appreciate ye assisting him." His tone darkened. "I understand ye went ta talk with the militia."

Royce pushed his hat back on his head and took a deep breath. "I wish I had better information. The captain in charge that day said every rifle was inspected, and none were fired. No one remembers seeing anyone take a shot. He can't explain it. I suspect the culprit managed to sneak off and clean it or change it out in all the chaos following. At any rate, somebody's lying."

James said grimly, "That's certainly disappointing."

"To say the least," Justin chimed in, joining the group.

Royce added, "Oh, I haven't dropped it. I might not get the truth, but that captain's going to feel the pain of my persistence."

"Appreciate that," Justin murmured.

Neil sat down next to James. "I'm glad to see you looking

like your old self."

"Duty gives me purpose."

"You'll be pleased—all demands have been met. Your men can get back to work at full pay in a closed shop. You'll have a say in choosing the new union rep. Caleb Redmond will work with you there; you can trust him. He feels as responsible to the miners as I do."

"That's grand. What about safety issues?"

"As you know, there's a lot of water to be pumped out before tunnel work can resume. Redmond wants to discuss implementing a bell system with you, as well as blasting innovations—dynamite is on the horizon." Neil glanced at Royce. "As I told you were our intentions, we've sold our shares to William Bourn. He's a good man, with vision. He's eager to meet you."

James scrutinized Neil closely. "What about the judge and his whelp?"

"Bourn means to have them out. He was outraged by recent events. Redmond will work closely with him to see it happen. He'll fire all managers that answered directly to Dutton."

James gave a fierce nod. "Speaks well of the man already. We'll start fresh on solid ground then." He tilted his head and asked, "Ye still in partnership with them?"

Neil sighed. "Not any more. It appears our core approach to people and business differs greatly. I thought I knew Dutton better than that—our families go a long way back."

James huffed. "Happens ta the best of us, that."

Neil smirked and looked at Royce. "I'm sure there's an 'I told you so' coming; my brother draws a lot harder line in the sand with people."

"Never liked him." Royce shook his head.

"Good instincts."

"On to better things," Neil said, patting his valise. "I have papers to go over with you if you're up for it?"

"Let's get to it." He looked at Charlotte. "Darlin', perhaps ye and Justin can show Royce around?"

Justin jumped in. "I'll catch up. I'm going over to the cottage to check on Mum."

"Aye. That ye should."

Charlotte smiled, inclining her head. "We can start with Banshee if you like?"

"Sure. Why wouldn't I like to start with the horse that skunked my favorite gelding?"

She laughed. "I'm glad to see you're over it."

She looked back as they walked away, happy to see her father engaged in mining business. She led Royce towards the main barn, saying, "This is really good for him. He needed a focus where he feels he can accomplish something for Sean."

"Justin said they were as close as brothers."

"It's been a horrific loss for us all," she said sadly. "You know he died trying to protect my father?"

Royce nodded solemnly. "Justin said that, too. It'll be hard for your father to get past that. How's Justin's mother doing?"

"Crushed." Her voice trembled. She smiled, though her eyes brimmed with tears. "Theirs was a long, complicated courtship, but, in the end, everything was just right." She looked down as they walked. "He and Justin had been close since we were little. I don't think the full weight of this has hit him yet, not while he's caring for Althea. I think he knows it."

"How are you doing?"

Her mind flooded with Sean memories, and she laughed. "He was like a favorite uncle, always making me laugh, joking around. When we were children, he was fun because he behaved like a kid, you know? He never met a stranger, never withheld a kindness—or a drink, my Da would say. A lovely, lovely man. I miss him greatly."

Royce hesitated. "I wish I'd known him. I'll never forget your

181

father's words at the funeral: 'Men have a need to find someone amongst ourselves to trust. A caring friend, someone we can touch and believe will be truthful with us. We yearn for someone who at least appears to be a little more than we are. Sean Miller was that man.' "

Touched, she looked up at him. "I can't believe you remembered all that."

He shrugged. "It was powerful. We all want people like him in our lives. It's more rare than we care to admit."

They stood in the barn's doorway, Royce searching deep into Charlotte's eyes. Banshee nickered from his stall.

Charlotte turned away. "Ah, your nemesis calls!"

Royce chuckled. "Then we should pay homage at once!"

They lingered while admiring Banshee, Charlotte stroking his velvety muzzle as Royce commended her ability to handle him. She detailed future breeding plans for the stallion as they continued wandering amongst the stalls and talked up the selling points of each occupant. Arriving at the end of the barn, Charlotte prepared to take him to see larger freight animals stabled in the next building. As they stepped out into the light, she saw Justin approaching. Royce took her hand.

"I wanted to ask before Justin got here," he began, "or rather to say . . . I know Sacramento was a temporary solution for you . . . but I would miss you . . . if you didn't come back. Adele says Mrs. Van Oss is already lamenting your absence . . . I hoped you might consider returning?"

"Oh." Surprised, she studied his face. His deep-blue eyes watched her most intently, making her uneasy. "I . . . really haven't had time to think about it." She looked off towards the house. "Da will need me here until he recovers, and Althea . . . I guess I've never thought about not being here."

"Of course, you're needed here for now, but . . . could I be so bold as to ask you to mull it over?"

"I . . ." The corners of her mouth turned up, and she fought a sneaking smile while contemplating her response. "I liked living in town—and feeling independent." She cocked her head at him and seeing Justin nearly upon them said, "We'll see."

He smiled broadly and turned to Justin. "Glad you caught up. Charlotte is educating me on the stock. Seems I saw more animals out in the pastures. Maybe we can ride out and look at the lot of them. You fill me in on the available ones, and I'll get you to work a couple of them out for me. How's that sound?"

"Perfect. I think Neil is about finished up; think he'd want to join us?"

"Sure."

Justin looked at her. "Charlotte, you coming?"

"Yes; let me get my gloves from the house."

Justin led the way back to the house. She saw Neil packing papers in his bag and her father standing by looking pleased. Althea sat in one of the rockers enjoying the sun on her face. Justin ambled briskly in front of them, not turning to see that Royce lightly held her hand as they walked. Closing the distance to the porch, Justin called out the invitation to Neil. She saw Da glance at them. She let her fingers drift away from Royce's hand, but not before she saw the jolt in Da's shoulders and knew he noted the gesture. His eyes darted to her face, but she focused on the doorway and bounded up the stairs to get her gloves.

She returned smiling casually and gave him a quick peck on the cheek, promising to return shortly. *"A successful escape,"* she thought to herself—for now.

James stood thunderstruck watching the foursome ride off to the pastures. He stared until they vanished from sight. He whirled around to face Althea, his mouth gaping like a fish. Her eyes twinkled as she stated, "I saw it."

He pointed off in their direction, still fumbling for words. His sandy-red brow knit tightly in a frown. "When? How did this . . . Has Justin spoken of this?"

She shook her head, smiling. "Well, she has been gone for a number of weeks. And, no, he hasn't mentioned it. I wouldn't be too concerned."

"Not concerned? With that lot?"

"I thought you liked the Colliers?"

"Liked that they stepped up ta do the right thing. Liked that they worked ta fix a mess they helped ta create. Liked that they gave Justin a good job. That doesn't mean I approve of that hubristic hulk sparkin' my daughter!"

Althea put her hand to her mouth, her lips tightly pursed.

"I swear ta God, if ye laugh at me now . . ." he roared.

She froze, her huge, crystal-blue eyes filled with mirth.

He pointed accusingly at the horizon. "Did ye see her breeze past before I cu gather my wits? She knew I would na like it!"

Althea burst into laughter. "Honestly, James! When have you ever liked *any* boy coming anywhere near her?" She held her side and tried to stop, but he saw the giggles had the better of her. She took a gasping breath. "Oh, it feels good to laugh."

He stopped his rampage as he realized how lovely she appeared in a happy moment. He ran the fingers of his left hand through his tousled hair and grumbled, "Och! I can na say ye didn't warn me!" He sighed and slumped into the rocker next to her.

She stifled a giggle. "That I did!"

"I should ha been nicer ta one of the local dunderheads. Ah, Thea. This will never do."

She put her hand on his knee. "And why not?"

He shook his head. "Ye know why. They are na like us, the rich. They don't value the same things. They discard what they become bored with."

"James, I refuse to look at that as a blanket assessment. If you keep growing this farm the way you want, people will be calling *you* rich."

"Och, it's na the same."

"If you can't explain the difference to me, then I very well doubt you can convince Charlotte."

"I *intend* ta discuss it with her."

"You'll be picking a fight," she uttered in a singsong voice. "She likes him. Justin likes him, and she trusts Justin's judgment. And you said it yourself—both of those young men did the right thing in very difficult circumstances. They fought for the right side."

He began to rock in his chair, sulking. "This is na over."

She sat back in her rocker. "I'm certain of that." She gave him a sympathetic smile. "Do you suppose we could put it aside for now? I'd like to rejoin the world, as hard as that is."

He glanced over. Her face was entreating.

"I looked forward to spending a pleasant evening with my friend," she coaxed.

He reached across and took her hand. They rocked quietly together holding hands, gazing out to the hillock, presiding over Thistle Dew.

★ ★ ★ ★ ★

Fall 1867

★ ★ ★ ★ ★

CHAPTER 29

San Francisco

Moonlight shimmered on the slick stone treads. The winding path descended to meet the crude jetty where small watercraft berthed. A host of stars and lack of clouds helped spread a generous luminosity over the water, revealing two Whitehall skiffs already en route to resting ships anchored well past the mud flats in deeper parts of the bay. Dutton questioned the wisdom of executing this small strike of vengeance on such a well-lit night. Even the giant seafaring vessels waited against a dark horizon as if anticipating a quick break for open water as soon as their human cargo arrived. He closed his eyes and allowed the soft slapping of the waves against the dock to ease his nerves. Opportunity seldom materialized at convenient times.

Gentle winds washed over him, carrying intermittent sounds from a multitude of down-at-the-heels dives in full chorus along the waterfront. Reedy songs of Melodeon dance halls beckoned sailors with tawdry promises of gyrating performances by scantily dressed women. Sporadic roars pummeled the air from scores of wine and beer halls—sightseers cheering the infamous entertainers known as Dancing Heifer, Roaring Gimlet, Lady Jane Grey, and The Little Lost Chicken. One such artiste professed the ability to sing in two keys at once. Rare was the critic to dispute her off-color shrieking as song.

The area surrounding Pacific Street, the first thoroughfare to reach the shores of Yerba Buena, now fed shabby backwater avenues of Montgomery, Kearney, and Stockton—where vice and crime prevailed. Just as Dutton grew restless to leave, he heard Tolliver's boots scuffing along the dock. He halted at Dutton's right shoulder.

"They're ready."

His father's minion had aged. His lank and greasy hair showed iron gray; his face appeared gaunt. The folds of skin around his neck hung loose, calling attention away from his distinctly damaged earlobes.

"You're certain about this?"

"Positive. Heard 'em tell their story meself. They're from Collier ranch, all right. One says he's the foreman."

"Did they see you?"

"Wouldn't matter, not where they're going. Naw. The pretty waiter girls do their job. Pinch of snuff, plug of tobacco in the whiskey—or sulfate of morphine—does the trick. Been out cold since we carried 'em over from the Deadfalls."

"Let's get this over with."

Dutton turned towards the warehouse behind them and stopped short; his face blanched. Standing at the land end of the wharf was a bald, behemoth of a man, blithely armed with a knife hanging on a lanyard around his neck, a revolver, a slingshot, and a pair of brass knuckles.

"Interesting new friends you've made since we curbed you here."

"That's Solly." Tolliver grinned. "For a small sum he'll sink a ship, or slit a throat. Mostly he's a runner for the crimps. But he gets his jollies rowing his passengers out to mid-bay and threatening to throw 'em overboard unless they pays double the fare. He'll see we gets you back to more respectable parts of town with no fuss."

"I feel immeasurably secure already."

Dutton stalked past his new guardian, eager to finish this

business, irritated that he was compelled to be in San Francisco at all. He felt jilted in Sacramento after the Empire mine shooting and made certain Tolliver disappeared into the shadows entirely. No sense in reminding anyone that they saw a man with cut-up ears. Miners were a cantankerous lot, particularly after the death of one of their own—especially a man as popular as Sean Miller.

But the cohesion of the Collier clan annoyed him most. His long-standing friendship with Neil suffered a major blow. Nothing illicit *proven* against him, yet a shaky trust evolved in the aftermath of fast paced acquisitions and stock manipulations. All strictly business. He and the judge had carefully orchestrated plans of dynasties for both families, and Neil was a vital political linchpin. The Colliers mustered for that insufferable MacLaren, prevailed upon Neil to weigh his options for public service, and all but drowned out Dutton's persuasive voice of reason. Adele, as the picture of fortitude and grace, he forgave, but not her priggish husband. Too young and insignificant, Celeste did not matter, but Royce . . . the overbearingly arrogant Royce blustered and bellowed throughout the family vote—ranting about the sanctity of their father's legacy. He became the rally point that bonded their integrity. As Dutton seethed, he felt ready for the task at hand.

He halted as Tolliver opened the warehouse door. Slipping inside, he heard a sharp, backhanded slap pierce the air. The harsh crack of flesh hitting flesh resonated high in the rafters before the strike of a second blow. He moved to a dark corner near the door, waiting for his eyes to adjust to the wavering flicker of a torch mounted well in advance of his position. The meager light flowed weakly onto center stage of the dank, dirt floor, the edge of its glow not nearly reaching into nearby corners, much less the rest of the crowded storehouse behind.

Tolliver and the monstrous creature he referred to as Solly

trudged into the dimly lit arena. The crimp moved on the first of two cowboys slumped against a tower of crates and grabbed his face. Struggling to wake, the man uttered a low moan and tried to focus eyes dull with the stupor of laced alcohol. The thug turned as the second man stirred, shaking off his daze. The man blinked and pushed himself up in a sitting position. Sudden comprehension jolted him, and fear flashed upon his face.

The crimp chuckled. "Probably saved ya self a beatin', mate." He delivered a vicious kick to the first man's ribs, causing him to groan and fall to his side. The second, eyes wide, shouted to his friend, "Hal! Hal, wake up!"

The man called Hal feebly lifted his head and vomited.

Tolliver shrugged. "That'll sober him some. Get the book, Solly."

"What's happening? Why are we here?" The alert prisoner looked from Tolliver to the crimp, then cringed at the sight of Solly returning. "Hal, are you all right?"

Hal spit, trying to clear his mouth. The crimp shoved him into sitting position.

"Glad to see you're back with us. You two had a helluva party. The girls said lovely things about ya both."

Tolliver snickered.

"We're meeting my brother. At the Cobweb Palace. He's goin' to be looking for us. You'd better let us go."

"Nice digs, the Palace. Serve a mean hot toddy. I was never much for the joint; ol' Abe Warner's fetish for lettin' the spiders decorate the place kind o' gives me the creeps. It's one thing to let the webs hang from the lights, the walls, and the ceilin', but when it starts covering the paintins' of the nudies . . . well that just interferes with the experience. I can say, though, the hoard of monkeys and parrots he buys from the sea cap'n's is impressive . . . collects walrus tusks and whale teeth, too. But not much on the female entertainment, which, I gather, was more o' what you boys was lookin' for, eh?"

Hal studied his captors, speaking with caution. "Listen, we ain't looking for trouble. We owe somebody money, is that it? I came to blow off some steam with Arvin, here. He's meeting his brother while he's at port, and he's gonna sign up for duty on his vessel. We just came for a good time before he ships out."

"Tell him, Hal. My brother's the first mate on the *Calypso*."

Tolliver looked over his shoulder into Dutton's dark corner. Dutton held up a single finger.

"Interesting." The crimp rubbed his chin, mulling this over. "Captain Hannigan's ship. Sails mostly into South America. It does seem if you two wanted to sign on with anyone it would be with your brother. Whatsamatter? Not that close? Was he Mama's favorite?"

"We're ranch hands. I have a job. Only Arvin is signing up, and only on the *Calypso*."

"I guessed as much by your duds. You'd be surprised how many cowboys yearn for more exciting times at sea. After all, who wants to spend life eating dust and looking at the dung end of a cow for the rest of their days . . . for so little reward when, instead, adventure on the high seas, travel, and exotic women await? You fellas made the better choice by signing on the *Reefer*. The Orient is far more thrilling."

Hal stood up. "I didn't sign on for nothin'."

The crimp snapped his fingers. "Solly, bring the book."

Arvin rose, plastering himself against the crate as he wilted under the giant man's glare.

Flipping through the pages, the crimp grumbled. "Well, you signed right here." He pointed to the middle of the page and looked up at his prospective sailors. "Hal Wittman, Arvin Michaels?"

Hal looked surprised. "Let me see that." He hovered over the proffered journal. "That's not our signatures."

"But it is yer marks." He tapped his finger above two shaky *X*'s drawn next to the names. "You made yer intentions known . . . gave yer names." He shrugged. "Just too drunk to sign."

"I want to talk to my brother! This ain't right!"

"I'm the foreman for the Collier ranch, and that's where I'm goin' back to. I ain't about to be taken on no Shanghai tour. The Colliers are important people, and my boss won't let this lie. Captain Hannigan's going to look for Arvin, too."

Tolliver grinned. He turned to catch Dutton's nod. He looked at Solly and began his retreat to the dark corner. "Wait for ya outside."

"Gents, I'll have you know I work for James Kelly, one of the biggest suppliers of sailors on this coast. He's got ways of dealing with those sufferin' with buyer's remorse. Tie 'em, Solly. Looks like we got a couple of possible deserters."

"I'm sailing on the *Calypso*!" Arvin shouted.

The crimp stepped up to within a couple of inches of Arvin, looking down his long nose at him, and smirked. "Rough luck, mate. You boys been passed out the better part of three days. The *Calypso* sailed yesterday. Noontide."

Dutton slipped through the warehouse door to embrace the night, Tolliver on his heels.

"There'll be no trouble with the brother on the *Calypso*?"

Tolliver laughed. "They don't know they only been in there a few hours. They'll be gone before they're missed. Captain of the *Reefer* is on his way to collect them and about twenty others in the warehouse next door. He makes his way inta high society from time to time, so's best he don't bump into you here."

"Unlikely we'd meet but not worth the risk."

"Solly'll be out, soon's he's tied 'em up for delivery."

"Nice work. Keep your ears open; never know what useful information you might stumble across."

"Always do."

Dutton stared out over the water, a mild satisfaction settling on his soul. Small strikes on an enemy provided a testing ground of their awareness. He was a patient man.

CHAPTER 30

Thistle Dew

"Let me see. Turn around."

Althea circled slowly, patting the thick, blonde coils of her chignon.

Charlotte stood armed with a fresh holly sprig, "Oh, very clever! You've braided the center bun with the ribbon but overlaid it with loose swirls of hair." She moved closer to examine Althea's design. Pulling the holly apart into three smaller pieces, she placed it around the outer twist and fastened the stems with hairpins. "That soft green is beautiful in there. Very festive!"

Althea smoothed the front of her pale-green velvet dress. "I suppose I favor pastels too much." She turned and took Charlotte's hands in her own, standing back to admire her. "Not like that bold plaid you're wearing! It's quite stunning."

Charlotte laughed. "I did that for Da. Not his clan colors, but the red and green seemed so cheery for Christmas."

She looked about her home at their handiwork of the last few days. Large red and white gingham bows joined long boughs of evergreen strung in great crescents around the walls of the main room; the fresh pine scent blended with the heady aroma of cloves and cinnamon rising from a pot of cider set on a grate in the fireplace. Clusters of mistletoe were twisted to form a wreath mounted on the stone above the mantle—a place where her father joked, "Will cause the least mischief."

The long oak table was set for eleven, with simple white china, dark-green linens, and beeswax candles encircled with juniper and red ribbon. The stately fir in the corner was dressed with bright strands of red, silver, and gold wooden beads she had painstakingly painted and boasted popcorn chains Justin complained about making even though he ate more than he strung. Lower branches were adorned with oranges and sweets for Vicente's children, as his large brood was joining them for Christmas Eve dinner.

"Well, your embroidery work is exquisite." She leaned in to study the intricate trail of holly and red rosebuds outlining the stark white inset on the front of Charlotte's dress. "May I tell you for the hundredth time how much I miss you in the shop?" Althea sighed. "And not just your work. I don't suppose I'll ever get you back now."

Charlotte squeezed her hands. "Don't say that! Without you, I wouldn't have my job, despite Adele Collier calling in favors."

"I think Mrs. Van Oss received the favor."

"It's worked well for us both, I think. But, I do miss working with you. You taught me so much, and it was fun. With her, I feel like I'm always under inspection. Not in a mean way, you understand. More . . . strict. I am learning new skills . . . just walking down the street in Sacramento I'm likely to see any number of new European influences amongst the wealthy set. Oh, and the fabrics that come in! Mrs. Van Oss travels to San Francisco for clients now that she has me to tend the shop. She brings back fabulous material, laces, and trim from France, Britain, Belgium. You should come for a visit, Althea. She said she would be happy to take you with her on one of her buying trips."

"That's very kind of her. And most tempting."

"She doesn't make offers lightly." Charlotte smiled. "I've taught *her* a thing or two, and she knows where I came by my knowledge!"

"Perhaps, I'll take you up on that . . . soon."

Her voice grew quiet, and Charlotte detected a slight shift in her demeanor. "I'm moving to town after the holiday." She turned and walked towards the stove as though remembering an urgent need to check on the goose roasting there. She no longer needed the walking stick; only a light trace of her limp remained.

Charlotte felt a jolt in the pit of her stomach. "Wait, what? Oh, but you can't! Da doesn't know about this, does he?"

"No." Althea whisked an apron over her head and tied it behind her. She snatched up a kitchen cloth and opened the stove door a few inches. "It's turning a beautiful golden color. Have you the flour and seasoning ready for the gravy?"

"Althea . . . Why? It won't be home to come back to, if you're not both here. Da will never sit still for this!"

Charlotte began to panic. With plans she was privy to in the offing, her mind raced to head off developments threatening to derail them.

"We've had the conversation before." Althea busied herself peeking into bubbling pots on the stovetop. "I couldn't bear to live in the home Sean built for us so soon after he died. My tenants are moving out, and it's close to the shop. Charlotte, it's been over a year. People talk. If you or Justin still lived here, that would be one thing. It simply isn't proper for me to be out here alone with your father."

"Don't count me and Justin out just yet!"

Althea shot her a skeptical look. "I work with *women*. It's been a year."

"No, it hasn't! *I* was still here for several months working the stock with Da until his shoulder recovered. And working in the shop! Everyone in town saw me."

"It wouldn't matter if you'd only left last month. Even a

week invites scrutiny for a single woman."

"You're a widow!"

"I'm weary of the whispers. It isn't considered respectable. And it will eventually hurt my business."

Charlotte scowled. "Pious peahens!" As she fumbled for her next argument, the front door squeaked open, and a nip of winter wind rushed in ahead of James and Justin.

Althea bolted towards them with her hand extended. "About time! What an awkward day for Caleb Redmond to call an urgent meeting in town. And to keep you this late! Our guests will be here any minute now. Justin, did you bring what I asked for? Is it snowing again? James, why do you have so much snow in your hair? Did you not wear a hat?"

Charlotte suspected Althea's flurry of exclamation was meant to cover a desperation to change the subject. Her father glanced in her direction as Charlotte raised her eyebrows as if to say *We have a problem.*

Justin handed over a parcel wrapped in brown paper. "Here it is." He, too, glimpsed Charlotte's animated expressions behind his mother's back. She locked eyes with him.

"Justin, could you help me pull the goose out of the oven? I need to make gravy."

"Sure."

Left to face Althea's inquisition alone, James gave her his most charming smile. "Mmm, smells heavenly in here! Well, where ta begin . . . the meeting concluded amiably, problem solved. We had ta wait awhile on yer package, so *that* slowed us a wee bit. No, tis na snowing. I removed my hat ta come inside when yer boy here stomped his boots on the stoop, causin' snow on the roof ta tumble onta my head. And Thea . . . how lovely ye look." He beamed at her.

With James holding Althea's attention, Charlotte leaned down to whisper in Justin's ear as he lifted the bird out of the oven.

"She says she's moving to town in a few days!"

"Again?"

"What! What do you mean—again?"

"I thought I talked her out of that."

"Well, apparently not!"

Althea turned around. "What's wrong, you two?"

"Nothing . . ." they chimed.

With a question forming on Althea's lips, James bolted towards the window and peered out. "Thea, looks like Vicente's wagon is heading down the road."

"Oh, dear. Charlotte, do you mind if I wrap this in your room? It's for Vicente and Ana."

"Not at all. Oh, the Christmas crackers are still in their box on my dresser."

"Dear me, I should have unwrapped those and gotten them on the plates already!" She bustled off to Charlotte's bedroom.

James hurried to the kitchen, calling loudly, "Need help, darlin'?"

"You could get out the carving knives . . ." Charlotte lowered her voice, "Did you get it?"

"Aye. He only finished it this morning. What's wrong?"

"She's all worked up about moving to the house in town . . . in a few days!"

"Och!"

"I wouldn't worry," Justin whispered. "It will all be settled tonight."

"Good Lord willin'." James grinned.

"Can I see it?"

James glanced at the bedroom door. "Best ta wait. We're all under enough suspicion."

"You're right. I better get this gravy going. How close are they to the house?"

"No guess. I dinna see them."

"What?!"

"Ye needed a diversion."

Justin moved towards the window. "Calm down. They're coming now." He shook his head and called out, "Mum? Do you want me to put the Christmas crackers on the plates?"

Charlotte rose from her seat at the spinet as her fellow carolers returned to the table, laughing and joking with one another over their lively combination of Spanish-English Christmas songs. All Vicente's children spoke English well, but a few oddly phrased old-English verses caused them to throw in the verbiage they knew best. They ended the sing-along on a reverent note, with James and Charlotte sharing a soulful duet of *O Holy Night*. An awe-filled silence followed Charlotte's soaring crescendo and the whisper-soft harmony of father and daughter in finale. Justin broke the reverie by quipping, "All right, everyone check your crystal for cracks." A burst of laughter erupted as all present recalled Charlotte's legendary birthday party performance.

"I do na think these qualify as crystal." James waved his glass.

"As I recall, neither did the ones in question," Althea added, smiling. "Hence, the demise of a small chandelier—into a punch bowl, no less."

Vicente shrugged. "People who make demands . . . sometimes get more than they bargain for, no?"

"In my defense, I performed as commanded by the hostess . . . Now, who wants plum pudding?"

Following Althea to the kitchen, Charlotte adjusted her purple paper tiara. She looked fondly around the table of smiling loved ones, each sporting a silly paper crown that had emerged with a bang from Christmas crackers, the brightly colored hulls of which lay spent all over the table.

Vicente's oldest boy, Rodrigo, sat next to Justin. The two were close in age and engaged in swapping mining stories, remembering their boyhood days as muckers in various tunnels. He was a handsome lad, taller than Vicente, but with the serious nature of his mother, Ana. Vicente had introduced both Rodrigo and his next oldest, Tomas, to hydraulic mining while he still worked up in the Sierras. Tomas and thirteen-year-old Luis each showed a great deal of talent and artistry with leather, and he hoped one, if not both, would take over his business one day. Luis had been named for Vicente's lost brother and possessed a wicked sense of humor. He had teased Charlotte unmercifully about her low placement of the sweets on the Christmas tree.

"Quien es los pequenos?" He reached a long way down to select a candy. He looked under the branches, *"No se?* Hmm, come little ones, we will share with you from the generosity of our friends." He put his thumbs under his armpits and strutted about as if he were very tall. Tomas smacked him on the back of his head. "He brays like a burro."

Fourteen-year-old Elena giggled the loudest at this, as she was most often targeted for their jokes. The youngest, Mariposa, gave only a slight smile. She was quiet and reserved—a pretty child, with enormous, doe-like eyes and wavy, black hair. Charlotte noticed she had scooted her chair even closer to Justin when they returned to the table. Ever since she was small, she followed him everywhere, and when she couldn't, her eyes did.

The individual conversations broke as Althea placed the sugar-dusted pudding in the center of the table next to the dessert plates. The sweet aromas of cinnamon, cloves, and nutmeg from the boiled confection elicited a chorus of appreciative "oohs" and "ahs." Charlotte winked as she set a large bowl of whipped cream directly in front of Mariposa and Luis. The girl's eyes twinkled, and Luis lunged with his finger set to attack the bowl until he looked up to see his mother shaking her head. He dropped the offending hand in his lap.

James chuckled. "Seems I have seen *that* move a few times in my day. Right, Justin?"

"When you're bold, you get the biggest scoop," he replied.

"Señor James . . ." began Rodrigo, "do you hear, we have now even *bigger* monitors at Malakoff? And strong! They tip them with steel . . . the nozzles are eight inches in diameter, the Giant . . . she is ten inches!"

"Yer father says ye live in North Bloomfield most all the time. What are ye working on in the cold months?"

"It is slow, working in the snow. But I am now apprentice to the surveyor. We look for new route for the flumes. Some older runs are damaged, and those we mark to fix when the snow melts. There is loads of repair work in winter."

"He patches much of what Sean and I worked on years ago," said Vicente. "The timber, it cannot support the constant force of all the water and rock but for a handful of seasons."

"That and the lower towns, they are complaining much about the tailings," added Rodrigo.

"Our old friends in Marysville and Yuba City . . ."

Ana poked Vicente in the ribs. "No. This is beautiful dinner prepared by our friends. *No politico*. The plum pudding *es delicioso*, Althea." She nodded at Vicente. "We will have happy talk."

He shrugged. "She is right." He gave James a look and patted his shirt pocket. "That is what cigars are for. Rodrigo and Justin, you may join us outside."

"*Ay, mi amor*. It grows late. Perhaps the families need to settle before Christmas day."

"I only bring the short ones. I want to be sure the boys can handle them."

Althea intervened. "Oh, I think there is time . . . for a short one. Besides, I do believe Charlotte brought gumdrops for the rest of us."

Rodrigo nudged Tomas, who rolled his eyes. "*Si*, I will save you some gumdrops."

"Good idea," added Justin. "It'll get the taste of cigar off your tongue." He looked at Charlotte. "Make mine licorice."

By Charlotte's estimation, the cigars must have been very short. Admittedly, Justin and Rodrigo did not finish theirs, but it gave them time enough to get politics out of their systems. Rodrigo commented that Señor James had puffed his with the determination of a man who thought he was igniting the smokestack on a steam engine and expected to go someplace. Vicente could take the hint, that something was up. As they waved good-bye to the Sifuentes family for the night, a calm settled on Althea—until she turned to face the stack of dishes and pots in the sink. James ducked out during the farewells and stood in front of her holding two glasses of sherry.

"Thought ye might like ta join me on the porch?"

"Well, that sounds delightful, but I refuse to leave you this awful kitchen to face on Christmas morning."

"Don't be silly, Mum—Charlotte and I will take care of this," put in Justin.

"Really?"

"Of course. You've been pampering us since we arrived."

"Go on . . . sit down and enjoy the quiet." Charlotte shooed them out the door. She closed it behind them and turned back to Justin, grinning. "How long do you suppose it will take?"

"Well, step away from the window before she catches on. Do you want to wash or dry?"

"Dry! Put some muscle into those pans, mister."

As soon as she was in range, he flicked her with water.

"Hey!"

After a few minutes of getting into a cleaning rhythm, he ventured, "So . . . be honest. How many questions has she asked about me?"

Charlotte chuckled. "A few every day. I know it's hard for

them, trying to imagine our lives somewhere different. What about Da?"

"Why do you think I asked? Constantly."

"She asks about your work. Is it dangerous? Is your boss as nice as you say? Do I think you will stay there forever? How often do we get to see each other? Do I know about any girls you might be interested in?"

He poured the goose fat into a large clay jar and dunked the big roasting pan into soapy water in the sink. "James has pretty much the same list. Though he seems awfully fixated on Royce."

"Your mother asks about him a lot, too—wanting to know if I think it's serious. I wondered how much was her initiative and how much is prodding from Da."

"I'd kind of like to hear the answer to that one."

Charlotte planted her hands on her hips, the drying cloth trailing against her dress. "What do you mean by that?!"

"Simple enough question. You seem to see a lot of him."

"Tch. I see him as often as one can see a very busy man running a large ranch. He sends *you* to town more than he gets there himself."

"He does that for my sake . . . and yours."

She felt her cheeks grow warm. "And I appreciate that. I see him every week or two weeks, I guess. He asked me to come stay at the house with Celeste when you bring me back to town. So we can go riding."

"How do you feel about him?"

"I haven't given it that much thought . . ."

"Bunk!"

"I can understand Da pushing, but why are you so interested?"

"Because I think he's serious about you."

She studied Justin's face. "What makes you say so?" Then she panicked. "You didn't tell Da that, did you?"

"Of course I did. Do you want him to think the man is toying with your affections? James intimidated every boy we grew up with if they looked sideways at you. Believe me, you don't want to give him a reason to be mad at Royce. And, as for you, any infatuations you had never lasted long."

"Da was right; they were pinheads."

"So . . ."

She sighed. If she didn't say *something*, his questions wouldn't stop. "I like Royce." She shrugged. "He's smart. He's honorable. He's respected. He's tough. Maybe a bit brusque at times . . . and opinionated . . . and bull-headed . . . . and *very* proud."

Justin smiled.

"What?" she demanded.

"Sounds like you *do* know him. Not too many stars in your eyes. Would you consider seeing anyone else?"

"I don't know. Like who?"

"Plenty of the hands want an introduction, but none of 'em are willing to buck Royce."

"Hmph. No gumption, then."

"That's not to say fellas from the other outfits wouldn't try."

"I suppose it would depend on the fella. This is all too pie-in-the-sky. I refuse to get mooney over a man that hasn't told *me* he's serious. Enough about me." She smirked at him. "I get hints from girls that see you come by the shop. They're always a lot friendlier when I say you're my brother. You might ought to hang around a bit after I go back in to work. There's a few I think might find a reason to rush in for 'new buttons' or such."

"Well, I wouldn't mind knowin' their names. Fat lot of good it will do for a while though. There won't be any time off coming up. We're running behind with no foreman."

"Is Royce still hoping Hal will turn up?"

"Nope. Pretty certain he and Arvin were both shanghaied.

Arvin's brother searched the waterfront, and, as a sailor, he knew where to look. From the few witnesses that saw bits and pieces, it's a sure bet."

"That's so awful."

"I liked Hal. Everybody respected him. He'll be hard to replace, and Royce won't hand the job to just anyone. A lot of us are shouldering more work."

"He trusts you . . . he could make you foreman."

Justin shook his head. "No, wouldn't make sense. I'm too young—which he might get past. He counts on me for horses. But, I'm still green with cattle. I'm learning, but nothing prepares a man like years of experience. Hal worked for Royce's father. He needs somebody all the hands will look up to without question." He sighed. "Sure has curtailed the men from wanting to cut loose on the waterfront. If they could get Hal, they could get any of us."

Charlotte hung the dishcloth on a peg and scanned the kitchen with satisfaction. "After I put away these pots, I think we've earned a sherry ourselves. While we wait."

"Agreed. I'll pour."

James had grabbed the blankets he left warming on the hearth. Althea wore one over her heavy shawl and the largest one across her lap. He saved a smaller one for himself to fend off the chill. The wind had died down, and a feeble snow sprinkled pinpoints of crystal to add to the collection on the ground. The night air felt both cleansed and sharp to his senses, a handy benefit after a heavy meal and the calming effect of watching the lazy drift of flakes. The porch rockers creaked with a protest of age—a sound he found oddly comforting.

He looked at Althea, her head resting against the back of the rocker, her glass of sherry sheltered in her mittened hands. She assumed a dreamy look, content, at peace. She glanced over at him and smiled at him watching her. Her pale-blue eyes exhibited a sparkle far beyond the starlight above.

"I miss this," she said softly. "You were right to suggest we brave the cold. The world and all its fuss seem to stop when we're out here. It's a perfect Christmas."

He chuckled. "Ye made it so."

"I had lots of help."

"Och, it has na just been this one. Thea, ye've been the glue that's held us all together. Made this a home for us all. Kept us a family."

She looked away and took a sip of her sherry. She stared down into the glass, looking sad. "And life keeps changing anyway. With the children away now, James, I . . ."

"No . . ." he blurted firmly. He sat straight in his chair, then turned to face her. "No," he said lowly. "I'll speak my piece, and after . . . if ye feel ye must, I'll hear ye."

Althea opened her mouth to protest but hesitated as she studied his face. He felt her reading him, and, as his oldest, dearest friend, she had the ability. He rushed to speak before she unraveled him.

"We've been through a time, lately," he began. "Your accident, my injury, the children stepping out on their own—too soon." He took a deep breath. "All the fightin' for the mines, betrayals . . . losin' Sean. But, we've faced it *all* . . . together. I've depended on ye, longer than ye know. Ye've been the strong sail guiding me through every tempest thrown our way. I've only ta look at yer lovely face, and ye bring me peace.

"I was a lost soul after Emma died. And I can na begin ta guess where ye are in that process with . . . Sean." He faltered, his voice now hoarse. "He . . . was a tremendous loss ta us both. Just like Emma.

"But, all the while, ye've been my closest friend. I knew yer fights, yer loves, yer disappointments, just as ye knew mine. I know yer heart . . . and yer spirit. Few finer have I e're known. Thea, in all this time, what I'm trying ta say—I've grown ta love ye. I'm so besotted with ye, I can na imagine life without ye by my side."

He saw her eyes glistening and grew nervous, not knowing if he touched her or if she dreaded to reject him. He stood. He walked over and took the sherry from her hands and set it on the porch floor. He dropped to his knee so that he could look full into her face.

"It's difficult ta separate feelings. A strong foursome . . . you, Emma, Sean, and I. And I believe, where we stand right now, they'd embrace us. It's never just you and I . . . they're built inta our very fiber. Ye can na separate us from them; it's who we are, now and forever."

He took a deep breath and reached into his coat pocket. "That's why I had Charlotte go through yer things ta find Sean's engagement ring." She gave a small gasp. "And I took Emma's ring. The jeweler in town made them inta one, because we are the sum of our parts. But make no mistake, Althea Albright. I love ye for the beautiful, exceptional woman ye are. I'd consider it my deepest honor if ye'd marry me?"

Her tears fell rapidly, and she opened her mouth twice to answer and could find no voice. She put one hand against his cheek, stared deep into his eyes, and nodded.

James broke into a grin. He took her left hand and tugged her mitten free. He placed the ring upon her finger. She stared down at her hand and saw Emma's wide, platinum filigree overlaid with Sean's thinner, gold band etched with roses.

"It's perfect," she whispered. When she looked up again, he leaned in to kiss her and found his welcome. As they began to part, she put her forehead against his and said, "I could not be happier.

"Oh!" She nearly pushed him over as she sprung from her

chair and stared at the house behind her. "Justin!"

He chuckled as he rose. "Now, ye did na think I cu attempt this without asking the lad's permission?"

"You did?"

"Of course. I asked them both. And I'm betting they're dying for us ta come inside and give them the news. Let's be on with it!"

The crisp January air pricked tears to James's eyes as they traveled up towards the Hallelujah shelf. He was comforted by the steady creak of saddle leather, soothed by the muffled rhythm of hooves thudding over snow as if through cotton. Charlotte urged Banshee alongside him as the path widened through the last of trees, their passage opening wide to his favorite overlook of the Bear River.

Each day, a pale dusting added soft layers to long grass cloaked in white. Afternoons warmed to melt encrusted surfaces of aspen branches, transforming them to clear coated fingers of ice, sparkling as they reached for a fleeting midday sun. As they approached the ridge, he saw across the expanse—hoary clouds over a distant sea of powdered evergreens spiked along the horizon. Below, a frosty mist shrouded the valley until an unseen current blew it aside, exposing glimpses of a deep bend in the river. Billowing snow showers rolled on, battered by a bullying wind.

On their ledge, gusts caused Charlotte to wrap her woolen scarf high enough around her neck to dive her face into its folds and capture the warmth of her own breath. Steam appeared in great puffs from Banshee's nostrils. Glancing at them, James felt a pang of regret. Expecting to find icy patches, he left Rusty behind—his old friend no longer sure-footed in rough conditions. From his stall, Rusty nickered complaints as James led out a dark-liver chestnut with four white socks and a thin blaze.

The leggy young stallion, eager and responsive, became James's new favorite. He decided to call him Knacker for the horse's mischievous nature, short for the Tommyknocker of Cornish lore. He habitually stole bandanas tucked in James's back pocket. Any tool, hoof pick, or currycomb James set down for only a second—Knacker plucked up with his teeth and tossed away. He kicked his stall door whenever anyone entered the barn, demanding first attentions. James liked his spirit.

His focus wandered back to Charlotte's face. Her sympathetic eyes peered over her fleecy red muffler. She reached up, tugging the covering below her chin. "It's no crime to exercise one of your new boys."

He chuckled. "I feel like I betrayed my best friend."

She smiled. "It was the right call—a steep ride. Rusty's earned a rest."

"Och, tell *him* that. He'd run on heart 'til it gave out."

He watched her lean forward to stroke Banshee's neck. The great silver beast shifted his stance, tossed his head, and gave a low, contented whinny. Aside from the nasty scar, Banshee's power and form had matured into a vision of grace and vigor, a far cry from the starving, mangled colt James rescued. He congratulated himself for detecting early signs of the animal's future conformation.

From first sight, he had envisioned the kingpin stud for his line of fine saddle horses; the first two foals were due this spring. He smiled, knowing this was the ace needed to draw Charlotte back to the farm. Banshee performed like a champion for him, but the animal adored Charlotte. She nursed him to health, and he followed her like a puppy ever after. In truth, her riding skills improved tenfold as she learned to handle his strapping size and speed. His eagerness to please pushed her to find new limits for them both.

"A sad thing, ta realize my daughter will miss a horse more

than her Da."

"Sorry, that's in my blood." She grinned. "Besides, I imagine you'll not be lonely. I'm leaving you in the best of hands."

He gazed out over the valley. "Aye, it's been a grand week. I can na thank ye enough for all ye've done. Only fitting, our last ride together for a while ends with a magnificent view."

He sat quietly for a few moments, reflecting on the perfect New Year's Day. He, Justin, and Charlotte agreed Althea would cringe at the thought of a large, fussy wedding. They planned a small, intimate affair in the formal parlor on the second floor of the Red Castle. John and Abigail Williams's four-story, Gothic-revival mansion perched atop Prospect Hill and afforded a grand vista of town. The house loomed high above the streets as a watchtower overseeing all the activity of Nevada City. Terraced gardens surrounded the perimeter, and a wooden stairway of two hundred steps sloped steadily to Sacramento Street and the plaza below.

Abigail and her daughter-in-law Caroline responded with delight to Charlotte's request. Both were terribly fond of Althea, for she cheerfully appeared at their disposal for last minute engagements. She created stunning new confections for them, secured the most discriminating accoutrements, and expressed the proper amount of awe for their exquisite Worth gowns. Considering themselves socially without peer in Nevada City, they appreciated her unfeigned gentility and felt no compunction to explain their bestowed friendships to anyone. James normally scorned such folderol, but these pillars of the community and their venue afforded his new wife all the elegance and provincial notions of respectability he felt she long deserved.

Besides Justin and Charlotte, a select few old friends attended their little ceremony—Vicente and Ana Sifuentes and, from Marysville days—Tim and Lucille Speeks along with Matthew and Ruth Cleary. Sadly, missing from the occasion was Matilda

Glenn, but there was simply no reconciling with Lodie.

He was certain that Charlotte could have described Althea's gown in glorious detail. James remembered only how lovely she appeared in the ice-blue silk that brought out the color of her beautiful eyes. Althea tossed her simple bouquet of hothouse paperwhites from the covered wraparound porch. Overhead, distinctive long peaks of milky icicle trim work hung from the high-gabled roof. Her laugh had been infectiously girlish, bringing his spirit to the summit of joy.

He glanced at Charlotte and sighed. If he didn't speak now, he might never get the chance. He hated to spoil an idyllic moment; his soul could be at peace if not for a nagging threat named Collier.

"Da, the view is breathtaking; I'm glad we came. I'll miss the snow in Sacramento, but I can do without frozen toes while riding at the Colliers'."

He suspected she brought up this topic to bait him into the very discussion he intended. Somehow, this annoyed him when he knew he should be relieved.

"I hate ta see ye go. Ye belong here. Ye love the farm. Half the reason a man builds anything is ta leave something better for his children—you *and* Justin. I hope ta see ye raise families right here. I'll watch ye all from my rocking chair on the porch."

She smiled. "That's a grand vision, Da. A lovely one. Who knows—perhaps when we've had our fill of seeing a bit more of the world, we'll both end up back home."

He shifted in the saddle. No. Oh, no. She would not end this conversation with simple platitudes. He pushed on. "Darlin' . . . I know it was I that sent ye ta Sacramento in the first place, ta keep ye safe during the mining troubles. I'm more proud than I can tell ye that ye found work and thrived. But there's nothing ye're doing there that ye can na accomplish here, with Althea.

With the advantage of growing inta yer rightful place running the farm."

"What about Justin?"

"Him, too. Of course."

"No. I mean you didn't question his leaving. You don't ask him when he's coming back. You can't get enough of Justin's stories about working on a big outfit and all the advantages, experiences of it. Why is it so difficult that I should want the same?"

"It's just *different* . . ."

She dropped her reins, jamming her fists on her hips. "Because I'm a girl!"

Startled, James shook his head. "Lord, ye looked just like yer mother . . ."

"And you *found* Mother on your travels, working various jobs, learning about yourself and what was important to you."

"My travels were na my choice."

"Nonetheless, it made you who you are! You discovered your passion."

He grew flustered at this turn in conversation and rushed headlong to his point.

"And . . . I . . . do na want ye ta think the first shiny nickel is the one ta select. I know Nevada City is pretty tame, and, in a bigger setting, the bigger fish is a more enticing catch."

She looked at him hard. "Is this about Royce?"

"I did na raise ye ta get caught up in the trappings of wealth."

"You raised me to appreciate a strong, honest family. Da— Royce isn't what you're picturing. He's like you, in that he spends all his waking hours outdoors building his ranch."

"Except for the big fancy house . . ."

"He doesn't care a fig for that. His parents built the house. He grew up there with his brother and sisters. I don't think he could name three sticks of furniture in the whole house, or tell you what color the drapes are. None of that matters to him."

"But he has a staff ta keep the place up for him? That's hardly how most people live."

"It *is* a big house. Neither he nor Neil can cook. I doubt Celeste can either."

"But to have people waiting on ye . . ."

"It's no different a job than hiring ranch hands because he can't do all *that* work by himself, either. He shoulders a lot of responsibility."

"Maybe. But he was born inta a life already made for him. *That* changes a man's values. It alters the way he looks at other people, how he treats them."

"Da, you're seeing ghosts that are not there . . ."

"Yer mother would never approve . . ."

"Are you serious? She'd have put my hand in Royce's and pushed us to the nearest church."

"Well, I raised ye different."

"Yes, you did. I've taken some of you both into my endeavors, but I'm doing it my way. Isn't that what you taught me?"

"He's just so damned sure of himself!"

Charlotte smirked. "Gee, I've never known anyone like that before."

"Ye watch yer tongue, lassie!"

Startled by the angry voice, Knacker threw up his head and snorted, backing up as if looking for a place to run. James circled him back around to face Charlotte. Banshee pawed the ground. Charlotte patted him. She stared at the ground for a few moments before looking up at him.

"I'm sorry, Da," she began softly. "All my life, I've heard your warnings . . . and I believe them to be just accounts of your experiences. I see the arrogance and sense of privilege in customers in the shop, in other families—I am aware there is a great deal of truth in what you say. But, Da . . . this cannot be a blanket evaluation of *everyone* with money, whether they spent a lifetime building it or were born to it. Look at yourself: Are you going to stop growing the farm when you reach a level where you feel affluent? Is it concerning if someone sees *you* as you see the Colliers? No. You'll expand, take your lumps when business is bad, and keep moving forward. The Colliers are no different. Royce's father began as you did; he just started a decade before you."

"I do na know that Royce thinks with a higher standard than others in his position . . . and that's a risk."

"But I do . . ."

He shook his head. "I think ye're naïve."

"You have to trust my judgment. Trust that I do listen to you."

"Perhaps, in time, ye'll see things differently."

"Maybe. I won't shut my eyes." She gave him a shy smile. "I was taught better than that."

"Just promise me—" he stared at her desperately—"that ye will na rush inta anything."

She shivered at a new rush of wind. "Promise."

He sighed. "I'm holdin' ye ta it." He gazed at her with pride. When did she become so damned independent?

" 'Tis getting late . . . and cold. We'd best be getting back, or Althea'll refuse us our supper." He turned Knacker's head, and, as he brought him about, Charlotte reached out and squeezed his hand.

"Don't worry, Da."

He winked and gave Knacker a kick. He faced the way home and thought grimly, *No worries, she says. Only I've just shoved her ten steps closer to the lad.*

CHAPTER 31

Sacramento

K Street, an avenue of commerce and recreation experienced best by strolling, originated near the Sacramento River. By the water's edge, a hub of transportation options culminated. Riverboat passengers came ashore in front of stagecoach lines positioned to whisk them away to their next destination. The Sacramento Valley Railroad expanded its platforms from Front to K Street in all-out competition with stage and freight lines. Lying in the crux of the Sacramento and American Rivers, the city became a hub for burgeoning wheat and cattle ranches. Despite a sudden slump in mining and unvoiced concerns of drought, prosperity was on the rise, steam traffic increased from San Francisco, and Sacramento awaited its final link to the Central Pacific to connect them with the rest of the nation.

For those choosing to linger in the city, a vast array of shops, restaurants, theatres, and amusements dotted their path. Interspersed with these, businesses coaxed industrialists, traders, magnates, and manufacturers to root themselves firmly in its escalating economy. A new era of society and sophistication set in, while Sacramento and San Francisco jockeyed for its crown.

The Golden Eagle Oyster Saloon occupied the first floor of the Golden Eagle Hotel on the corner of 7th and K Streets. The three-story brick structure with its granite, Italianate façade was a favorite haunt of well-heeled ranchers, businessmen, and

217

politicians. Its location across the street from Sacramento's famed horse market drew significant agricultural patrons, while sometimes annoying the professional elite with its rustic odors and occasional impromptu horse races down K Street to assess the agility of a new mount.

The hotel continued its reign as the rally point for local and national politics, gaining a reputation as a garrison for the Republican party. The attentions the Golden Eagle staff lavished on patrons of all persuasions fulfilled all they desired and provided the finest fare. It was here that Dutton invited Neil to join him—a first step towards repairing the damaged trust of an old and deep-rooted relationship.

Knowing he faced an uphill battle, he carefully set his stage and perfectly timed his players. Upon entering his arena, he glanced down at the contents of the chinoiserie umbrella stand, noting the distinctive silver wolf head on the cane resting within. As usual, he arrived early and positioned himself at a table with the most advantageous view.

Pushing grand schemes aside, Dutton had to admit he missed their easy rapport. He cultivated alliances, and Neil's friendship was a rarity in his world. Befriending those that one meant to control raised unnecessary complications. A tenuous, nostalgic link remained between them, which he hoped to improve over time.

Now an enterprising member of the upper house in the California State Legislature, Neil had cautiously sidestepped the Dandridge-created vacancy in the governor's office. After the deadly fiasco at the Empire mines, Governor Burke bore the brunt of an outraged public calling for his head. Judge Dandridge's smokescreen to cover stock-jobbing involvement was also a carefully plotted path, an organized maneuver to punish his puppet governor's disloyalty and replace him with a more Dandridge-faithful public servant. Dutton had watched agog as Neil not only refused to fill the niche prepared for him but worked for a respectful transition in power. The man humbly took the lower role stumped for, allowing the Democrats to reclaim the governor's chair.

Neil built a reputation for quiet candor and level-headed thinking—garnering high regard from both sides of the aisle. Dutton smiled. He could use that. He quelled his father's fury, urging him to watch events unfold. He noted, Neil wasn't just the candidate they were looking for, but the contender *everyone* was looking for. Now, if he could ingratiate himself to his former position as the bug in Neil's ear, he felt representation of certain Republican interests would thrive.

Sitting across from his former Harvard roommate in the crowded restaurant, Dutton felt an exaggerated distance. The buzz of camaraderie and enterprise filled the room, and their part in it was lacking. He lifted the goblet in front of him. "Are you certain I can't entice you to try the champagne? Truly, it's the perfect balance of bubbles and brine."

The waiter hovered by Neil with the heavy bottle poised over a fresh glass. Neil waved him off politely. "Thank you, no. I'm quite happy with the white claret."

"As you wish; the white claret *is* exceptional, a specialty here. Although I want to toast you and Beth. I hope Father expressed my congratulations and regrets. It was his fault for sending me to London on business," he joked. "To wedded bliss!"

"Thank you. I highly recommend it." Neil smiled, showing a glimpse of their old repartee. "*You'd* find marriage quite rewarding, but I'm not sure if I'm willing to sacrifice any of Beth's friends to promote your future happiness. You'll never extract yourself from your ventures long enough to actually *woo* a woman. Besides, *I* . . . have lived with you." He smirked. "You're quite moody, you know."

Dutton laughed. "Yes . . . perhaps you were the only one who would have me."

He picked up a pearl handled oyster knife and wedged its short, thick blade at the hinge between the two valves and twisted until he heard a slight pop. He slid the blade upward to cut the adductor muscle and release his prize. After a soft slurp, he tossed the vacant shell into a bowl on the table.

"Northwest Pacific nectar," he said, grinning.

Neil shucked three stony mollusks before dousing an oyster in mignonette.

"So . . . London?"

"Indeed. Productive trip overall. Father sold some San Francisco properties he's held since the fifties." Dutton sighed. "His age is beginning to tell on him, particularly after the stroke. Certainly not up for overseas travel—despite his feisty persona."

"No quiet retirement in his future?"

"Never! He sees California's prosperity as his legacy as much as his time on the bench. His hobby and his passion. Probably he'll outlive us both." He poked into the bucket of crushed ice with tongs and refilled his plate. "Given your role on the senate committee for business and economic development, you might find this interesting . . ."

"To be honest, I've spent more time with agriculture . . . Given the family's status in ranching, I have a ready flock of constituents. But with the transcontinental nearly completed, possibilities are endless." Neil sat back to study Dutton. "I am curious about what prospects you're developing overseas."

"Ah! The potential contacts could be useful to you," he said, nodding. "The world is amazingly small when it comes to commerce." He waved the oyster knife in a circle, scanning the room of smartly-dressed men, pressed elbow to elbow in their various packs. The deep droning of voices with an occasional burst of raucous laughter all but drowned out their conversation. "Just look around. Can't flip a coin in here without hitting someone important."

He pointed the tool's flat edge toward prominent tables bathed in sunlight by the arched windows overlooking the street. "There's the old boys' club. Contemporaries of Judge Dandridge and Garth Collier. Pioneers, notable for their speculations and survival. Those will be our seats one day," he said, winking.

"A lot of gray heads over there; I can wait my turn." Neil gazed in their direction as though trying to picture his late father amongst them. He looked back at Dutton. "Speaking of trailblazers, I believe I passed Sam Brannan on my way in. Sacramento hasn't seen him in ages."

"Yes, I spoke with him. Busy managing the significant part of San Francisco he owns, I imagine. Brannan's responsible for prying open markets into China, a passion of mine, as you might recall. Which, incidentally, ties in with my London trip." He sat forward, intent on his message.

"Neil, California is in a unique trade position with ports in San Francisco and the transcontinental head in Sacramento. I've signed a joint venture with a British import/export business. Britain has a long track record with China—rice, silk, tea . . . markets well explored by Father's London contemporaries. We'll build warehouses for distribution of these commodities and others. Trade opportunity for us in China is largely untapped, and this deal ties us in to a larger model—tremendous potential.

"Former governor Frederick Low advises me concerning his prior experience as collector of the Port of San Francisco. He's now taking the role of United States Minister to China. Also intriguing to our London partners are my ties to Collis Huntington, having worked closely with him at the Department of Transportation in Washington during the war. Huge interest at the moment in Chinese steel—the war drove up the price, causing shortages, and now it must come from somewhere.

Both Huntington and Durant are scrambling for enough to complete their rails." He smiled. "As you see—a small world."

"Dutton, this is astounding." Neil sat bolt upright, riveted to his recitation.

Dutton gave his old friend a sly look. "I've been busy."

Neil shook his head. "I shouldn't be surprised, but good heavens, man! The foresight in bringing the moving parts together—impressive."

"No small part of the credit goes to Father. He's a master at laying groundwork with relationships." He glanced around for the waiter, then grabbed the champagne bottle from the silver bucket and helped himself. "I can only imagine the ramifications of this would benefit you in committee work. I'm happy to make introductions."

Neil looked down at the table. Dutton noted his hesitation with disappointment.

"That's . . . very kind . . ."

"But?"

"I'm not certain what to say here."

"Ah." Dutton sighed. "Time has passed, and much has gone unsaid between us."

Neil nodded silently.

"Let me just say: I regret any past misunderstanding; I've always been in your corner. I hope someday you'll see that. However, I remind you—Father and I brought you to the public servant role because you're perfectly suited for it. We believed in you then; we believe in you now."

Dutton's voice softened; he gazed off into the distance. He was quiet for a time and, uncharacteristically, non-defensive.

"Neil . . . Why do you think we chose you . . . to back, I mean? Plenty of bright, successful, wealthy, capable men out there. Why you?" His voice remained quizzical.

"I suppose you'd have to tell me," replied Neil. He glanced

up as a server refreshed his claret.

"Honesty. Humility. Unbelievably intelligent—a creative thinker. Most important of all, your touch with people—it's a rare quality, Neil. A politician can get along without it, but with it? Unstoppable."

Neil frowned. "And some interpret that to mean I'm soft."

Dutton gave way to a slow, lazy smile. "That's good. They underestimate you. People who know you best will know the stuff you're made of. Why do you think I didn't run myself?"

Neil laughed. "I've often wondered."

"Because I *knew* you'd be better at this than me. I like making deals, as it turns out." Dutton gave him a direct look. "Qualities you possess, I, shamefully, do not. I'm not sure many men do. Your father did—strength combined with compassion. He worked harder than every man in the room and then turned to see whom he could help. Garth never wanted fame or prestige, but he focused on building for the future.

"Whereas the judge saw the muck of society from the bench—says it ruined him as far as empathy goes. People never fail to disappoint. He strove to curtail the short-term opportunists and point California in the right direction. It made him hard—but he always, *always* had his eye out looking for the right type of leaders. He knew I wasn't suited for it; he raised me to watch for the negative in people. Like it or not, he produced the cynic I am today." He bobbed his head and continued, "Lord knows, California's had its share of wrong men for the job but touted their successes anyway. Look at Broderick—if he hadn't died in such a sensational dual, I shudder to think where we might be today. What a driven man—so capable and intelligent, and still one of the state's most celebrated political figures. Yet he was savage in his approach, ruthless in achieving his objectives. He accumulated such individual power, no new stars on the political horizon rose without his endorsement—unless, of course, certain kickbacks were guaranteed.

"You see, he forgot his reasons for wanting to lead . . . he drifted. He let power consume him. The man thought himself untouchable—agreeing to a dual showed the height of hubris! No doubt Broderick's stranglehold on the future of our state was a frustration leading Father to abandon the bench for the private sector. As long as the Vigilance Committee ruled, Broderick purportedly detached himself from Vigilantes and their opponents, the Law and Order Party. Yet, he managed them both to his advantage."

Neil sat back in his chair, frowning. "I hear disapproval in your words, yet a touch of admiration in your voice. Are you saying I should be like Broderick? That's the model?"

"Certainly not! The man grasped control of the San Francisco political machinery for nine years! Name one piece of legislation with his name on it during that entire time with any lasting importance. He kept the system oiled and working, but beyond that he capitalized on California's growth rather than enhancing it. You're the antithesis of what he represents!" Dutton shook his head with a defeated air. "I won't pretend I'm not disappointed that you didn't step into the governor's office after Burke was ousted. What an opportunity for change we lost."

Neil sighed. "I think we both know . . . I wasn't ready. Politics has a steep learning curve, and my education is just beginning. At my current level, I'm inundated with requests, complaints, ideas . . . all with merit. I love the interaction, the magnitude of prospective projects . . . But, frankly, I'm overwhelmed trying to balance which interests best serve the majority, because there's still a percentage of the population ignored. And, sometimes, majority *shouldn't* rule. And selfishly I wonder . . . how *does* one make this a career? Anger the majority, and you no longer have a job, no longer have the ability to speak for anyone."

Dutton nodded. "Many times the electorate is blinded by prosperity. The *greatest* representative serving during an economic downturn may not have a snowball's chance in hell to show a positive legacy or get re-elected. But everyone loves a scoundrel spreading wealth around. Somehow his sins seem more palatable." He cast a sympathetic look. "Neil . . . I think you need to narrow your focus. What *one* issue screams at you, 'this needs doing!'? Gather support and run with it. Don't stop until it's done. Nothing is more frustrating to the public than a promise half fulfilled; it's neither a victory nor a defeat. Look at the problems with vice on the Barbary Coast, for example. It gets cleaned up from time to time when whoever is in office suffers a bout of civic virtue, but it's never wiped out. So, it appears nothing at all has been accomplished."

He watched as Neil sat in deep contemplation. He decided to lighten the mood.

"Worst of all . . . you let a *Democrat* take the throne."

Neil burst out laughing. "They aren't so bad, you know. Most of them anyway." He smiled. "I have to admit, as always, you manage to ask questions that pierce my mind into a different way of thinking."

Dutton shrugged. "It's why we're a good team—always were. Could be again."

"I'm not sure my family would agree with that."

"Your family, friends, supporters—we all have different roles, Neil. Your family is your backbone, your heart, your core. All good, but seriously . . . do any of them have the legal minds or legislative expertise to guide you through a political battlefield? No. They're your background; they illustrate what you stand for, but they can't help you once you're in the job.

"You know as well as I do: high minded morals are terrific— what everyone wants and all you need, if only your opponents played by the same rules. But they don't.

"Look how Durant pushed Stanford in this race to claim the biggest part of the railroad. Who knows what Durant's illegal antics forced Huntington to do, to negate the damage.

"Fortunately, Huntington is a man with his finger on the pulse. He was there to back up Stanford. Who can help you navigate through legal ramifications and political growth? Adele and Stan? Their causes are admirable and invaluable to the community, but they won't help you when up against a private interest that wants to take their orphanage land or support and funnel that state funding into their own pet projects.

"It's ugly, but it's the way the world works. You need savvy outside counsel. You think Royce can help you conquer opposition, with his temper? Yes, he'll call a spade, a spade; but he cultivates more enemies than allies because he's incapable of compromise. No one gets it all one way, Neil, no matter how righteous the cause. You have to pick the parts that mean the most to you and be willing to give something of importance to the other side.

"It takes tolerance, negotiation, relationship building, *and a lot of digging* to find out what makes an adversary tick. These elements build a patient man's success story. But he needs a solid team around him . . ." Dutton paused. He looked at Neil and gave a soft chuckle. "I'm ranting, aren't I?"

Neil smiled. "A bit. But, clearly passionate and as astute as ever."

"Look, I'm not suggesting anything other than my being a sounding board; I have too much on my plate already. But I do have an outreach"—he brushed his fingers against his collar in a braggart's gesture—"and quite the nose for information, if I do say so myself."

"No doubt!" Neil laughed.

Dutton glanced up at the bar, searching for the eyes awaiting his cue. The man set down his drink and strolled towards their table. Dutton returned Neil's smile and raised his goblet for a sip of champagne.

"Mr. Dandridge, isn't it?"

"Well, my goodness!" exclaimed Dutton.

"Pardon the interruption . . ."

Dutton stood to shake the man's hand. "Not at all! How fortuitous! Neil, if you haven't yet had the opportunity, this is a gentleman you would like to meet. He's new to the state assembly and making quite a name for himself on the committee for labor and employment. You share many common values."

Neil stood and extended his hand. "Pleased to make your acquaintance. Neil Collier."

"The pleasure is all mine," said the tall man with the kind blue eyes. "Lodie Glenn."

CHAPTER 32

Hearing a jingle at the door, Charlotte looked up from bolts of fabric spread over the surface of a worktable. Mrs. Van Oss continued her musings as she rearranged the rolls in her preferred order. A young woman, richly dressed in purple, stood just inside the door waiting to be noticed.

"Charlotte, bring me that dark-blue silk brocade I left on the counter, please?" Mrs. Van Oss pointed behind her and then called out to a customer in the dressing rooms, "I'll be there in just a moment, Harriet . . ." She peered over the top of her spectacles to address her client. "Miss Solinger, how good to see you. Was I expecting you today, dear?"

"Ah," the woman strolled forward a few paces, removing her gloves. "No, no . . ." she said breezily. "I have several events in upcoming weeks and thought perhaps a few new things might be in order."

Charlotte approached with the brocade and a welcoming hello, only to be met with the briefest of dismissive looks before the woman turned her attention decidedly upon Mrs. Van Oss. "I understand you recently returned from San Francisco. Any exciting ideas from Paris?"

The shop owner smiled. "Of course . . . always. I'm with Harriet Ledbetter at the moment, dear." She scooped up a bundle of fabric and some trim trailing off its card. "I don't believe you've met my new assistant, Charlotte MacLaren—she can show you samples of some delicious laces that just arrived.

I brought back some darling hats, too. Charlotte, this is Miss Iris Solinger. Miss Solinger works on many, many committees in town and is in such high demand at so many functions, she is one of my very best customers." Mrs. Van Oss scurried towards the dressing area. "You're in good hands, Iris. Coming, Harriet!"

"Pleased to make your acquaintance, Miss Solinger." Charlotte pulled out a comfortable cushioned chair and gestured. "If you'd care to sit down, I will bring some bits over for you to browse through. Perhaps we'll find something that piques your interest."

Iris moved slowly around to the chair, taking great care to arrange her skirts while studying her. Charlotte felt her searing inspection from head to toe and offered, "Shall we begin with the Belgian laces?"

She sighed heavily. "Whatever will fill the time."

Charlotte moved to gather a variety of Parisian passementerie and laces of highest quality, aware of her new client's lofty expectations and apparent disappointment that Mrs. Van Oss declined to cater to her personally. She turned to inquire, "Some of the new French selections come with a delicate colored embroidery in them. Do you have colors you favor?"

Iris began to remove her hat, a sign she intended to stay awhile. "Just bring them all."

"Of course." Charlotte smiled politely and pulled several cards of delicate trim from the shelf. She turned to assess the woman's coloring. Iris's deep-blonde hair resembled a shade of ripened wheat. Given their narrow, feline slant, the color of her eyes was difficult to see but appeared to be soft hazel. She possessed sharply defined cheekbones, adding to the catlike impression. At least a few years older than herself, Iris's grand mannerisms suggested the refinement of a pampered woman. Charlotte thought her quite pretty and suspected she had been told so often enough to draw confidence and satisfaction from it. Given the combination of beauty and money, she considered Iris an ideal client. Just the type to demand unique style and allow Charlotte's creativity to run wild.

Charlotte brought over the fluffy stacks and fanned them out on the table. She selected a brilliant white and a softer cream and held one to each side of Iris's face. Iris plucked the white one from her hand. "I prefer white."

"As you wish." Charlotte swept aside all choices without white backgrounds and spread the remaining ones out for Iris's inspection.

"But you don't think that's the correct choice?"

"It's largely a matter of personal preference, sometimes dependent on the color of the material you select and how they work together."

"Yes, a fairly obvious observation."

Charlotte ignored the remark. "Is this to be an evening event?"

The woman fingered the samples. "Most of them are. But there is an important luncheon for the new orphanage. I will require a suitable afternoon dress."

"Oh, at Adele Hensley's in a few weeks. I shall be there myself."

She looked up abruptly. "You know Adele?"

"Quite well. She's been so kind to me and my brother when we first arrived here."

Iris sat forward with renewed interest and appeared to scour her. "I see," she said finally, slumping back into the chair. "I suppose Adele could use the help. You're presentable at least, almost attractive really . . . aside from the groveling."

Charlotte straightened and leveled her gaze at the woman. She left an awkward few moments of silence, yet felt not the slightest bit uncomfortable. "I don't confuse manners with groveling."

"Don't be silly. Everyone does it at one time or another with their betters."

Her father's prejudices against the privileged fought for space in Charlotte's mind. Uncertain as to why this woman took such an instant dislike to her, she knew her options were limited. As she grappled for an appropriate response, Mrs. Van Oss appeared from the dressing area and placed a hand gently on Charlotte's arm.

"Charlotte, dear—Harriet is ready to be pinned. If you wouldn't mind taking over back there, I'll see what we can do for Iris. Oh, I see you've brought the best of my new finds . . . very good."

"Yes, of course." Charlotte turned to withdraw as Iris called out to her,

"I'm sure you'll work out just fine around here."

"Interesting to meet you, Miss Solinger."

"Well, now." Mrs. Van Oss motioned to the laces. "What are we thinking here?"

"First of all, I'm thinking I'll require you to handle my gowns personally." Iris's look darkened as she stared after Charlotte.

"Good to know I'll always have my regulars, dear." The older woman leaned forward in a confidential manner. "But she is one of the most talented dressmakers I've ever come across . . . does beautiful work—so innovative! I'm rather afraid soon I'll be reduced to doing the books and sipping tea." She busied herself with the lace samples as she allowed the words to sink in and added, "Harriet just loves her!"

Daylight began to dim as Charlotte worked to put the shop back in order for tomorrow. She enjoyed the diverse female interactions, getting to know Sacramento from differing parts of its community. Most of the socialites needed no strokes to boost their egos. For the most part, these clients found her straightforward, yet polite, and her gentle approach opened them to her suggestions. But it was the women lacking confidence that Charlotte loved most. Looks of genuine surprise as they discovered styles that suited them or made them feel beautiful delighted her. Mrs. Van Oss produced women's staff uniforms for several of the major hotels in town. She found these employees often arrived shy and feeling out of their element; but, as they warmed to her, they left Charlotte in giggles with anecdotes of working with the public. Their tales made her wonder if she'd ever feel prepared for the haughty discontent that caused some people to feel the need to quash a simple shop girl.

As she did at the end of each day, Mrs. Van Oss thanked her for her work. While Charlotte stood on the ladder putting up heavy bolts of fabric as handed to her, her employer broached the subject of Miss Solinger.

"You know, Charlotte, in this business it is imperative to make sure the customer always feels important. Even when they are unpleasant."

Charlotte glanced down from her perch. "I thought your timing was highly coincidental today."

"With certain customers, I always stay on my toes. Surely, you ran into this sort of attitude in dealing with the public before?"

"Not as much as I thought," she admitted. "I worked in town when Althea needed me, but mostly she brought piece work home for me. My responsibilities on the farm took most of my time. I grew up knowing the high and mighties in town, so I expected pretensions from them. *She* took me by surprise." She looked at Mrs. Van Oss earnestly. "This is your establishment. I'm surprised you let her behave with disrespect—even if she hides it under syrupy words."

"Her reticule holds enough reasons for me. Oh, don't look so shocked . . . It isn't just her business; it's the amount of business she influences in town. If egos are bruised and a customer chooses to go elsewhere, I lose. I don't have the luxury of expressing personal opinions or entertaining gossip in such a way that I add anything to the conversation. If they want to vent while they are here, I listen, sympathize, and, when all else fails and I feel pressed for an opinion of some sort . . . I find the need to hold a mouthful of straight pins while I work on them so that any answer is undeniably impossible."

Charlotte chuckled. "I understand."

Mrs. Van Oss looked at her sternly over the top of her glasses. "I hope so, because I expect you to do the same. Your respectability is not determined by her, but by your own actions."

"Yes, ma'am."

"Well . . . good enough. Thank you, again, for your help today," she said, turning away. "But you might remember, dear: if someone gives you the gift of anger, and you refuse it . . . whose does it become?"

Royce was late. Again. She avoided pacing across the shop floor. Mrs. Van Oss's eagle eye missed nothing, and she had the uncanny ability to express opinions without saying a word. Charlotte loitered in the back room, studying the rack of dresses in progress for various clients.

Three of the garments belonged to Iris Solinger, who arrived for each fitting smartly dressed in European designs. The first day she entered in a fashionable, braided Zouave-style cutaway jacket, tailored shirtwaist, and wide belt. The next, she appeared wearing a bowler-like hat wrapped in a scarf and a russet colored outdoor walking costume of a loose fitting jacket and matching skirt. The third, she flounced in wearing a stunning black-and-cream-striped day dress dripping with wide lace on bell sleeves. Charlotte openly admired each ensemble, giving Iris opportunity to drop the name of the finest salon in San Francisco.

Her taste was richly impeccable—until she attempted to adapt styles to her own ideas.

Unable to dissuade her from notions of grandeur, Mrs. Van Oss proceeded as the client insisted. Charlotte pulled the dress Iris intended to wear to Adele Hensley's from the rack, wrinkling her nose as she examined it. The deep-mauve fabric was a popular color choice but not one that suited her. Iris imitated a London creation featuring "a row of adorable little bows" tapering down pagoda sleeves. Additionally, she demanded large silk bows cascading down her skirts in lines spaced a handbreadth apart. Current trends abandoned hooped petticoats in favor of the crinolette for a narrower silhouette; however, the overly-flourished, poufy bows easily negated the effect. Her two unfinished gowns took a more sophisticated tone, more in keeping with the elegance she projected.

Charlotte found outings in the Collier circle demanded higher refinement. She began enhancing her own wardrobe, taking care to remain understated as Althea taught. Most clients could not afford the level of attire Miss Solinger presented. Yet, as a walking advertisement for her work, she found ways to balance exceptional details with finesse. Today, for her lunch with Royce, she wore her new favorite—a delicate buttercream colored dress with a high neckline trimmed in a pale-yellow silk-satin. The dress featured a modest train, gathered low in the back with a large bow before making its fall to the floor. She sported a dainty hat tipped forward over her forehead with a jaunty air.

Feeling annoyed, she peeked through the doorway for a view out the front window. Charlotte heard the familiar hurried pounding of Royce's boots on the planked sidewalk. She forced herself to walk slowly from the back, appearing just as Royce yanked the door open. He poked his head in, his hat in hand at half-mast, neither quite on his head nor fully removed as he entered the shop. Mrs. Van Oss glanced up from her perch behind the counter to assess the male intrusion, giving him a slight nod upon his greeting.

"I'll be taking lunch now, if that's all right?"

"Certainly, dear. Take your time." She returned her attention to the catalogue in front of her, though Charlotte felt certain that her eyes were upon them as they left.

She stepped outside, greeted by a persistent coolness in the air and an admiring look from Royce.

Grinning, he offered her his arm. "What a lovely break in my day!"

She raised an eyebrow, and he hastened to add, "Sorry I'm late. I've spent days doing nothing but mending fence and mid-wifing cows, and now pressing new opportunities have come up. I'll explain once we sit down. Forgive me?"

"Depends on how compelling your story is."

"Lunch at the Orleans Hotel?"

She laughed. "You know I love the gumbo there."

"I'm not above bribery."

"Good to know. Heavens, the streets are busy today." She noted he wore a frock coat and tie, probably for his business dealings, but she still enjoyed the approving glances thrown their way from passersby. There was no denying they made a striking couple. As they weaved their way through the assorted business strollers, shoppers, and occasional panhandlers, he tightened his grip on her arm, pulling her closer to him. After several vigorous tugs, she protested, "Royce, I'm quite capable of not colliding with people."

He gave a warning scowl to a dust covered construction worker who veered too closely while shifting the weight of the tools he carried.

"You object that I'm protective?"

"Not generally, but as the situation warrants." She glanced at the workman, envisioning Clancy or any of a dozen miners she

235

knew merely going about their business.

"Let me be the judge of that."

"Do you assess each person on approach, or do you have some innate ability to separate wheat from chaff?"

"There's a lot of chaff on these streets."

"That's a rather bleak outlook. And unfair, I should think."

"If it were just me, no one would even stand out. But I have you to watch out for."

She nodded to her right. "What about that fellow over there? Does he pose a threat?"

"You tell me. You don't think he looks a little rough?"

"Rough isn't a threat."

He stopped, giving her hard look. "Now, you're worrying me. There's a lot of riffraff here, and appearances are deceiving. I need to know you're wary of your surroundings."

"If it makes you feel better, I'm very cautious of which streets I take and what time I am out and about. But I don't look at every stranger as an enemy."

"Well, you should until they prove otherwise," he said gruffly.

"But you don't know . . ."

The disheveled man Charlotte had just pointed out turned and vomited on the sidewalk ahead. A group of walkers scattered to avoid him. He staggered, trying to support himself against the building. Royce pointed with a grand swooping gesture. "You were saying?"

"Okay, so he's a bad example."

"A very bad example." He offered her his arm.

She took it, then poked him in the ribs. "You knew him."

"Of course I did; he's a beggar and a drunk."

"All right, so you knew he was a drunk. Not all beggars are, you know. Sometimes they have families to feed. Royce, I've seen men so far down on their luck they've had all hope beat right out of them."

He gave her a sympathetic smile. "You're caring and tender hearted. You're also pretty gutsy, and I appreciate that, but you can't take on the concerns of strangers all alone. There are plenty of women's benevolence groups . . ."

"Have I missed some general rule of life somewhere, or is it just the Collier family creed that charity is a woman's concern?"

"What?"

"What your family does is commendable, of course, but does it buy you the right to walk around with your eyes closed? Not to feel compassion for another human being? Your mother fostered a dozen different causes, and Adele works tirelessly to get this orphanage off the ground."

"I didn't realize I was asking my social conscience to lunch."

"I'd hope you at least care what I think. Every now and then you need to step out of that world of yours and see what the rest of it's about."

"Oh, come on. I'm in the *whole* world every day, working with all kinds of people. I have to look at things from all angles."

"Perhaps you're right." She stopped and gave him a sweet smile. He softened. Still smiling, she gave a quick nod and walked ahead calling over her shoulder, "Looking and seeing are different, you know."

Startled, he stared after her. In two strides he caught up, ready to sputter out a new argument.

"Look, Mr. Miller's adding to his store," she stated.

Distracted, he glanced up, then realized he didn't want to continue with this conversation either. He raised his brow. "You like having the last word, don't you?"

"Well, if I can't win outright, I might as well have satisfaction, eh?" She looked at him sideways, smiling so that her dimples showed deep. He moaned and laughed.

"Are you making fun of me?"

"Yes. Clearly it's something you are incapable of doing

237

yourself, so *someone* needs to do it for you. It is a skill, you know. But also something that must be practiced."

"Probably like humility. I haven't had a lot of practice there either," he countered.

"Very good. Ability to laugh at one's self shows a higher level of intelligence. But perhaps I could help you out with that humility problem as well."

He laughed heartily. "I am quite sure you could at that."

She slipped her hand through his arm and allowed him to escort her into the Orleans Hotel.

Once settled at their table, she found herself simply enjoying his company. Time together had been sparse these last few weeks. Even now, with a first course in front of them, he seemed distracted and fidgety.

"Which gallant steed did you ride today?" she queried.

"Jughead."

She laughed. "I can't believe you gave him such a mean name. Most undeserved."

"He's stubborn and a klutz."

"Ah, the one that throws out with his left hind foot."

He looked startled, then impressed. "I forget whose daughter I'm dealing with sometimes." As if he remembered something, Royce yanked at his watch fob, glanced at the time, and stuffed it back in his pocket. "I think you know more about horses than most of my hands."

She nodded. "Goes without saying."

"But"—he held up a finger as if heralding an announcement—"today's meeting was all about cows. Do you remember me boring you with a lot of details about my plans to improve our stock?"

"Let's see: you've been rapidly increasing the number of Herefords and feel they're the future growth of the ranch. While phasing out your stringy, ornery Spanish cows, you still have a fascination with crossbreeding them with . . . oh, give me a minute . . ."

"Durhams!" He leaned forward in his excitement, spilling details at a rapid pace. "I've been corresponding with a rancher from New Mexico Territory for a while now. He's in town visiting family here in Sacramento, and we met this morning. He's had great success with Durham cattle. As you know, I've been researching this for some time, and I'm convinced the benefits of a selective breeding program could produce a superior animal. Larger, sturdier body structure, improved carcass quality, more fertile, easier calving, milder temperament. The possibilities are endless! He's invited me to visit his outfit, and, if all goes well, I intend to buy a prize bull and some heifers."

"Royce, that's wonderful. Your strategy is in motion."

"It's still experimental, but you can't expand if you're not willing to try new ideas, right?" He glanced up, catching someone's eye, and waved. He looked at her regretfully as he rose from his chair. "And, unfortunately, I have a last minute meeting with the bank to discuss the business loan to pull this off . . . and I have a Cattleman's Association meeting after that."

Charlotte turned to see Celeste approaching their table, then gaped at him in surprise.

"But you've hardly eaten anything."

"I'll be fine, but you stay. It's why I brought Celeste; you two have a nice lunch on me." He stood, pulled out the chair for Celeste, then took Charlotte's hand and kissed it. "I'll make it up to you later, I promise."

Celeste smirked. "Ah, the pledge of busy ranchers everywhere. How often did I hear Father drop that one on Mother? Hi, Charlotte. I'm glad to see you, even if I am a stand-in."

Royce shot his sister a look. "Not helping."

"And, yet, you'll buy me lunch anyway," she giggled.

Charlotte stared at Royce's retreating form and sighed. "A

239

little notice might have been nice."

"In his defense, which is a position I rarely take, the fellow from New Mexico sent word to the house last night that he was here . . . apparently an uncle died or something. Royce wolfed down his dinner and threw papers around in the study for hours last night preparing for this meeting. He didn't want to cancel on you altogether." She cocked her head with a sympathetic air. "Which is why *I* shall *never* marry a rancher! Always at the beck and call of smelly beasts and living *miles* too far from civilization."

The waiter arrived with two hot bowls of seafood gumbo.

"Ah! Dear brother at least got my order right."

"Well, that should have been my first clue. He doesn't care for gumbo, yet he ordered it." Charlotte shook her head. "Tell me what's new with you? That dress looks lovely on you, by the way."

"Of course it does; you made it. And I love my dress for Adele's luncheon! You may well see a great deal of me in the shop. Oh! Maybe you could go to San Francisco with us! Now that I'm finished with school, Adele and Stan are pushing me for so many decisions!"

"What sort of decisions?"

"I'm to find something worthwhile to do with myself." She rolled her eyes. "I could stay with Neil and Beth here in town and further my education . . . which has great appeal apart from the education bit. I could remain at the ranch, pretend to be of help to Royce, and pick up some of Mother's charitable causes. Or, I could go to London to stay with Aunt Agatha and travel Europe for a year. It would be so much more fun if Adele could take me, but her children are so young. She did agree to take me to San Francisco to shop for the trip. You should come with us!"

"That would be fun, and how exciting for you! It sounds as

though you've decided then?"

Celeste dallied her spoon through her soup. "Most likely . . . I wouldn't mind dragging it out a bit."

"Why?"

"I'd like some time without responsibility for a little while longer. Just for me. Once all the commitments begin, it never stops. Also, I need time to figure out where my place is. Stake a claim before I go, so to speak."

"I don't think I understand."

Celeste feigned a worldly smile, a look seasoned well beyond her fifteen years. "You'd have to grow up here to fathom all our layers of society. The more deeply rooted the family, the more ensnaring the social mores. Pioneer stock carries the most weight, but even then you have pastoral geneologies—the 'outer city belles' versus the more metropolitan or political families of 'society matrons.' One's selection of a husband becomes quite serious in regards to standing, so it's incredibly important to visualize your future." She shrugged. "Not that one is necessarily better than the other; it is a personal choice.

"*That* said, the outer city society belles are often more dangerous than established society matrons because they *aspire* to be city belles. Old Sacramento families have nothing to prove; their very names say it all. But for the county up and comers it can be a vicious fight for acceptance. First, they conquer their own area of countryside to be deemed worthy to enter Sacramento society circles.

"Now the Colliers have long been included in all circles due to Father's influence. My mother, Eugenia, didn't give a hoot but was a truly gracious woman, and her interest in causes was heartfelt. Neither of them accepted praise or recognition for their efforts—they forged their own way, and their legacy stands because of it."

Celeste glanced up as a waiter neared to clear their plates. "I

241

don't suppose you have any of your divine lemon cakes?"

He bowed. "Of course, miss."

"Charlotte?"

Charlotte stared at her in astonishment.

"Charlotte?"

"Oh. Yes. I'd love one."

"Two, please."

"Very good, miss."

As the waiter withdrew, Charlotte ventured, "Aren't you a little young to be . . . planning a marriage? And to whom?"

"Oh, certainly. But it's never too soon to start weighing my options, casting a few lines in the water. And establishing my standing with various groups of women."

Charlotte shook her head. "I'm finding it hard to grasp the scope of what you've just said. And you . . ."

"Know all of this? Well, it's all anyone talks about at a prestigious girls' boarding school." She sighed. "It used to annoy me if I was going to live somewhere else, that I was so close to home. After all, Neil went to Harvard. But weekends on the ranch, with the family, gave me time to relax, regroup, gather my wits."

"I feel fortunate to have some distance from all that."

Celeste gave a low chuckle. "You think so? Ah-ha. I hope you're ready for Adele's luncheon; the haute monde are lining up like hungry cats."

"You must be joking! Adele is so gracious."

"It isn't Adele, darling. She quite relishes her country doctor's wife role. It's her connections. This is a fundraiser. Whom do you think has the funds?"

Charlotte sat back in her chair. She felt an odd sensation of readying for a fight come over her. "Well, this *is* enlightening. Believe me, I've seen haughty women's tactics before. Largely, I give them a wide berth and don't engage. Althea is a master at grace under pressure, and I always admired her for it."

Celeste plucked at the tablecloth as if deciding whether to say more. She cocked her head and studied Charlotte's face. "Iris Solinger will be there with a bevy of her followers."

Charlotte met her gaze, weighing her response. "Mrs. Van Oss is working on her dress for the occasion . . . and several other events. She . . . comes in wearing the most beautiful fashions from abroad. I enjoy studying her clothes, seeing new trends . . . so I can duplicate them with ideas of my own."

"Smart. She hates you, you know."

Charlotte smirked. "Have I not kowtowed enough? Celeste, that's a rather harsh assessment."

"Yes. But true, nonetheless."

"I can live with it—but don't tell her I'm studying the dresses."

"She's jealous—you're prettier than she is, and *you* have Royce's attention."

"That's silly. She's very attractive."

Celeste gave a cynical chuckle. "She'd never *admit* she was jealous—that would imply she believed you to be superior in some way, and that she doesn't believe of anyone. She'll put you down, quietly, but publicly." She leaned in with an incredulous look. "You really don't know how this prima dona game is played, do you? Whispers behind the hand, statements that on the surface seem to have no meaning at all but hint at a defect. Remarks most women in the game immediately take as deliciously derogatory, but most men wouldn't think twice about. But somehow, the implications stick." She pushed away the half-eaten lemon cake.

"Gossip."

"A tool as old as time, but still effective. Charlotte, I tell you this because I care. Make no mistake, she'd claw him away from you in a second. She's been on the prowl for a suitable match.

Had her eye on Neil until he and Beth got married."

Celeste sat stiffly straight, an uncharacteristically hard line settled on her face. "Iris doesn't know it, but I can't stand her. I've heard a few nasty remarks about Beth attributed to her. *Nobody* . . . speaks ill of *my* family.

"But . . . we run in the same circles, and I know she's got a dangerous tongue. I smile and giggle, but I watch her—she thinks I'm simple, and I let her think so. She's a petty and vindictive woman who wades in amongst other women with interest for only herself."

Charlotte was silent . . . shocked that one so young possessed such a cynical outlook.

"Surprised, huh?" Celeste smiled. "You didn't know my mother. Charming, kind, strong—a pragmatist in every way, and you didn't cross her. Adele got most of her gentler attributes; I got a double dose of the last."

Charlotte looked at her fondly. "I don't know about that. But, I recognize that look. I feel protective of Justin."

Celeste gave her red-gold curls a dramatic toss. "Oh, now don't tell me you're going to spoil my fun. He's so entertaining to flirt with. Obviously, he sees me as a girlish nuisance"—she raised her eyebrows provocatively—"totally unaware that one day he'll be head over heels in love with me!"

Charlotte burst into laughter.

"Darling, this has been lovely, but I need to collect my shopping and head for home."

Charlotte rose to walk out with her. "And I have work waiting."

Celeste leaned over and pecked her on the cheek. "Tuesday at Adele's, then? Oh, and of course I'll see you at the barn dance Saturday next. Tell Justin, I'm claiming at least two reels!"

Charlotte frowned. "What do you mean, 'see you there'?"

"Well, you are going with Royce."

"Did Royce say he was taking me?"

"Sure, last night at supper."

"Oh." She turned away, deep in her own thoughts.

"Something wrong?"

"No. It's just that he forgot to ask me."

"Oh." Celeste shrugged. "Well, must have slipped his mind. He'll be by."

CHAPTER 33

Nevada City

The smell of new leather never failed to quiet James's spirit. In its clean, heady scent lay a promise of beginnings, future projects, and fresh starts. Knowing he needed only to replace two hackamores, he allowed himself to be enticed by rows of assorted leads, lariats, and harnesses. He heard Vicente bid his customer good day, then turn to instruct Luis in rapid-fire Spanish to come watch the counter while they met.

Vicente chuckled as he watched James run his hand down a sixty-foot reata. "You can not throw that far, amigo. You are too old."

"I cu na throw that far when I was young. Tis why I learned ta whisper sweet nothings ta horses and make them come ta me."

"Come to the back." Vicente beckoned. "I have hot coffee and something sweet Ana sent with me. We will talk."

James scooped up the hackamores he had set aside and dropped them on the counter as he passed. He winked at Luis. "I think yer father intends ta sell me that fancy saddle he's working on in the back."

Luis nodded. "Someday."

Vicente placed two steaming mugs on a small table next to a plate of cinnamon and sugar-coated churros. James stopped in front of a work in progress. There on a tree stump, leveled for use as a work surface, was a cowhide pierced with an awl and a

246

knife in close proximity. By drawing the cowhide in circles around the knife, Vicente created a single continuous strand of leather for braiding. A small, razor-sharp knife lay nearby to strip the hair from the string.

"Four strand?" asked James,

"*Sí*, I prefer. Is stronger."

"How long?"

He shrugged. "For you . . . maybe twenty-five feet."

"I'll thank ye ta be kinder ta yer elders." James sat on one of the three-legged stools by the table and reached for a coffee. "I wanted ta talk ta ye about Rodrigo."

"He does a good job?"

"Aye, hard worker. He's well liked by the crew in North Bloomfield. I seek him out when I have ta go up there on union business. He's got a sharp mind, yer boy. Keeps me apprised on flooding issues, the men's concerns . . . good eye for detail and such. I was thinkin' . . . he's instinctively good at this work . . . it would be advantageous for him ta be more involved."

"How?"

James paused. "As ye well know from experience . . . miners appreciate quality workers. But they're clannish. They are na always fair ta laborers that are na white."

Vicente sighed. "I prospered . . . because I had Sean to shield me."

"Exactly. Tis my hope that, one day, the union will welcome all men inta the brotherhood. Voices like Rodrigo's should be included. My thinkin' . . . is ta appoint Rodrigo as an assistant of sorts ta me as union chief—along with men from other areas. These men will continue ta work at current jobs but take on added responsibility as eyes and ears for me. He can na be a full member, but he'll be involved and visible. I believe it's a first step for acceptance."

"I . . ." Vicente's voice cracked. "It would be an honor for

247

him. I am grateful, my friend."

James gave him a fretful look. "I ask ye, because it may na be without risk. Times are better than when ye first started out at the rush, but . . . there are always a few dunderheads threatened by their own ignorance."

"This, I understand. It is important that he stand up to be counted as a man." He smiled. "Do I tell you . . . he wants to get married?"

"No!"

Vicente chuckled. "*Sí, es verdad*. Beautiful girl. Even Ana approves."

"Congratulations!"

"My heart is full. And now, with this good news that you bring me, I feel guilty that I ask a favor of you."

"We do na keep count of favors between us. What is it?"

"You go to the horse market in Sacramento soon, no?"

"In about three weeks, aye."

"Would you mind if Tomas travels with you? He needs experience selling at the market."

"Of course; I'd like the company." He smiled, and then his face took on a burdened, faraway look.

Vicente studied him. "Ah. You are thinking of her today."

James looked up sheepishly.

"Thinking is good; worry is not."

"I can na look out for her from here. I am worried."

"As a father, I guess why. She is grown, my friend. You have raised her well. It is up to her now. *El corazon* has mysterious ways. One day you look into the eyes of one who makes you feel as though their soul is your own . . . and the heart pounds with a strike so large it almost stops. Was it not so when you met Emma?"

He grimaced.

"Well? And Althea?"

"Althea snuck up on me."

"But even then, undeniable. Yes?"

James frowned.

Vicente shrugged. "I know these things." He pointed at James. "And so do you."

"He's na right for her."

"Only she can say this. Go home and let your wife explain these things to you. The women always know more than the men in these matters. Ana swears she picked out the right girl for Rodrigo four years ago. She just waited for him to notice."

James laughed. He shook his head. "I suppose it's time ta go pick Althea up for home. I ha enough worries ta save for another day." He stood and embraced Vicente. "I'll be lookin' ta talk ta Rodrigo in the next few days."

"Very good, my friend."

James picked up his purchase and bid Luis good-bye. He sighed as he walked up the hill towards Althea's dress shop. He expressed pretty much the same concerns with her last night. He could find no allies in his cause as he mulled over their conversation.

"Wish I cu be certain which was turning her head—the man or all the pretty things that come with him."

Althea answered quietly, "I wouldn't worry so. Besides, you can't blame a girl for wanting a comfortable life—don't you remember how difficult it was for Emma and me to give up things in Boston?"

"I recall ye were fairly eager ta leave that house."

"I had great reason. I watched Mistress Margaret become more attached to Justin every day. I wanted to get as far away from that family's claims on him as possible."

"Would ye really fret over a few indulgences? For ye, it was soaps, tea, materials. Leftovers—scraps of fabric and fine lace."

"I wanted all I was entitled to; Charlotte's welcome to more.

Why should she not have it?"

"But ye grew up in a household where ye saw all the snares of such a life from the beginning. She has no such knowledge; she does na see the hook."

"I also remember before that—a home that was cold in winter, a lack of food, where my parents were too exhausted to lavish us with attention. Where my overburdened family was only too willing to send me off to lighten their lot and know that I would be better for it. And, even so, it still pains me."

James came to a halt outside the dress shop door. Before he entered, he knew he had to push his brooding aside. Althea had certainly heard enough of his reasoning and remained unmoved by his case. He couldn't surrender the thoughts. He would soldier on alone.

CHAPTER 34

Sacramento

Royce didn't appear until Friday morning. He came into the shop with his arm behind his back and his most dashing smile. "How's my best girl?"

Charlotte continued putting away spools of thread. Mrs. Van Oss sat at a distance behind the counter sewing, tolerating his presence because of the early hour.

"Am I?"

He breathed deeply. "Okay, I should have been here sooner." He whipped the flowers out from behind his back as a peace offering. "Of course you are." He tilted the bouquet towards her.

"Perhaps, you should save those for whomever you're taking to the dance."

"Well, you know that's you," he said.

"Unfortunately, I did not know. Therefore, I said yes to Luke Wilcox when he asked me the day before yesterday."

"Luke Wilcox! That sneaky . . . ."

"Actually, I think he was surprised to find you hadn't asked me. Sweet of him to ask, since he thought he'd be turned down."

"Well, I'll have a talk with *him* and get this thing settled."

"It is settled. He asked, and I said yes. I wouldn't dare have the bad manners to back out on him now, and I suggest you act accordingly. If you'll excuse me, I have quite a lot of work to do."

"Charlotte, you don't mean this."

He was talking to the back she had turned to him. She was mad, but she realized he was furious. He flung the flowers on a table next to her and stormed out.

Mrs. Van Oss never looked up from her sewing but stated, "Bravo. Good girl." Charlotte wished she felt some sort of victory.

Justin paid his two bits for the cause and leaned against a post with his beer to watch the revelers.

The barn dance was in full swing. He felt the pulsating stomp of stoutly clad feet on rough puncheon boards as if emanating from his chest. The joyful song of fiddles, the shouts of the caller, the whoops and whistles of exuberant dancers rang out all around him. He granted himself a breather from the festivities, as he had been scuffing up the floors with the best of them. He had no special girl but chose instead to dance with several of the girls from church, hoping to get to know them better. After services left time for only brief conversations and inviting smiles. He took a sip of his beer, thinking he might try to catch that pretty, soft-spoken Melissa Hobson between partners.

This fundraiser for the new orphanage was a community effort—a celebration to break from the cycles of torrential winter storms, spring rains, and melting mountain snow that converged to spill the Sacramento River and her tributaries into the valley. He himself felt the pain of it, as he spent his morning wading in to free cows bogged down in mud. The last one had panicked and was stuck nearly up to her nose. Fearful of putting his horse in the same state, his partner pulled the rope encircling her horns while Justin yanked up on her tail trying to get all four feet moving at once.

The overwhelming force of water barreling out of the mountains, engorging rivers to flood state for up to a hundred miles, was an expected, annual event. As years passed, increasing mining debris carried along in the onslaught further jammed rivers in sharp bends. River bottoms filled with tailings, making passage for boats and ships nearly impossible. Fights exploded in every direction—farmer versus miner, neighbor versus neighbor, upstream versus downstream. Arguments on how to control it varied from levees bordering natural embankments, to allowing overflow to spill into a defined bypass system. Flooding, exacerbated by mining—particularly hydraulics—remained a hovering, unreconciled concern. But nothing, he suspected, as bad as the storm to come.

Justin gazed at paired-off partners grasping hands and wheeling in circles. He took delight in the maze of patterns created by the dancers, the kaleidoscope of gay colors whirling by, and feet skipping as if on air in a sense of pure, light-hearted glee. With so much laughter and good humor, it was difficult *not* to notice the one soul fuming in a corner. He watched Royce soak up every smile on Charlotte's face, the flush on her cheeks as she spryly wove in and out of the path of fellow merrymakers, and her carefree spirit that she now shared with Luke Wilcox.

Throwing back the rest of his beer, Justin put down the mug and made a beeline for Royce. He noted the cluster of Colliers behind an information table with a large easel depicting an artist's rendition and plans for the orphanage.

Adele and Stan were stalwartly behind the organization and fundraising of the effort, pulling in help from both Neil and Celeste. Adele had assembled her army of society women at the luncheon, and from Charlotte's stories it seemed to him a lot of these women needed something constructive to do with their time. Adele intended to scatter them amongst Sacramento elite to solicit donations. The price of admission for the dance went towards the cause, not to mention proceeds from the pie auction. As if the sweet confections were not enough, the high bidder for each pie won a picnic lunch with its baker—to be shared after tomorrow's church services on the back lawn. Each dessert was labeled with a number and the flavor of the pie. Though hints could be given by the decoration on the pastry, identities of the bakers were strictly secret. Knowing sweethearts were likely to pass along clues, Adele hoped to create a few bidding wars in the name of charity.

Justin placed himself directly in front of Royce, blocking his view. "Boy, I tell you, did we have a morning!"

Instinctively, Royce jerked his head to see past this obstacle but smirked as Justin's words sunk in. "Heard you went swimming."

"That I did. Tough to get a good stroke going while paddling through mud."

Royce chuckled. "Low man on the ladder always gets wet."

"I was hoping to move up that ladder pretty soon."

Royce gave him a joking punch on the arm. "You're doing just fine. Takes a while to earn the trust of experienced cowpunchers. You're gaining a lot of respect. Bank it."

Justin nodded his thanks. He began a slow turn towards the information table. "Those the plans for the new orphanage?" he asked. He took a few steps in that direction, causing Royce to turn with him.

"Yeah. Looks like it's really coming together. Stan and Neil have been going over the building codes, so tonight's success could go a long way to get us to groundbreaking."

Now standing in front of the table, Justin said earnestly, "I can't think of a more worthy cause. Did I hear this was all Adele's idea?"

Royce responded with pride, "Yes, she and Stan. He hears about a lot of cases firsthand through his patients, those that know of loss amongst their neighbors. Neil's trying to get a handle on the kids alone loose in the city trying to beg out a living. He's working with law enforcement to find them."

Justin caught Neil's eye. "This is impressive. How's the fund-raising?"

"Going very well, thanks for being here to support us," replied Neil. "We should be able to break ground in a week or two."

Justin watched Beth and Adele answering questions and pointing to the diagram of the building. Celeste hovered in the background, straightening piles of pamphlets.

Royce studied the floor plan of the main building and looked at Stan. "So how many kids can you house in a place that size?"

"About forty, comfortably. Of course, I have plans for an addition if need be."

"Since when have you been the least bit interested?" sneered Celeste.

Royce looked startled. "I know I stay pretty buried in ranch business, but I'm not totally oblivious to what else goes on. If it's family business, I'm always interested. I was just curious to see if you needed anything."

"Help, from you?" Celeste mocked.

"What, is that so unheard of?" he demanded.

Adele and Neil glanced at each other. Adele responded, "We have a team ready to start, but if you could spare a few men for the ground breaking some of the other ranchers might follow suit."

"Sure, I can spare a crew. Can spare myself, too."

"Royce, that would be outstanding!" exclaimed Stan. "It would really pick up the pace of the whole project. With you there personally . . . well, I couldn't ask for a better endorsement."

Royce began to back away from all the fuss. "Yeah, well . . . just tell me what day to be there." He circled around to scan the crowd.

Neil mumbled to Adele, "Now, what do you suppose brought that on?"

255

Adele smiled. "Perhaps it was *who* brought that on. I think I like it."

Justin grinned to himself. Neil moved between the tables until he stood just behind Justin, who in turn was watching Royce.

Neil spoke in a low tone. "I take it you haven't encouraged him to get out there and dance? He's been doing an awful lot of skulking about."

"Nope, not touching that one."

"I believe he's brooding over your sister."

"Yep, she specializes in puncturing the egos of men."

"Especially the prideful, I take it?"

Justin chuckled. "Remember you said that. I'm just a hired hand."

Celeste strolled over, cocked her head, and challenged Justin. "I believe, sir, you owe me a dance?" She scooped up one corner of her skirt as she moved closer, casually exposing her petticoat and an enticing glimpse of her ankles.

"Do I, now?" Justin observed that Celeste bestowed practiced expressions on men. She was far too young, a colossal flirt, and the sister of his employer. That being a dangerous combination, it led him to treat her as he did Vicente's youngest, Mariposa— kindly and politely. Where Mariposa was shy and reserved, Celeste was boldly coquettish.

Behind him, he heard Royce's angry voice soar above the noise of the crowd. "Is that right?"

He turned to see him facing Luke with a grim set jaw as if weighing his options before throwing his weight into battle.

Luke wore a sneering frown and appeared to enjoy taunting his rival. "The lady made her choice, Collier."

The very tilt of Royce's head was threateningly direct. He stood, shoulders thrown back, chin jutted out, thumbs looped through the back of his belt as his chest prominently thrust

256

forward. He looked as if he were just itching to launch himself at Luke.

Luke carefully held his gaze, gently taking Charlotte's elbow to turn her away. Charlotte glanced anxiously about until she saw Justin and threw him such a beseeching look that he muttered a hasty, "Maybe later" at Celeste and bolted for the tight and testy circle in front of him.

Justin pushed himself into their midst with boisterous tidings. "Boy, howdy, you fellas been to see the pie table? I don't think I've ever seen such a spread. Royce, come have a look—I'll give you a clue which one is Charlotte's." He gave his boss a playful nudge.

Royce's stance suggested he meant to hold ground. He kept his glare focused on Luke and stated, "I just asked the lady if she would like to dance," he growled. "But this melon-head seems to think he owns her, like his ticket bought her for the night."

"I think she expressed herself loud and clear." Luke's voice dripped with contempt.

"You didn't even let her speak!"

Justin put a restraining hand on Royce's arm and said lowly, "Will you cool off?"

"Someone has to open that loaf that sits on his shoulders!"

Justin moved to change the point of the conflict. "I think we'd all be better served to settle this at the silent auction. Put some of this energy to use for the orphans. That is why we're all here, isn't it?"

No one moved. "C'mon Royce—like I said, I got an inside track to the pie table."

Royce looked at Luke as he spoke to Charlotte. "I was hoping Charlotte would give me a hint herself." He positioned himself at an angle as if to come between her and Luke.

Charlotte gave a nervous laugh. "Ah, that would be cheating.

Perhaps if you go take a peek with Justin you might be able to guess. I certainly left a clue for you, if you look closely."

At the mention of giving him advantage, he relaxed a little and looked down at her face. She placed her fingertips gently on his arm and said, "I'll see you soon . . ." Justin tugged his other arm, but he did not look away from her face. She nodded her reassurance, and at that he reluctantly allowed Justin to pull him away.

After making a few yards of headway, Royce began to unravel. "Now why exactly should I walk away here? He's got no claim on her."

"Royce, think about it. She doesn't want a scene, and you can't win any other way. If you press yourself as if *you* have a claim, you'll make her mad for the rest of the night. If you back her in a corner, she will come out swinging."

He gave a slight grin. "I could take that as a challenge."

"I wouldn't."

Royce did a double take.

"Look, you don't *want* to fight with her, and if you fight him, you'll make her mad. Let her deal with Luke. Give him a break; he's only trying to save face a little."

"I'm not interested in saving his face . . ." he fumed. He began to think of his rights and turned back towards them.

"No, but if you're interested in hers, you'll let them be." He grabbed Royce's arm to jerk him back around. "If you want to be the hero here, you'll be patient."

Royce glowered at him, and he continued, "I *guarantee* you'll reap the rewards if you'll just set still." Royce's shoulders relaxed a little. "Guarantee," Justin repeated.

Royce shrugged in reluctant resolution. "Well . . . what are we waiting for? Let's go look at that pie table."

Justin slapped him on the back. "Now you're talking."

They stood before the silent auction, looking down the gaily decorated table against the wall, pies of every variety running three deep down the length of it. Numbered bid sheets lined the edge. Bows and flowers, fruits and trinkets adorned the pastries. Royce scanned the rows, looking for anything at all familiar.

"I thought you said you knew?"

Justin inspected each one methodically. "I know Charlotte."

"Well, that's a big help . . ."

"Wait!" He smacked Royce's arm with the back of his hand. "*There* it is!"

He turned to Royce triumphantly. "She said specifically she left you a clue."

"Yeah?"

"Well, who besides you and me know the name of the farm?"

Royce searched the table again and began to laugh. There on the second row sat a beautiful strawberry-rhubarb pie. In the center of it sat the prickly, purple flower of a thistle, fashioned out of twisted bits of cloth starched into the proper form. He rubbed his hands together with glee. He turned back, grinning, to look at Justin, then over to see Charlotte standing in a group of her friends, chatting happily. "Thank you."

"All's well that ends well."

"And this . . . ends right here." Royce picked up a pencil and scrawled his name on his bid. He put down an amount that ensured it would be the only one. Luke might be able to compete with him on many things, but not this.

"Maybe you could return the favor and help me figure out which of these belongs to Melissa Hobson?"

"Melissa, huh? I could ask her sister."

"*I* could ask her sister."

"You don't think that's awkward? Choosing between sisters?"

"Good point."

"You ever notice she wears an awful lot of pink? I mean,

almost always."

Justin located a pie sporting a large pink bow. He pointed. "You think?"

Royce spotted Luke. He inspected all the bid sheets until he found Royce's name. He grimaced as he read it, and his face turned red. Royce smiled with satisfaction. Luke walked towards them shaking his head, and Justin braced himself.

Royce crossed his arms over his chest and waited. Luke ambled up and chuckled bitterly, "Well, I guess we both know now who bought Charlotte."

Justin interjected, "This is for charity, Luke. Let's just all enjoy the rest of the evening."

Royce rocked back on his heels, looked down at his boots, and said calmly, "You know, Luke, I've really tried to be a gentleman about all this . . ."

Luke snorted his contempt.

"But, that's it!" Royce reeled back and threw all his weight into the punch landing squarely on Luke's jaw.

Justin made a mistimed grab for Royce as Luke sprawled to the floor. Royce was already in motion as Luke scrambled to his feet and lunged for his middle, setting him off balance. The two rolled on the floor, struggling for position, each landing blows that couldn't miss at this proximity.

The crowd scattered at the commotion. Women screamed; men rushed in—first to see who was fighting, then to try and separate them.

Royce leapt to his feet and landed a hard strike to Luke's cheekbone. He appeared dazed. Luke's two brothers broke through the pack and charged Royce but were caught by a group of men shouting for an end to the fight. Royce, distracted by the rush of brothers, suffered a backhanded belt to the nose as Luke somewhat recovered. Justin briefly managed a hand on Royce, but he jerked away. He turned to glare at Justin and saw

Charlotte standing to one side, shouting for him to stop. Still in it, he glanced back at Luke, who had his arms pinned back by two bystanders.

He straightened, felt his nose, and discovered blood. Justin jumped in front of him, yelling, "That's enough, Royce. It's over." He looked past Justin at Charlotte. Her expression switched from fear to rage. She whirled about and darted for the door.

Charlotte sank into the worn armchair, eyes closed, head leaning back, too emotionally weary to change out of her clothes for bed. She sat quietly in the dark for a number of minutes before an incessant pounding began on the front door of the boarding-house. An uneasy feeling hit the pit of her stomach. Moments later she heard the scurry of slippered feet in the hallway and a rapid tapping at her door.

Mrs. White pleaded with her. "Won't you *please* come down? He'll wake the whole house. I should go and get the sheriff. But, in the meantime, he'll disturb the others."

"Of course. I'm very sorry, Mrs. White."

Angrily, she put her shoes back on, grabbed a shawl, and headed downstairs. She stopped at the bottom and glared at him. He stood dusty, disheveled, with his hair hanging in his eyes and a telltale trickle of blood from his nose.

Royce cleared his throat. "Maybe we should go out on the front porch?"

She slid icily by him, head erect, and didn't speak. She stalked to the railing and stared into the night.

He closed the door behind them. "I guess I've made a mess of things, haven't I?"

"Oh, indeed you have!" she snapped, not turning to look at him. "And I suppose Luke is right behind you, and the two of you will embarrass me at my residence as well?"

261

"No, Luke was out cold. I think his brothers took him home."

She felt a pang of guilt that Luke had been caught between them. "Is he hurt badly?"

"No, he'll be all right. Probably have a pretty good headache tomorrow though."

"I guess you're proud of that?"

"I'm not . . ." he faltered. He stepped closer to her, speaking in a low, deflated tone. "I'm not proud of much of anything right now, Charlotte. I've got much to apologize for; I'm not sure where to start."

"Beginning is always good."

"Beginning with not getting myself to town to ask the lady I most admire to a dance in a timely fashion. I guess I forgot she needed to be told that she's . . . very important to me. And, being so important, I couldn't let go of the fact she turned me down. I acted with my gut and not my head. I know . . . I'm bad about barreling along with my own plans without thinking about other people." He tentatively placed his hands on her shoulders.

"I want you to be a part of my plans. I'm sorry that I take it for granted that you'll just be there . . . or even that you would want to. I'm hoping you can find it in your heart to take pity on somebody as hard headed as me and maybe forgive me while you're at it. Generally, I don't much care what other people think. I guess I proved that well enough, making a fool of myself at the dance. But what *you* think . . . that matters to me." He left a long, quiet stretch before admitting, "And, well . . . I really don't know what else to say."

She listened, softening as she realized he spoke from his heart. His touch on her shoulders sent a shiver through her. She waited in silence to let it all sink in. She turned to him and sighed. "Now, why couldn't you have said some of this earlier?"

"I'm new at this. Nobody ever mattered enough to me before.

Forgive me?" His eyes pleaded, soft and hopeful.

"Unfortunately, sincerity always works on me. Fortunately, you hide that pretty well most of the time."

"Hey," he protested.

"Sorry, I shouldn't have said that. A good mad is hard to let go of sometimes." She smiled tiredly. "It's been a long night."

"I meant what I said."

"I know you did."

He looked deep into her eyes. She felt mesmerized by the intensity of his gaze. Maybe it was the power of his words, maybe the feeling as she looked at him stripped of pretense. Maybe she was too tired to think. He bent to kiss her. When she didn't pull away, his hands went ever so gently to her waist and pulled her closer. It was a long, gentle kiss. When they parted, both were silent, yet he held on to her right hand. As if not wanting to push his luck, he said, "I'd better let you get to bed."

She nodded.

"Can I see you tomorrow?" he asked.

"I suppose you will after church. You did buy a pie, after all."

He squeezed her hand. She could tell he was debating on whether or not to pull her in for another kiss. She took a step towards the door.

"I'm glad you came by. Good night, Royce."

She saw he watched her go inside and lock up. Too exhausted to sort out the evening's events, she decided to leave tomorrow to sort out itself.

CHAPTER 35

San Francisco

"Let me help you with that, Mother."

Dutton took the tray laden with fruit and chocolates from her and followed her into the judge's study.

"I just need to get your father settled." Mary Dandridge minced into the room, selected the largest pillow from the sofa, and plumped it to her satisfaction. His father lowered his significant bulk into a large overstuffed chair with some difficulty. He groaned as he lifted his calf with both hands and waited mere seconds before his wife whisked the cushion under it to rest on the footstool.

Judge Dandridge eyed the tray Dutton placed on a side table. "Where's the port?"

"Now, Walter, you know the doctor said that alcohol aggravates your gout."

He pulled a face and grumbled as Mary kissed the top of his head.

"I'll leave you boys to your business." She turned to kiss Dutton's cheek. "I'm going up to bed shortly."

"Dinner was superb, Mother. Thank you."

She patted his face, looking at him tenderly. "I'm so happy you had time for a proper visit. Good night." She pulled the double doors behind her as she left.

The judge waited for less than a minute, pointing to the edge of his desk. "Dutton, grab that whiskey decanter and a couple

264

glasses, would you?"

Dutton raised an eyebrow, and his father snapped his fingers and continued to point.

"Cigar?"

"Heavens, yes! Your mother worries too much. It's my little pleasures that get me through the aggravation of age. And make that a double."

Dutton cut and lit his father's cigar as the judge reached in his jacket pocket for the list.

"I suppose we covered at dinner the normal business successes fit for your mother's ear."

"Mmm." Dutton puffed the tobacco until its end glowed a fiery red. "On to politics, I take it?"

"Now is the time to decide on our particular business needs going forward, and which illustrious candidate is most likely to help us fulfill them. Where are we on Neil?"

"A delicate balance, but making progress. It's best that I remain removed from the situation. Neil's vulnerable, but cautious. More appropriate that I appear consumed by my own business dealings and somewhat disinterested. Let him come to me . . ." A smug sensation came over him as he blew a long, slow line of smoke. "It's why I've deployed Congressman Glenn. He's my eyes, ears, and mouthpiece when necessary. He conveys our plans with such an altruistic tongue, I almost believe him myself."

His father nodded. "Of course. We've indoctrinated him. He's an extremely grateful specimen . . . been awhile since we've had a man so agreeable."

"As you say, he's been well trained."

"And is Neil aware of Lodie's ties to you?"

"Not really. We played it as a passing acquaintance at the Oyster Bar, a friends of friends sort of thing. They've met several times, found all the relevant connections of where they might be of political support to one another, and not one mention of my involvement anywhere. Lodie understands fallout after the Empire mine disaster, so he grasps my uphill battle with Neil. He faces the same with his former partners. Being simpleminded sorts, I don't imagine they'll *ever* forgive."

His father's mood darkened at the mention of Empire. "Though we profited handsomely on the mining stock's ride back up, I'll not forget the blight Bourn cast on our good name by pushing us out. He turned a pretty penny on his purchase of Collier stock, yet his implications towards us were insulting. This round went by quietly, but I'll remember *him* when the tables turn, and, believe me, they always do."

"That may come quicker than you think." Dutton swirled the whiskey in his glass, eyeing its golden color with admiration. "I've been investing in a new commodity . . . quicksilver. I'm about to close on the last of available sources. We'll see how well Bourn can process his gold without it. I predict . . . a shortage. I'm certain we'll eventually come to agreeable terms." He raised his glass to his father and watched the slow smile steal across the judge's face.

"Well done."

"I thought so. And, by the by, our congressman has secured an invitation to the Collier soiree you're invited to at Cornelius Cole's."

"Excellent! You'll be attending, of course."

Dutton frowned. "I think not. It's a major coup that Neil has garnered a United States senator's patronage, and his stellar reputation needs protection. He's being pulled into the inner circle, and there will be a number of fat wallets he needs introduction to before the real campaigning begins again. Your presence is far more essential, as you've been friends with the man since the organization of the California branch of the Republican party. My relationship with Collis Huntington is well-known to the senator, and it seems *their* friendship is suffering some frayed edges."

"I've heard nothing of the sort! And the railroad so close to completion!"

Dutton gave his father a hard look. "I'm not supposed to be privy to this myself, but Huntington is getting ready to sever ties with him completely. It seems Cole is suffering from a bout of ethics. He no longer sees the vision of bending principles—a difference in defining 'serving the greater good.' Huntington pushed him through that last amendment to the Railroad Act of '64—permitting the railroad to issue their own mortgage bonds on up to one hundred miles of track before it was built . . ."

"A brilliant move, actually."

"Yes, but Huntington waits a minimal amount of time to push his way back to the till. Government is beginning to resist his grasp for more funding, no matter how urgent his plea. Cole doesn't like being caught in the middle. He's decided he prefers being a statesman rather than a railroad tycoon."

"Tough call, that one. I'll pass on your regrets. As you say, it's best to appear too busy with your own affairs. But you *are* attending the party at the Collier ranch this Saturday?"

"Yes. Probably good you had a conflict. This is more a thank-you for past support . . . best not to overwhelm with our presence. Now that Neil's given to doubt my motives, he listens with a much keener ear. I'll have to be more guarded, while appearing nonchalant. He needs me, and he knows it; he just doesn't want to. Time will cure that if no mistakes are made."

"It's a formal affair . . . are you taking anyone?"

Dutton chortled. "That sounds like Mother talking."

His father sighed. "It is; I promised I would ask. But she has a point. It's time you start thinking earnestly about finding a wife. A family anchors one in a community with a halo of respectability. Not to mention, I would like to see the Dandridge name carried to the next generation before I pass on."

"Ah. Point taken." He refilled both their drinks. "You know, as a young man, I fancied myself with Adele Collier." His father nodded approvingly. "I haven't met the woman that measures up to my image of her. But I'll make a point of scanning the partygoers to see whom I may have overlooked."

"That's all I ask. Believe me, it's to your advantage to find someone before your mother takes it on as a project."

Dutton laughed. "That's a serious threat."

His father shifted in his chair. "Take it seriously. I need you settled. Neil needs to be ready by the next election, and that means strengthening ties with him. We will require federal patronage with the port collector and customs house once our warehouses are completed and while the treasury department here in San Francisco is still amenable to our proposals on mutually beneficial growth. His ties to the committee on economic development are a necessary link for us."

"I'm not sure I follow . . ."

"The customs house provides the federal government's main source of revenue in the state, so it is tightly watched. A few customs officers are known to be willing to 'expedite' imports for a price . . . Golden State Freight and Finance gets *very* 'special treatment.'"

"Ah. I remember their attempts to block railroad funding with the banks. How they strive to manipulate the competition! Your quick note to Sam Brannan thwarted that one."

"Yes. I've made some inroads with those same officers in reference to our Chinese investments. A few good men on the inside will assist in the difficulties we've experienced with imports. It seems my contacts stumbled onto quite the duty evasion scheme by our own dear Golden State F&F. That information provided helpful leverage in explaining to certain customs officials why they might also want to be accommodating with us."

"Well, now. We'll have to keep our finger on the pulse there . . . perhaps there's some influence we might also wield in convincing Golden State to transport goods to some of our more far-flung outposts? How grand a scheme did they run? And can we imitate it?"

"Most certainly. The gist of it is they avoided the higher express charges on merchandise in order for their goods to reach the market first. Shippers must clear boxes individually. Their arrangement in New York allowed them to clear eight thousand packages at once. When their wares reached Panama, the agents placed all small boxes into locked packing trunks. They had their own messengers keeping a lookout on the progress."

Dutton's mind raced with the possibilities. Certain Chinese commodities required discretion in their handling. He glanced up, feeling the judge's steely gaze upon him. He found it difficult to quash the rising feeling of guilt. He saw that his father read his face as easily as when he was a child.

The judge cleared his throat. And waited. Almost as if he anticipated that Dutton might speak first and tip his hand. *Wily old devil, he still unnerves me.*

"Dutton, I leave Chinese negotiations in your capable hands. You have a savvy rapport with the celestials. They appreciate a mathematically quick mind, and negotiation is nearly a sport to them. You play their game well. But . . . I cannot stress strongly enough . . . Keep us out of the opium trade."

He answered coolly, as if it were of no consequence, "Father, there's nothing illegal about it, and the profits . . ."

"It's immoral! And if the rumblings I hear are true, it will be illegal, and I don't want to be sitting on a mountain of product we cannot move—or have our name sullied."

Dutton hesitated, thinking, *Ah, but that's when the profitability really soars.* Plans already in motion must follow their natural course. Not ignorant of the rumors, he had taken great pains to bring merchandise in quietly. No need for public record on where to find an illegal substance when he could have a nice stockpile tucked away. Just a precaution—it could take years before laws went into effect. Opium was definitely not a clean venture, and a tarnished community standing was a risk.

"Not an enterprise to build reputations, to be sure. Plenty of business opportunity staying within the guidelines of the Six Companies."

His father did not blink, nor did he relax. His voice held a hard edge as he said, "I'm holding you to that."

Dutton supposed the time always came when fathers and sons parted ways in thinking, particularly when more progressive measures came to light. He lifted his glass to the judge.

"Of course."

CHAPTER 36

Collier Ranch

The scant number of errands sending Justin inside the main house left him with an impression of its stateliness. His purpose for being there was usually urgent, so it had not occurred to him to pay attention to his surroundings in the boss's home. Even when he and Celeste served as chaperones, riding with Royce and Charlotte, they returned to spend time in the library. Though impressive, it was a more comfortable, masculine-feeling room, and his focus had been drawn to the billiard table.

And now he found himself in a crowd of preening peacocks, elegantly dressed, sipping champagne and swaying to the sophisticated scores of the orchestra positioned at the edge of the enormous drawing room. A grandeur that overwhelmed. Not an understated elegance, but a determined statement of power.

He tugged at his stiff, starched collar, looking for familiar faces and wondering why he was here. Even the formal evening clothes he wore were provided by his hosts. Hard for a man to feel at ease in this setting, especially when he couldn't wear his own clothes. Well, he knew why he was here. As a favor to Neil. The party itself was a lavish gesture of thanks to friends, neighbors, and supporters at a time when he needed nothing from them. He wanted to remind them that he was approachable and seeking to serve. It was hard to fault the man for sincerity; Justin both liked and respected Neil. And, moreover, he felt respected by him—all the Colliers, really.

Hence, the favor. He came to escort Celeste. She did not wish to choose amongst her admirers for such an important event. Nor did the family feel it appropriate, knowing Celeste's penchant for drama. Justin was the steady choice, with the added bonus of company for Charlotte. He wondered when either of them would make an appearance.

He glanced over at the grand foyer table—elaborately carved, with eagles' heads on its triangular pedestal base, their beaks screeching forward in warning like sentries on watch. Dozens of sparkling champagne flutes covered the highly polished surface of the table. He decided standing alone in one place made him feel awkward, and bubbly was an excellent way to remedy that. He picked up a glass and glanced at the imposing curved staircase. No sign of the women still upstairs dressing, so he edged his way between encircled groups of guests into the drawing room.

He regarded the room dominated by French rosewood furniture—the dark, intricate fretwork of which raced and curved its way around the edges of the sofas and settees, set off by a plush, coral-pink velvet. The cushions were luxuriously stuffed and plumped; the cording, a twisted combination of coral and deep red. A fine Persian carpet graced the floor, flowing nearly to the edges of the room. Rose and peach pinks, touched with soft yellow and sage, danced across its open, creamy surface.

The fireplace centered in the room was a massive, putty colored marble, veined in greenish hues and braced with enormous corbels to support the mantel. Carved seashells and acanthus leaves splayed out across its face. On the mantel sat a domed Austrian clock, and, on each end, vibrant enamel vases rested, in rich blues and dotted with rosebuds. Over the mantel was a magnificent, black-lacquered mirror, European in origin, despite its Asian style. Its top corners were accented by complexly carved pagodas strutting out from the framework, the center of which featured a Chinese temple, anchored by foo dogs. Above the mirror, stretching towards the impressive crown molding, the fireplace wall was painted with twin columns rising from behind the pagodas in browned Chinese reds and deep forest greens, which joined over an arched painted scene of the exterior of the Collier house—poised in the center and encircled by ivy.

Justin drew in a long breath. He had the impression of being smothered by his surroundings. He looked for escape. He gazed past the orchestra, through the French doors to the veranda—even this portal to outdoors was weighted down by heavy draperies and silk tassels. The prominent center seashell of the cornice overhead would have made Poseidon proud. As he pondered the opulence closing in around him, an odd thought crossed his mind. He wondered if this was like an English manor . . . one like his father's. The idea of him soured his mood.

"Justin!"

He turned as Royce's voice boomed behind him. Royce clapped him on the shoulder.

"Looking dapper, my friend." He smirked. "So glad you could join us."

Justin tipped his glass. "Looking pretty spit shined yourself. Nice to be invited."

Royce leaned in. "Is it?"

Justin chuckled, nodding. "It's a lot to take in."

Giving the room a perfunctory glance, Royce agreed. "Now you know why I prefer the library. All this . . . stuff; it was Mother's favorite room. Adele would kill me if I tried to change it—not that I'd know how. Actually, seeing Neil back here for the party, the house would suit him and Beth a lot better than me. Maybe after she tires of city life and political demands, they'll settle back here. I've got a ridge picked out where I'd like to build something more comfortable." He reached to snag a champagne glass on a passing waiter's tray. Arriving guests continued to fill space around them. "You haven't seen the girls, have you?"

"No. I was about to ask you the same."

Royce grimaced. "No doubt, Celeste is making Charlotte redo her hair for the tenth time. I barely saw your sister yesterday because mine monopolized her with dresses."

Justin looked around at the room peppered with men in regal evening garb, women in resplendent gowns of every color. "Certainly looks like everyone pulled out all the stops." He saw Celeste glide into their midst, the smile on her fresh, young face dazzling. Her strawberry-blonde hair was swept up and her curls captured from underneath by a large gold comb embedded with seed pearls. She wore a gown of cerulean-blue silk and a triple-stranded pearl choker at her throat. He felt a grin creep across his face and bowed low before her in order to hide it.

"Now see there . . ." she smacked his arm lightly with her folded ivory fan as he rose. "You're a lot more charming when you smile."

Adele appeared, a bit out of breath. "Celeste, you look lovely, dear." She nodded her approval and peeped about, searching. Her tone was pinched. "Has *anyone* seen the servers sending food out yet? I sent Stan to the kitchen a few minutes ago to check on them . . ."

Royce pulled her over and kissed her cheek. "Relax; it's going fine. Everyone is enjoying themselves, and you look beautiful, by the way. Just remember to send out the spirits before Neil makes a speech."

She threw him a piercing look. "Are you mingling with the guests? You're supposed to be greeting people."

274

"Adele, I was the first one at the door and have stayed on the opposite side of the room from Neil, as instructed, talking to people, until this very moment." He glimpsed over the crowd. "There's hardly ten I haven't spoken to. Now, why waste that gorgeous dress on us? Stand still for five minutes and let Stan admire you. Or, at least take a stiff belt of something to calm yourself."

Adele sighed. "You're incorrigible."

"I do my best."

"Where is Charlotte?"

Celeste pointed to the staircase behind them. "There."

Adele turned and uttered softly, "Oh, my."

Justin looked up to watch Charlotte descending the curved stair. Her chestnut tresses were pulled back and elegantly woven into a loose chignon at the nape of her neck. She wore a thin, pounded-gold necklace that belonged to her mother, unusual in its simplicity as it encircled her neck with a gap at the front before one side of it trailed enticingly down towards her décolletage. Her burgundy and gold silk gown appeared to float around her, her skirt flaunting an overlayer of sheer fabric called *illusion*. Its delicate, gossamer sheen projected an ethereal effect, particularly in tandem with the light wrap of the same, draped over her arms.

In a room full of hothouse flowers, she was the rose of Sharon—strongly rooted, with pure white petals as smooth as her aristocratic skin. Yet, there was a wildness in her rosy, pointed edges and a flame of character sparking from the center, proving her to be much more than just a thing of beauty. Justin glanced at Royce. He was mesmerized.

Before Justin could comment, Royce strode off into the crowd. A tall, blonde woman standing nearby smiled slyly at him as he approached and rested her hand briefly on his arm. Briefly, because Royce's eyes never left the vision on the stair, and the woman's hand slid away unnoticed. Charlotte looked up as he neared, and her eyes danced. He placed one arm formally behind him, and gave a slight bow as he reached to take her hand. Reaching the bottom of the stair, she placed her hand in his. He tucked her hand onto his arm and led her proudly through the roomful of guests, stopping to make introductions along the way.

"Goodness, they make a striking pair," said Adele. "Now that she's here, Royce is more likely to interact with our guests when he's parading her around." She looked past where they stood and exclaimed, "Finally! Here comes the food."

Once Charlotte and Royce disappeared into a group of Neil's patrons, Justin caught a flash of raw hate the blonde woman aimed at Charlotte. Her attention returned to her group, and she laughed gaily at something her escort said that she only halfway heard. He looked down at Celeste and noticed a smug grin on her face.

"Best comeuppance I've seen all week."

He raised a brow. "Who is she?"

"Iris Solinger. Come show me off around the room, and I'll tell you all about her."

Justin studied Celeste's worldly expression, thinking what a curiosity she was. She made no bones about setting her sights on the most lavish of lifestyles, yet she could poke fun at the absurdity of it all, too. He had to admit she was entertaining. He offered his arm. "It would be my honor."

"And, perhaps, a dance later?"

Justin scoffed. "Where?"

"They've cleared all the furniture at that end of the room, silly. And there's plenty of room on the terrace. You *do* waltz, do you not?"

"My mother insisted cotillion would come in handy one day."

"Wonderful!"

Justin watched with amusement as Celeste worked the room. She flirted coyly with at least half a dozen helplessly charmed sons of ranching and industry. She chatted and flattered every well-heeled and influential old friend of her parents, making them feel like long-lost aunts and uncles. She introduced him with confidence, treating him as important as anyone else. As they walked on to the next guest, she gave him the backhanded story on the last one; some she regarded fondly, others . . . she laid their secrets bare.

They were standing with a group of Collier neighbors when an older gentlemen asked Justin what line of work he was in. Celeste noted Iris within earshot and quipped, "He's in ranching!"

Justin chuckled and looked the man in the eye. "I work on *this* ranch. Mostly with horses."

The man winked. "My favorite part of ranch work when I was young and my back could take the pounding. Say, you're Royce's trainer? He surely brags on you. I've got a stallion that's a real head scratcher. I've been meaning to convert some of Royce's poker losses into a trade for your services."

Justin nodded. "You work it out with Royce, and I'd be happy to take a look."

Looking over Justin's shoulder, he called out, "Well, let's just ask him now!"

Royce moved in with Charlotte in tow. "I believe you're maligning my good name," he joked. "Harrison, Justin came as a friend tonight, and, as I recall, our poker account is square."

"Can't blame a fella for trying."

"Nope, but I've heard you complaining about that horse for a while now. Why don't you bring him over next week?"

The man winked again. "Just like your daddy. A good neighbor."

Charlotte reached up to hug Justin's neck. "I haven't seen

you all evening."

"Celeste keeps me busy."

Iris edged her way into the circle. "Celeste! How are you, darling? Hello everyone, good to see you." She nodded to the assembled couples, cut her eye towards Charlotte, and ignored Royce. "Best be careful, Celeste . . . I believe this one's after your fellow . . . I don't believe we've met?" She fawned at Justin.

Celeste smirked. "I'm not terribly worried. This is Justin Albright. Justin, Iris Solinger."

She looked at him intently. "Delighted."

Charlotte and Celeste exchanged amused glances. Iris gave Charlotte a once-over, pointedly examining her dress. "Well . . . it seems our little *seamstress* decided to buy European after all." She cocked her head. "Must have set you back a year's salary, dear."

Charlotte leveled her gaze. "No, no. I made it myself."

"I've not seen anything like that in the shop!"

"Of course not. I'm always experimenting with new ideas. I keep a few garments tucked away for myself. And my more adventurous clients."

Celeste piped in. "It's true, she's made a number of gorgeous dresses for both me and Adele. If you can describe something you've seen, she can recreate it."

Harrison's wife stepped forward, touching the illusion shawl on Charlotte's arm. "I had no idea you made this; it's just stunning!"

Another woman joined in. "Lydia, she works at Van Oss's dress shop."

"Where did you find the inspiration for it?" asked another.

"I study engravings of the latest trends. Parts of this dress were featured in *The Englishwoman's Domestic Magazine,* from a gown worn by Empress Elisabeth of Austria."

278

A chorus of "Ah's" arose as women crowded around Charlotte.

Justin muttered to Celeste, "Miss Solinger looks ready to boil."

"Doesn't she, though!" She giggled.

Royce glanced over the gaggle of women and shrugged at Justin. He leaned in behind Charlotte's ear. "I'm going in search of more champagne. When I return, I expect another waltz."

She nodded, her eyes twinkling.

Miss Solinger stalked away in disgust.

Seeing Celeste engrossed in conversation, Justin moved closer to Charlotte.

"Enjoying yourself?"

She beamed. "I'm having a marvelous time. And you? You look very distinguished."

"Pretty extravagant bash." He gave her an odd look. "Far easier to look the part than play the part."

"What are you saying?"

"It's a far cry from where we came from. Fun for a night, but this society stuff . . . I prefer when people say what they mean."

She scoffed. "I see this behavior every other day at work." She nodded towards Iris. "Especially from that one. And I don't have the luxury of responding in kind."

He shrugged. "Just so you don't get lost in it." He frowned. "Who's that dark-headed fella staring at you?"

She glanced in the man's direction. "No idea, but I noticed him, too. He's been hovering. Goodness, I'm parched! Must be the dancing. I wonder if Royce got caught in a conversation."

"There's a table with water over there. I'll bring some for you and Celeste."

"Thank you!" She tried to attract Celeste's attention, but the girl was so busy telling a story she missed her signal. Charlotte nearly bumped into the devilishly handsome stranger.

"Oh! You startled me!"

"Forgive me," he said, bowing. "I've been trying to get close enough to make your acquaintance all evening, but you've been preoccupied. Perhaps you would care to dance?"

Charlotte hesitated. "Well . . . I am waiting for someone."

"His loss, I'd say. I'm Dutton Dandridge."

She drew in a quick breath and stared, just for a moment. She hesitated, then smiled prettily. "Yes, I've heard a great deal about you. I'm Charlotte."

"I'm utterly charmed."

"Could you . . . turn around for a moment?"

He laughed, looking confused. She circled her finger in the air indicating she wanted him to rotate.

"Anything to oblige a lady." He chuckled and gave her an exaggerated spin. "Will that do?"

"Quite." Her smile faded. "I was merely checking to see if the dagger was as well hidden for this encounter as it was in the last."

"I beg your pardon?"

Charlotte peered over his shoulder to see Royce and Justin, both standing with a glass in each hand and mouths agape.

Dutton's face darkened. "I'd really like to know what I've done to provoke such a reaction."

She spoke plainly. "Mr. Dandridge, for Royce's sake, I'm quite certain I owe you an apology." She lowered her eyes, searching for words. "I'm sure in a complex world, there are many things I don't fully understand. So, to my way of thinking a situation may not seem right, where to Royce, he might say, 'That's just business; sometimes things run in your favor and sometimes they don't.' "

Calmer, Dutton nodded as if he understood. He reached over to pat her arm, but she stiffened to avoid his touch. She looked him dead in the eye now.

"But *you* shouldn't take this as an apology. I'm a miner's daughter, Mr. Dandridge. So, you see, there's an awful lot I do understand—even about profits and losses. I understand owners like you profit greatly, no matter what loss of life occurs to the miners. My father helped drive you out of Empire, but I imagine your newer enterprises are not familiar with your history. Workers enslaved to a job they cannot afford to leave? Or safety callously disregarded, expertise ignored, in favor of the dollar?" Her eyes took on an angry glint. "Yes . . . I did overhear your earlier conversation about your labor problems, and I was not at all impressed. Because that I do understand, probably far better than you do. You think *I* overestimate my knowledge in these matters, sir? Well, perhaps I should tell you my name is Mac-Laren. It tends to be known in mining circles. It's probably one you'd rather forget."

He stood eerily still. "I'm very sorry to have troubled you." He turned on his heel to find Royce shooting him a black look. He uttered an exasperated sound and pushed past, jostling him as he departed.

Charlotte took a deep breath as she cooled down. She noted the open space and amplified silence between her and the two men standing shoulder to shoulder holding drinks.

Justin leaned in to Royce. "See, here's the thing about Charlotte . . . the gentility of her mother always seems to be at war with the frankness of her father. You never know when the two sides of her'll switch. Sometimes it's her mother—all soft . . . sweet. Other times, it's James . . . marching up to stomp you."

"That so?"

"Seen her do it. She doesn't give in to temper much, and it's a long way to the line and then some—but if you push her far enough to cross it . . . well, *nobody* can help you then."

"Very funny." She was not amused.

"Seems like I did see that once."

She couldn't tell what sort of look he sent her, but it was steady.

"Oh, you're an angel!" Celeste rushed over to Justin to claim a glass of water. She looked up towards the foyer, "Is that Dutton Dandridge? Is he leaving?"

They each looked at Neil speaking with Dutton by the door. They shook hands, and Neil turned back to the party.

"Thankfully, without incident," Royce muttered. "You . . ." He nodded at Charlotte. "Come with me." He handed her a champagne flute and led her towards the terrace.

"What?" Celeste poked Justin. "What did I miss?"

"Oh . . . just Charlotte remembering to play her part . . ."

The terrace was filled with couples dancing, nearly to the balcony. Royce glanced around, then guided her down the stone stair onto the grounds. They walked a short way along a garden path lined with lanterns. When they reached a small gazebo, he let go of her hand. He circled around to face her. He threw back his glass of champagne in one gulp, set it on a bench, then shook his head. He turned away from her again, rubbing his jaw as if frustrated.

She stood quietly, holding her glass with both hands, realizing she had created something of a scene.

"You're killing me; you know that?"

"Royce, I'm so sorry . . ."

Her mind raced to find words. She saw he must be angry as she watched his shoulders tense. And then they shook. She blinked. "Wait . . . are you . . . ?"

He couldn't hold his breath any longer and burst out with an uncontrollable belly laugh. He turned to see her stricken face and howled even louder.

"I don't understand . . ."

"Because it was *Dutton*!" He kept chuckling. "God, I've always hated that bastard . . . sorry, language." He started laughing again. "But there really isn't any other word that fits him so well." He burst out laughing once more. "Ah." He wiped his eyes, trying to get past the humor. "Honestly, I don't know whether to scold you or congratulate you."

She sighed and tipped her glass to him as she took a long sip to calm her nerves.

"However," he said, growing serious, "this is Neil's party, and it's important to him. He and the Dandridges fell out, but he and Dutton were close friends for many years, not that I ever understood it. Our fathers were staunch allies. To be fair, they helped him get where he is now, and both are very important in the community and business world. He can't ignore them."

"I understand." She felt a touch defiant. "I'm *not* sorry as far *he* goes, but I understand it was not my place."

He grinned and moved closer to her. "You'll not spoil my mood tonight."

She brought the glass up between them and sipped at the edge. "Oh? Certainly not my intent."

He advanced, taking the glass from her hand, and set it on the bench. "I'm grateful to be right here, looking at the most beautiful woman I've ever seen. Challenging, but beautiful."

She tilted her head. "You are wont to gloss over my opinions at times, particularly ones you disagree with."

"Dear lady, mounting a defense for that ruins a perfectly congenial frame of mind. And, I don't get to see you often enough." He captured her hand and tugged her to him. "I don't intend to spoil the opportunities I'm given." Their foreheads nearly touched. She dared not look up, lest she invite a kiss. He bent down and kissed her anyway.

His fervor was all consuming. He took her breath away, leaving her feeling flustered and unsure. She found him overbearing and yet was powerfully and oddly attracted to him. Did his intensity overwhelm her, or coax her own latent feelings out of hiding?

He leaned back, looking at her. She was certain he read a thousand questions on her face, yet all she saw were unspoken answers in his eyes. Her hand nervously clutched her necklace, twisting it between her fingers. When he moved to kiss her a second time, she dropped it, her hand opening with the palm nearly flat as if to signal him to stop. Her hand touched his shoulder twice before she allowed it to rest there. Encouraged, he encircled her and drew her close, kissing her deeply. She warned him with pressure from her hand that she would momentarily flee. He relaxed his hold.

Understanding, he said, "Let's walk awhile."

They strolled the grounds together; Chinese lanterns strung through the trees overhead shared a soft light as they enjoyed the quiet. The chatter of guests and orchestra music drifted to the back of her consciousness as she took in the heady scent of jasmine blooming all around them.

"I must say, you're different tonight."

"Different? How so?" she asked rather dreamily.

He leaned in as if parting with a secret. "Docile, maybe?"

She smirked but did not look over at him. "Are you trying to change that?"

"No, no." He chuckled. "Just enjoying this rare moment of truce between us and wondering what brought it on."

"Must be the music. I've enjoyed it."

"Ah, I'll remember that. I myself enjoyed the dancing. With you, of course. Must be those sprightly feet."

"Well, you do whisk them around rather nicely."

"A compliment from the lady . . . this is my night, indeed."

They stopped at a small hedge separating the garden from a pond below. The moonlight shone full on their faces, and they gazed at stars, saying nothing, but each very aware of the other.

Charlotte heard the orchestra strike up "The Emperor Waltz" in the distance. She smiled. "Oh, this is one of my favorites."

Royce extended his arm. "Then we can't let it go to waste."

"Here?"

"Why not?" He smiled. He took her in his arms, and they waltzed around the grassy grounds as elegantly as in any ballroom. The music wafted from the house, accented only by the sound of the crickets chirping. The moonlight, stars, and jasmine combined to create a fairy-like theatre across the lawn. As they completed a turn, Royce brought them to a gentle halt.

"Why did you stop?" she whispered.

"Because all at once I couldn't hear the music. All I'm aware of . . . is you."

As he was yet holding her in dance position, he pulled her in. She came willingly. Just before their lips met, her eyes closed, and her head tilted back. He lingered a long time, savoring the sweetness of her mouth. Whatever he communicated at that moment she returned in full. As their lips parted, he still embraced her firmly. Her heavily fringed lashes opened, and she stared into a sea of Collier blue. He seemed to find something in her eyes that he had searched for all along. "Marry me," he said.

Her eyes grew wide. Her mouth formed a perfect *O*, and she murmured, "What?" He continued to clasp her tightly. "Now that we've come this far, I don't want there to be any confusion as to what I'm after. I said, 'Marry me.' I'm not letting go, and I'm not dropping to one knee until I hear 'Yes.' "

She continued to stare as if not comprehending. "Royce . . ."

"Do you love me?" he demanded, giving her an additional squeeze.

"Yes . . ." she said breathlessly.

"Good enough." He dropped to one knee, held her hand, and continued boldly. "Charlotte MacLaren, I hereby declare my undying love and devotion to you. I humbly ask if you will do me the honor of becoming my wife?"

Her eyes filled with tears as she looked down at him, posing with that silly grin on his face, and began to laugh. "Yes, I'll marry you."

He rose at once and took her in his arms, declaring, "I do love you, Charlotte. You've made me incredibly happy." Feeling entitled, he went after and got another long and lingering kiss. When he pulled away, he jerked his head back towards the ballroom and said, "Say, we've got an announcement to make."

"Oh," she began, flustered. "Royce, I need to compose myself a minute."

"You look great," he said, beaming. "Besides, I want everyone to see that you're mad for me."

CHAPTER 37

Sacramento

Charlotte fingered the violet-blue sapphire on her left hand. It felt peculiar, foreign, and most decidedly obstructive when she worked. All day it flashed constant reminders of her explosive happiness, and her secret anxiety.

Barely two days had gone by, during which she was overwhelmed by jubilant Collier welcomes and Justin's affectionate delight. But not two minutes past saying "yes" did she balk on their way to make the announcement. She had stopped short of the stone step, looked uneasily at Royce, and asked, "Have you spoken to my father?"

He apologized and told her he planned to ask permission ahead of time but was overcome by the moment. He assured her they would go to Thistle Dew together on Friday.

She was relieved to go soon, for the coming weeks were packed with demands. Senator Cornelius Cole was hosting a political function for Neil. Adele and Celeste insisted Charlotte accompany them to San Francisco to shop for Celeste's trip to Europe. They teased her about the wedding dress inspirations they would find. She hoped Althea might join them. Their jaunt would coincide nicely with Royce's cattle buying trip to New Mexico. He planned to take Justin, a testament to his growing importance to the ranch as well as a future brother-in-law.

Royce's friend Carl and his girlfriend invited them to the theatre tonight, and she was grateful for the distraction.

She remained thoughtful as their carriage meandered through the finer Sacramento neighborhoods; resplendent homes all jockeyed for position of most elevated. Each tried to crowd out the rest with superior standing and garish detail, like a woman overdressed for the opera. Moldings, cornices, ornate carvings of nymphs and gargoyles all attempted to put their best face forward to smile upon the bustling, haughty city that embraced all their occupants stood for.

Once inside the theatre, they settled into a more festive atmosphere—anticipating the performance.

"I can't believe I let you talk me into this, Carl."

"Where's your sense of adventure? Aren't you curious? Besides, the girls are excited. Aren't you, Trudy?"

"Heavens, yes!" Trudy all but bounced in her seat. The motion of her springing curls only accentuated the ridiculous. "Mother took me to New York just last year, and we saw real actors there. Now we have *real* theatre in Sacramento. I mean, the orchestra here is nice and all that, but true theatre—Shakespeare, even! Now that's culture!" She clasped her hands together.

"Culture?" snorted Royce. "What kind of culture do you expect to squeeze out of a bunch of hobos living out of wagons? You notice how many towns get robbed blind when these vagrants come through?"

"Sacramento's more sophisticated than that, Royce," said Carl.

"Bad as gypsies. Things just disappear," he muttered.

"Royce, this is a family troupe," protested Charlotte. "I'm looking forward to it, Carl."

"Uh huh. Family, same as gypsies. And how do you know that, anyway?" he demanded.

"I read it on the poster outside. You've been listening to too many granny tales. These are decent folks trying to perform an art they love! There's no grand scheme. They're no different than half the people in this town."

"If that were so, they'd live in a town and not three jumps ahead of the law."

Charlotte shook her head. "You boys are too fat and well fed. Your families have been flush so long that you haven't the faintest idea of what it's like to scratch out a living." She pointed at the stage. "They're no different than I am."

Royce leaned over her chair. "Lower your voice."

She gaped at him in surprise.

"I won't hear you put yourself in the same class as charlatans, or bring ill association to the family name," he growled.

"You're being silly." She looked the opposite way towards Carl. "Did I ever tell you my mother was a gypsy?"

Carl caught the twinkle in her eye. "That would explain why Royce here is so bewitched with you."

"She was not! Charlotte, stop saying such things before people who don't know better hear you!"

"If someone is ready to ban me from society for that, then I don't think it's a society I want to be part of."

"We'll discuss this later," he said harshly.

She turned away, annoyed that he was going to turn this into an argument.

Trudy attempted to lighten the mood. "Look, on the program it does say four of them *are family*. They're from a theatrical group in San Francisco, so they're hardly hobos, Royce."

"Bunch of vagabonds, scoundrels, tramps, and thieves," he insisted.

Charlotte fretted. She wondered how it was so entrenched in Royce's nature to confront anything appearing as a threat. She embraced new experiences. It was her honest belief that she was not defiant, as he suggested, but forthcoming. He presented quite a conundrum—bold, unconventional, and bullish in his approach to all things, so the fact her vocalized opinions somehow bothered him did not make sense to her.

As the curtain rose on the stage, and the house lights dimmed, a calm settled on the group as they became lost in the performance. Charlotte even heard Royce laugh a few times, and her tensions disappeared.

Afterward, their foursome strolled to a nearby cafe for a light, late supper. The restaurant bustled with theatre patrons, and a high-spirited ambience abounded. Carl sprung for champagne, and he and Trudy toasted the newly engaged couple. Royce's celebratory mood returned.

Trudy gasped and pointed at the door. "Look, it's that woman! The one that played Lady Hortense!"

A distinguished looking couple stood at the front, waiting to be seated. The woman's gray hair was streaked with black, rather than the other way around, and she had kind, sparkling eyes. She struck a dramatic pose, holding tightly to her husband's arm. As diners looked up, they began to applaud, and she favored them with a deep curtsy. Her husband grinned and tipped his top hat. As they paraded through the restaurant to their table, Trudy tugged on Carl's sleeve. "Oh, can we please go ask them to autograph our programs?"

"Why not?"

"Charlotte, hand me yours, and I'll have her sign it. Unless you want to go, too?"

She didn't bother to look at Royce as she passed it over. "Thank you, Trudy, that's very kind."

As they walked away, Royce grumbled, "And what are you going to do with that?"

"The point is . . . it makes Trudy happy."

He shrugged. "I enjoyed the play, all right? But all this fuss over adults playing make-believe? Those folks should give legitimate work a try."

"Honestly, I don't know if you're annoyed because you believe all that hogwash or because I disagreed with you."

"You need to learn to temper your opinions in public."

"I don't say what I don't mean or don't believe in. I won't bat my eyes and act simple."

"You don't *say* whatever comes to your mind."

"You do if you're honest."

"I'm not asking you to be deceitful. In these circles it isn't necessary to take a stand on everything. It's particularly unattractive in a woman to take on strong views."

"*Really?* And how *is* the view from up there on Mt. Olympus?"

He scowled.

"Besides . . . *Adele* does."

"Adele," Royce sighed, "has grown up in this community. People already know where she stands on most things, as they knew exactly how my parents felt about issues. Yes, she's strong and opinionated. But if you'll notice . . ." He reached over the table to take her hand. "She's usually the last one to give her opinion, only stepping in if she needs to set something straight. She listens to everyone in the room first, and, if they've already covered her feelings, she doesn't speak at all. A lot of her clout comes from staying in the background."

Charlotte thought about this and realized it was true. Adele didn't need to speak to be heard.

Royce watched her mulling this over. The anger was gone from his eyes.

"I suppose you have a point."

"That wouldn't be your way of saying that I'm right, would it?"

She raised an eyebrow. "Partially, maybe."

He grinned and squeezed her hand. "Okay, stubborn, I understand . . ."

"As you say, if your feelings have already been covered, I

shouldn't have to say you're right at all, right?"

"You're not supposed to use this stuff against me." He laughed. "It takes time, Charlotte. Let people get to know you . . . before your opinions, hmm?"

Trudy appeared by the table, handing Charlotte her playbill. "William and Cora Huffington. They've been on stage for over twenty years! Even performed in London, once, or at least she did. Her husband handles the business end. And . . . they have a daughter and a nephew that are also *thespians*—how's that for a word?" She giggled. "Their daughter was the pretty girl playing the fairy that lived in the garden. The nephew played Charlie. Ah, their lives must be so exciting, don't you think? They plan to travel all the way to the East Coast. I should like to travel like that!"

Royce looked at Charlotte. "Very nice of you, Trudy. It will make a great keepsake."

CHAPTER 38

Sacramento

James anticipated an easy journey home. The wagon bed, once piled high with saddles, harnesses, and other leather goods, lay bare, an indication of a successful trip. He found Tomas needed little help from him in the art of selling; his demeanor was warm and engaging, he calculated figures rapidly in his head, and he was not bashful in negotiation. Vicente taught him well. All he really required was the security of James at his back. The boy was grand company.

James sold both pairs of matched freight teams before noon and spent considerable time strolling the grounds of the market sizing up his competition. Some may beat his price, but not his quality. He spoke to a fair number of future customers who stopped to admire his string. He made his final round back to the wainwright he'd been haggling with all morning. Tomas shadowed him, nodding his agreement as James closed in on his final bid. He considered it lucky the man agreed to shake his hand at the end of the deal, as their parley became heated at several points.

"So, what do ye think?"

"She is beautiful. Althea will love it. It is a surprise, no?"

"An early birthday present."

They stood admiring the light, two-wheeled trap with red bullion fringe and overstuffed leather seat. "I've been meaning ta get her something easier ta handle for some time now. And I have just the sassy little mare ta get her along."

"I will secure it to the back of the wagon, if you wish to visit Charlotte?"

James pulled out his pocket watch. "I best hurry, if I'm ta catch her before supper. Ye'll be all right, then?"

"Sure, sure."

"Good lad."

James whistled as he headed towards Mrs. White's boarding house. He figured to surprise her as she arrived from work. Perhaps she and Justin could travel home for Althea's birthday and make a proper celebration of it. It would be good to have them all together again.

He settled on the porch swing, thinking how pleasant it was to sit down. He and Tomas traveled most of the night to be in Sacramento in time for the market's open. A hot meal and a good night's sleep would put him right before traveling home.

He looked down the street as the face he adored came into view. He watched her stroll towards the house, deep in thought. He grinned, waiting for her to notice as he continued to sway back and forth. As she reached the top stair, she stopped short, blinking twice as if she didn't trust her eyes.

"Da!" she squealed, launching herself as he stood to catch her.

"I've thought of this hug all day," he said, laughing.

"You should have told me you were coming! I'm so glad to see you! Were you at the market today?"

"Aye, me and Tomas. Vicente wanted the lad ta get some experience. I head back the morrow. I thought I cu take ye ta dinner."

"Yes, how lovely! Can I get you something to drink?"

"Just had a beer with Tomas a bit ago. Let's sit. A long day on my feet."

She tucked her skirts under as she sat beside him on the

swing and swept an errant lock of hair away from her face. He
snatched her hand in mid-air, frowning at the dark-blue stone.

"What is this?"

She panicked, trying to yank her hand away. He held fast.
She looked at him ruefully. "Da, we were coming to the farm
on Friday . . ."

"What does this mean?"

Dismayed, she stammered, "I . . . know how this looks."

His chest burned. He fought the fury of a storm rising. "It
looks as though someone does na ha the respect for ye nor me
that he should."

"Da . . ."

"Ye're marryin' him?"

She took a deep breath and, with great effort, steadied her
voice. "This only happened a few days ago. He planned to speak
to you first, honest he did. We were attending a big party at
their home for his brother, and he got caught up in the moment. We both did. It was all . . . so very sweet. Justin was there.
We were coming to tell you together on Friday."

"Ye promised me, ye'd come ta me first."

"I promised to take it slow. We've been seeing each other a
long time now."

"Ye canna rely on him, child. The promise of a wealthy man
is like a toast—given in a moment of fullness because it suits
him ta do so. In the end ye'll be left with an empty glass and
dependent on him ta fill it, if and when he chooses. It's na a
partnership . . . ye'll be a bauble that he claims."

James's agitation grew as he saw the icy look form in her
green-gray eyes that so mirrored his own.

"What *you know* is: His family behaved honorably in an awful
situation. He's a friend to Justin, has given him a wonderful job.
And his family has money. You've made no effort to get to know
him. He *loves* me. You can't see anything but wealth that you

view only as evil. I'm sorry, Da. That's not what I see."

He shot up from the swing. "When the eye is clouded, the heart is untrue!"

She sprang to her feet and squared off before him, "We want a life together!"

"Ye'd *defy* me, in this?"

"In this? Yes. You've made no attempt to be reasonable."

His hands shook, and his face felt as stone. "Then *go*. Go ta him. Ye've chosen yer family now."

He spun on his heel and stalked down the walk to the street. He smashed the gate open with his fist and charged the road ahead without a backward glance.

CHAPTER 39

"The California Republicans *and* Democrats are battling over the spoils of corruption. Now the trick is, to strike on something big while the public is engaged in a scandal committed by the opposition—against the tide and all that. At least when the Republicans were in control we moved forward! If it had not been for their staunch leadership, we wouldn't have overland mail service, overland telegraph, and, biggest of all, the damn railroad would never link the country. Our entire communication and commerce is dependent on forward thinkers."

"Well, Governor Haight is far too sympathetic to farmers and workingmen. He's crippling business efforts; but, at least he may calm down the miners. Lord knows we could stand to get some distance from the whole Empire debacle. Give the little man a few victories and perhaps quiet down the angst that seems to follow their every overblown outrage."

"Oh, it isn't so bad—the governor's role has been a bit disenfranchised as of late. There are many ways corporations and entrepreneurs surge ahead."

"How do you figure that?"

"By burying the good governor in his own machinery. He likes government overreach? Good for him. He's spending so much time on boards and commissions, *much* escapes his notice."

A burst of baritone laughter arose from the tight circle where she stood, Royce to her left, Beth and Neil to her right. Char-

lotte smiled politely, if not a little sadly. A rather stiff-necked affair from her point of view, one where she dressed her part and
followed Royce meekly through countless introductions. But the
point of it being that Senator Cole noticed Neil for an honest,
altruistic servant of the people—and that was important. To
publicly receive the blessing of such a stalwart man was to
become integrated amongst the power brokers supporting his
ideals.

Charlotte glanced around the crowded ballroom of the
Golden Eagle Hotel, hoping to glimpse Celeste making rounds
with Stan and Adele. She could use an infusion of the girl's
inappropriate social commentary to cheer her up. A wave of
despondency struck her as they entered the hotel, directly across
from the city horse market. Royce squeezed her hand, which
put her in greater danger of losing the tears she fought to hold
back.

She was still in shock. She flew to Justin, dissolving into a
puddle of misery after her father left the city. They talked for
hours, agreeing James needed time to cool down, and they
considered how to avoid engaging Royce's temper at James's
slight. Two immovable forces, each possessing unbending will.
And they both loved her. Just remember *that,* Justin urged.

They decided to wait until Justin and Royce returned from
New Mexico. In the meantime, he would write Althea for advice.
She was certain to have heard an earful. Justin hoped she might
see signs of James easing his stiff-necked position. Still, Charlotte couldn't muster much confidence in their plan; never
before had she felt deserted by her father. Ever.

The flock of guests began closing their circles, directing their
attention towards the front of the room. She saw the portly
form of Judge Dandridge in the first row. Royce had pointed
him out as a forewarning. She made it her mission to avoid the
man at all costs, but, if confronted, she had practiced enough

meaningless platitudes to fit the occasion.

Senator Cornelius Cole made his way to the podium amidst a shower of applause. He was a distinguished looking man with swept-back brown hair and sported a brushy mustache and beard that rounded his chin and cascaded onto his shirtfront. His deep-set eyes sought out a number of colleagues amongst the front rows, some of them congressmen from his years in the United States House of Representatives. He smiled, acknowledging his thanks for their presence.

He possessed a firm, pleasant speaking voice, so much so that Charlotte's attention waxed and waned throughout his speech.

". . . So vilified was the first California legislature, they left ample room for improvement—or so one would think. These pioneers were of brilliant mind, and any with an eye for exploiting opportunity soon discovered they had very little where-with-all in which *to become* corrupt. *Corruption*—would come with progress . . . by its people . . ."

She struggled to pay attention. The room was exceedingly warm, and the enthusiastic crowd seemed to press in on all sides. Sleep had escaped her for many days now, and she definitely felt the lack of it. She smiled and clapped as those around her did.

"Decline of government reputation increases when political parties create extreme partisanship and divert interest from legislating to campaigning. Legislators devote excessive attention to *one* of their roles to the exclusion of others, thus corrupting the process. Lobbyists take a hand in drafting legislation and rewarding those voting in their favor. Conflict of interest is not an unknown concept. The line between public welfare and private gain has been blurred, and *it . . . must . . . stop!*"

A cheer went up from the room. For the snippets she heard, Charlotte wholeheartedly agreed with the senator and grew irritable at her lethargic mind. Perhaps a drink of water would help. The wait staff seemed to have disappeared. She felt stifled. She noticed the doors to the balcony were open at the back of the room. Listening, she realized he was nearing the end of the speech. Questions would follow, and she could slip outside unnoticed.

"We are headed in a dangerous direction—I can not stress strongly enough that this partisan strategy only leads to infighting, and progress is thwarted on all counts, for both sides. The fight is no longer about what's best for the state, but what's best for the politician. The need to cultivate senators and congressman with new blood, untainted by manipulations of the system that came before them, without duty to tycoons and robber barons contesting for federal patronage, is more important today than it has ever been in California's history . . ."

The clamor of enthusiasm aided her escape. She tugged Royce's arm and nearly shouted in his ear, "I need some air; I'm going to the balcony."

He nodded, looking to accompany her, and she assured him she wouldn't be long.

She pushed her way gently through the spirited tide, feeling better as she broke from the back of the crowd, better still when the light breeze of outdoors caressed her face.

She breathed deeply. Standing on the shady side of the building brought added coolness, and the bonus of facing St. Rose of Lima Church instead of the city horse market. She gazed up at the bell tower inside the steeple, watching what appeared to be swallows circling the brass bell. She heard snatches of conversation through the French doors and the scurry of waiters as service began again.

The speech must be over. She heard a man's footsteps behind her and turned, expecting to find Royce. Instead, a chill went down her spine as she faced a tall, white-haired presence as familiar to her as a long-lost uncle.

"Hello, Charlotte. It's good to see you." Lodie stood expectantly waiting. For what, she could not imagine.

She gave a short, bitter laugh. "I don't know why it never occurred to me that I might run into you here."

"I've gotten to know Neil Collier, working for the state . . ."

"I'm guessing he hasn't gotten to know you."

He looked down, to break the piercing look she gave him. "I had hoped our meeting again wouldn't be this way. I regret the rift between our families. I've seen you—a number of times on the street, on your way to work. Matilda . . . really misses you. She's tried to work up her nerve to go and see you at the dress shop."

"I have no grudge against Matilda. She's as welcome as anyone, though there's much unpleasantness, none of *our* making, that stands between us."

"One can be fueled by their mistakes, Charlotte, and go on to do great things, important things. This job is who I am; I'm doing what I'm meant to do."

"And that gives you peace? It erases the wrongs committed to get there? I'm glad you know who you are, Lodie, and grateful that now *we all know.* An awareness of the risks involved in a duplicitous relationship with you is a life and death distinction."

"The shooting was not my fault! There is no way I could have foreseen that!"

"But you know who did it?"

His face blanched. She turned pale at the implication. "You *do* know?"

"I didn't say that."

"I know you as well as family, Lodie Glenn! So, *do na think I ca na read yer face!*"

"Charlotte, you don't . . . understand how these matters work." He struggled to lower his voice as his eye shifted to the

301

people drifting onto the balcony, listening to their conversation. He checked himself, seeming to shift to a public persona as his expression took on a look of benign compassion. "Of course, I'm sympathetic to the tragedies at the mines. You're . . . a bit of a lost lamb when it comes to understanding the bigger political picture . . ."

"Better a lamb than a wolf posing as a guard dog!" She glared at him through her father's eyes. "*Politically,* I find no comfort in your representation."

She felt a firm hand on her arm. Royce stood behind her. "It's time for us to go, Charlotte." He gave a short, curt nod to Lodie.

"Gladly."

She allowed him to lead her through the ballroom, grateful for escape. They made their way downstairs, and, as they passed an empty gentleman's smoking lounge on the first floor, he pushed her inside.

"What . . . do I have to say to get through to you?" he demanded.

She blinked at him, uncomprehending.

"We just *had* this conversation about watching what you say in public. Yet here we are, again at a huge function for Neil, and there you are telling off an invited guest!"

"How much of that did you hear?" she challenged.

"Enough to know you were attacking the man."

"That . . . was Lodie Glenn!"

He stared at her silently. He sighed. "I . . . only know him by name. I never saw the man before."

"But you know who he is, to my family?"

"Yes . . ."

"Does Neil? Because Lodie says they're quite chummy."

Royce shook his head. "I suppose it makes sense that they would know each other through their government roles. But

Neil has never mentioned him; it's possible he didn't make the connection. I'll talk to him." He frowned. "But, Charlotte, this behavior can't continue. We all have our responsibilities to *this* family. You belong on my arm and by my side, and I'm proud to have you there. But you're forcing me to leave you locked up at home when something this important comes along."

She drew a sharp breath, almost as though she'd been slapped.

Royce grew flustered. "You know what I meant."

"I'm afraid I don't."

"You have to ignore these people; they don't matter."

"Apparently, they matter to you."

"Charlotte, we *all* lost a great deal at the Empire mine! Neil forfeited huge political standing. Our reputation suffered. It will take us years to make up the financial deficits."

"It's not the same."

"How do you figure that?"

"Because no one *died*! *You lost no one!*"

He stood mute.

She began to tear up. "Nothing. Nothing makes up for Sean. I nearly lost my father. And Althea, as we now know."

"We did all the right things, once we knew," he said quietly. "We assisted in every way we could."

"You did. And, yet, you let those snakes wind their way around your brother as if none of it mattered."

"What do you want me to say? I mean, is this what we're doing? Setting my family apart from yours? *Your father* has certainly driven a huge wedge right in the middle of us."

"I think you need to take me home. Right now."

"Charlotte . . ."

"Right now." She spun and walked out of the lounge.

The carriage ride to Mrs. White's boardinghouse was silent, but Charlotte's mind raced. Panic attacked all reason. She heard

Justin's voice: *"It's easier to dress the part than play the part."* Her father's admonitions about falling for a man who didn't value her pounded in her head. What *if* he was right? Oh, Royce warmed her blood clear to boiling, made her want to cling to him. But she could see in him the pride, the smugness in having vanquished all comers, holding her up as his prize . . . did he actually value her? Twice he had lashed out and vented his temper on her. She endured his assaults out of love, but this third time proved the least forgivable.

Royce pulled the carriage in front of Mrs. White's. They sat quietly in the twilight until she broke the silence, though she couldn't look at him.

"Royce . . . I'm beginning to think we've made a mistake."

He still glowered with anger. "What mistake?"

"I think . . . maybe . . . we're just not well suited."

"How can you say that?" He grabbed her hands. "Charlotte . . . I love you."

"What if that isn't enough? Look at us. I'm always doing the wrong thing in your eyes. You're always angry with me. Neither of us can be happy like this." Her voice began to quiver.

"What? No. This? These are bumps in the road. We're still finding our way around each other; we'll be fine. Once we've married, everything will work itself out."

"Not if we're too fundamentally different. I can't live my life on guard that I might say or do the wrong thing. And I need to be involved . . . with things that matter *to me*. I get the feeling you're going to set me up on a shelf to take down and admire me when it suits you. I can't live like that."

"Sweetheart," he said, grasping both of her shoulders, squaring her to him. She refused to look in his eyes. "Okay, maybe I've gotten more worked up than I need to. My temper gets the best of me sometimes. But, I don't mean to be so hard. Time is all we need." He spoke in a soothing voice, rubbing her arms.

"We can work this out . . . no more talk of calling it off, hmm?"

She accepted his caresses but was silent.

He grasped her chin gently and raised it until she looked at him. "I would be insane without you now. I can't see any future without you in it. You're the only woman I've ever loved. Ever could love." She saw the softness in his eyes and knew he meant it. Belief allowed hope to flicker. She nodded.

He kissed her forehead. "And I'm going to win your father over. Might be the hardest thing I've ever done . . ."

She smiled. "Might be an understatement."

"It'll be worth it." He stroked her hair. "I'll walk you to the door. And I'll see you . . . just before we leave, all right?"

In the few moments between sleeping and waking, when dreams are filtered through morning light, the belief in something good rises first. It was Charlotte's nature to find fresh cause for optimism.

She bustled about the early hours of morning, dressing with great care and packing the last few small items in her valise, setting it beside the larger suitcase. She ate breakfast and waited in the parlor for Justin and Royce to come say their good-byes.

Justin came in first while Royce waited with the horses. He gave her all the encouragement she expected and helped redirect her doubts. He assured her James would come around and that she was overthinking.

"In trying to be ready in every circumstance, you're not seeing what's right in front of you," he cautioned.

"Isn't that what we were taught to do?"

"Yes, but Royce *is* who he is; he hasn't changed one iota since you met. You can count on that. The promises he makes are solid. Stop borrowing tomorrow's worries." He grinned. "Now go and have a good time with his sisters. You've earned some time off."

"I will. And be careful, the both of you. It's a long journey." She hugged him knowing she wouldn't see him for a long time.

Royce strode in smiling in his usual commanding manner. He went straight to her, scooped her up, and squeezed her until she couldn't breathe.

"I'm missing you already," he declared. "Here, I've got something for you." He handed her a box tied up with a large red ribbon. "Open it!"

She eyed him suspiciously, smiling as she tugged off the top. Inside was a small wooden music box, the lid beautifully painted with songbirds. She pulled it out and lifted the latch. The tiny teeth rotating on the notched wheel under the glass began playing "The Emperor Waltz." The underside of the lid was inscribed *All My Love, RC.*

Surprised at his sentimentality, her eyes filled with tears. "Oh, Royce. You remembered the song."

"I'll never forget it." He cocked his head. "You still want to spar with me?"

She shook her head *no* and nuzzled up to his chest. He smiled and held her close, her head tucked neatly under his chin.

"I never wanted to spar with you at all," she said softly. "Sometimes, we just . . ."

"Don't start," he laughed. "Let's just enjoy the moment. This is what I want to remember while I'm gone."

She stood on the porch for a long time after she waved goodbye. The first step up the stairs to her room seemed too monumental to take. At last, she moved. When she reached her room, collapsing into her worn chair, she wept.

Despair whispers lies. She awoke that morning, feebly hoping optimism would win. Her spirit had been battered between the two for the last three days. She had already let her father down. She couldn't bear the thought of consummating her dishonor by failing Royce, too.

306

Yesterday, she went to the headquarters of stagecoach lines—a block from the waterfront and steamboat passages, even spur railroad routes might provide her means of escape. But where to go? For some odd reason, Boston kept coming to mind, perhaps because her mother had loved it there.

She had wandered into a tearoom in the Union Hotel and ordered a pot of oolong and a slice of lemon cake. She needed time to weigh her options. As no other destinations came to mind, she focused more on Boston—far enough away to make finding her tedious. She stifled a sudden sob as she realized the finality of what she considered.

Her soul filled with dread as she realized Royce would never give up. He would trail her, or pay someone to find her if he couldn't. Her mode of transportation must change drastically and often, creating a route suggesting several options at each junction. She could put up smokescreens, but it would only buy her time. Because, at the heart of things, he loved her. They drove each other mad, but, God help them, there was passion between them. If he found her . . . she would crumble. She knew it as certainly as every argument that ended with her in his arms.

She had to disappear without a trace. She sipped her tea, glumly staring out the window at a happier world waltzing by. Like the scream of a boiling kettle, a plan jolted her awareness. The only way. She had gotten up, paid her tab, and strode outdoors to take control of her life.

And now it was time. She brushed the tears from her face. She hesitated, looking at the music box in her lap. She folded a blouse around it and put it inside her valise. She pulled four envelopes out of her bureau and laid three of them out on the bed. Mrs. White expected her to be gone to San Francisco with Adele and Celeste. She wouldn't look in her room for a couple of weeks. One to Justin, one to James, one to Royce. She picked up the suitcase and her valise, carrying them downstairs to put beside her trunk. The hired carriage was here. He drove her to the appointed destination. She paid him for the trip and to deliver the fourth envelope to Adele, explaining she had gone home to visit her family.

Charlotte stood behind the theatre at the back of the last wagon, watching the bustle of the company as they loaded and secured trunks and boxes. She smiled bravely at the woman with the gray hair, streaked with black, now approaching.

"Hello, dear. Welcome." She kissed Charlotte on the cheek. "Are you ready for a voyage of adventure?"

"Thank you, Mrs. Huffington." She took a deep breath. "Aye."

ABOUT THE AUTHOR

Kalen Vaughan Johnson, author of *Robbing the Pillars,* is a historical fiction writer living in Raleigh, North Carolina. Graduating from UNC-Chapel Hill with a BA in mass media, she worked in television for eight years. Together with her husband, Gary, she has raised three children on the move in Tokyo, Chicago, Sydney, and New York before returning to her southern roots.

The employees of Five Star Publishing hope you have enjoyed this book.

Our Five Star novels explore little-known chapters from America's history, stories told from unique perspectives that will entertain a broad range of readers.

Other Five Star books are available at your local library, bookstore, all major book distributors, and directly from Five Star/Gale.

Connect with Five Star Publishing

Visit us on Facebook:
  https://www.facebook.com/FiveStarCengage

Email:
  FiveStar@cengage.com

For information about titles and placing orders:
  (800) 223-1244
  gale.orders@cengage.com

To share your comments, write to us:
  Five Star Publishing
  Attn: Publisher
  10 Water St., Suite 310
  Waterville, ME 04901